About *The Eternal Kingdom*

After King Saul and three of his sons are killed at the battle of Gilboa, the way seems open for David to assume the throne, but Abner crowns Ish-bosheth, the weak, fourth son of Saul to rule over the tribes north of Judah. When the elders of that tribe crown David king, the stage is set for civil war.

Assassinations and betrayals are the order of the day, finally leading to David becoming king of all Israel, although he is not implicated in any of the treachery.

However, it will be David's own actions that will prove to be the greatest threat to the kingdom.

"Watch biblical history unfold and come alive on the pages of *The Eternal Kingdom*, Gary Ivey's highly anticipated third installment in 'The Age of the Kingdom' series. Another well researched saga, with wonderful character development. It's a winner!"

Bill Barley, BS, JD, Pastor, Living Stone Church

"In the third volume of this biblical series based upon the books of Samuel and Kings, we once again find the Bible coming alive through the engaging characters and dialog carefully crafted by the author.

"For example, the story of Uriah the Hittite, one of the more confounding back-stories in the King David saga, is wonderfully fleshed out in a way that connects the reader memorably and intimately with the character of Uriah.

"Reading the Bible is one thing, but there is a lot of ground to cover in very few pages. Gary Ivey's volumes fill in the gaps between what the Bible covers in 'shorthand'... A must-read for anyone who wants to bring the Bible to life in the most human way possible."

Brett Goldberg, BA, author, A Psalm in Jenin.

Other Novels in This Series

What people say about Christian Book Awards winner and American Book Fest finalist _Quest for a King_.

"Gary Ivey brings the Bible to life through vivid and intricately crafted characters.... I read it cover to cover in one sitting... it is impossible to put down. I wish I had had this growing up. I would have understood biblical history so much better!" _Brett Goldberg, BA, author,_ A Psalm in Jenin.

"... a remarkably ambitious saga exploring the lives of a complex array of Biblical and non-Biblical characters... as their lives are swept up and overturned by the move of God and the forces of history." _Terry Freeman, BA, MBA, CG, Genealogist, Historian, Author._

"...like an Old Testament _The Chosen_."
Bill Barley, BS, JD, Pastor, Living Stones Church.

What people say about Christian Book Awards winner _Exile of the King_:

"After reading _Quest for a King_, I couldn't wait to continue the riveting sequel in _Exile of the King_. If you love to read well-researched historical books that bring scripture alive, this book does not disappoint! I didn't want to put _Exile of the King_ down 'til I'd read the whole book!" _Ruth Arthurs, MSW_

"I loved this second installment in the Age of the Kingdom series. Gary Ivey takes the Biblical narrative of the emerging Kingdom of Israel and makes it come to life with a book that's hard to put down. Can't wait for the next volume of this saga!"
Bill Barley, BS, JD, Pastor, Living Stone Church

"The Bible's tales have always been timeless, but now [In _Exile of the King_] they are made both timeless and immediate through the unswerving use of vivid detail. David's years in the wilderness, while spanning a few chapters in the Bible, are here given their due as the backbone of an entire novel."
Brett Goldberg, BA, author, A Psalm in Jenin

Other Novels by Gary L. Ivey

BACKLASH

BACKLASH 2: JUSTICE DENIED

A conspiracy of activists and politicians threatens the livelihoods of hundreds of thousands of people, so Jacqueline James finds herself in the midst of a national controversy. To save her company, her employees and her stockholders, she must launch a daring response called "Operation Backlash."

"It was fabulous!!!! I was so intrigued by the plot... environmental terrorists, murder, politics, moral integrity, a female heroine, hard-core work ethics, and a splash of love made for a great read! (ah...and the evolution/creation thread!)." *L. Z., Facebook post.*

"I found myself cheering Jacqueline on, as she took on Washington and her stockholders throughout the book. The storyline kept me wondering 'what next?' The author meticulously conducted his research, reminding me of a well-developed Grisham-like novel." *D. J., Amazon.com review.*

"Get Ready for a Wild Ride! *Backlash* can be enjoyed on many different levels. As a page-turner, it keeps you on the edge of your seat...but Backlash has a deeper subtext, almost a platonic dialogue being conducted between the lines, that addresses many of the key political concerns of our time." *B. G., Amazon.com review*

www.backlashbook.com

THE ETERNAL KINGDOM

Age of the Kingdom Series
Book Three

By Gary L. Ivey

Published by
Studio IV Productions, Kailua Kona, HI 96740

ISBN: 978-0-9993968-6-5

www.garyivey.com

Front cover design by Gary L. Ivey using stock photo resources from pexels.com, elements.envato.com and wikimediacommons.org, plus original art (David's palace) and work from Artificial Intelligence (AI) platforms like Adobe Firefly and Runway.

❦ Acknowledgements ❦

I'd like to sincerely thank those who helped me with this third novel in the series. Approaching people about reading a book before publication is a "big ask," but their input is invaluable.

Once again, friend and business associate Brett Goldberg saved me from a "Freudian" mistake in wording. He has been very supportive to me in this effort. He holds dual U.S. and Israeli citizenship and speaks 11 languages fluently, including Hebrew. He has first-hand knowledge of the geography of the Bible lands and knows well the history of the Jewish people from Antiquity to today.

My pastor, Bill Barley of Living Stones Church in Kailua-Kona, Hawaii, has now read all five of my novels, four of them prior to publication. It was he who said the novels of the Age of the Kingdom series were "like an Old Testament 'The Chosen,'" which I had thought, too, though I started writing well before "The Chosen" TV series appeared.

Ruth Arthurs, former leader of the Living Stones Church writers' group, has now read all three of the books in this series and offered valuable feedback, calling my attention to awkward wording and finding typos I failed to catch through many passes.

And once again, my wife, Toni Ivey, suffered through my reading the manuscript aloud and called my attention to inadequately explained backstory, nonsensical timelines and confusing character references. This process always helps me find things that somehow eluded me while reading my own writing on a computer screen.

The Eternal Kingdom

The heroic stories about King David are among the best-loved in the Bible. They are also some of the most detailed, recording events that happened 3,000 years ago. Yet the purpose of the Bible is not the same as a novel, so there is much the Bible doesn't tell us about the interrelationships of the characters and the personal and political motivations which caused them to do what they did, not to mention the emotional turmoil which preceded and then resulted from their actions. That is what historical fiction tries to do; to discern the unspoken emotions that eventually break out into action.

There are fascinating relationships that the Bible doesn't quite tell us about directly. Only by reading and rereading the accounts do some of those connections and the pressures they must have caused become clear. Some of the events are shocking and worthy of the seamiest romance novel or scandalous tabloid. They give the lie to the fiction that the Bible is prudish and irrelevant to the lives of real people.

This third book in the Age of the Kingdom series, even more than the two preceding it, is about relationships and how they are challenged by events and clashing personalities.

But it is also about the kingdom, an idea that is a thread running through the Bible from beginning to end. When a prophet tells David his kingdom will endure forever, it is difficult for him to get his mind around it. Some might look at the prophecy and see it as a failure, because even though descendants of David sat on the throne in Jerusalem for 500 years, the dynasty was not eternal in any sense.

For that we must look to the New Testament, where we see Jesus of Nazareth being often referred to as the "Son of David." That was no idle nickname. The Jews of Jesus' time looked forward to a king in the mold of David who would finally restore sovereignty to their nation and usher in a new golden age of the kingdom.

When Simon who would be renamed Peter testified "You are the Christ," he was saying, "You are the anointed one of God," using the Greek word that is the same word as "Messiah" in Hebrew.

But while Jesus embraced the titles of "Son of David" and "Christ," He never intended to raise an army and defeat the Romans, who were just the latest – not the first or last – oppressors of the Jewish people. Instead, His was to be, not just an eternal kingdom, but a universal one. It would not be just for Jews but for all people of all times. He called it "the Kingdom of Heaven" and commissioned his followers to "make disciples of all nations."

In the last couple of chapters of the Bible, we learn how the eternal kingdom will culminate in the final destruction of evil. A new heavens and new earth will fulfill all the promises made to the people who call on the one true God.

In this third novel of the Age of the Kingdom series, I have once again included features not always found in novels, like the genealogical charts and the map.

Since Exile of the King was published, I also started a YouTube channel as a platform to discuss a lot of the issues raised by these books that I can't deal with in the text of the novels, because the characters do not have the benefit of our hindsight from the 21st century, not to mention a great many inspired writings. You can subscribe at https://youtube.com/@AgeOfTheKingdomSeries.

Gary L. Ivey

THE FAMILIES OF SAUL & DAVID

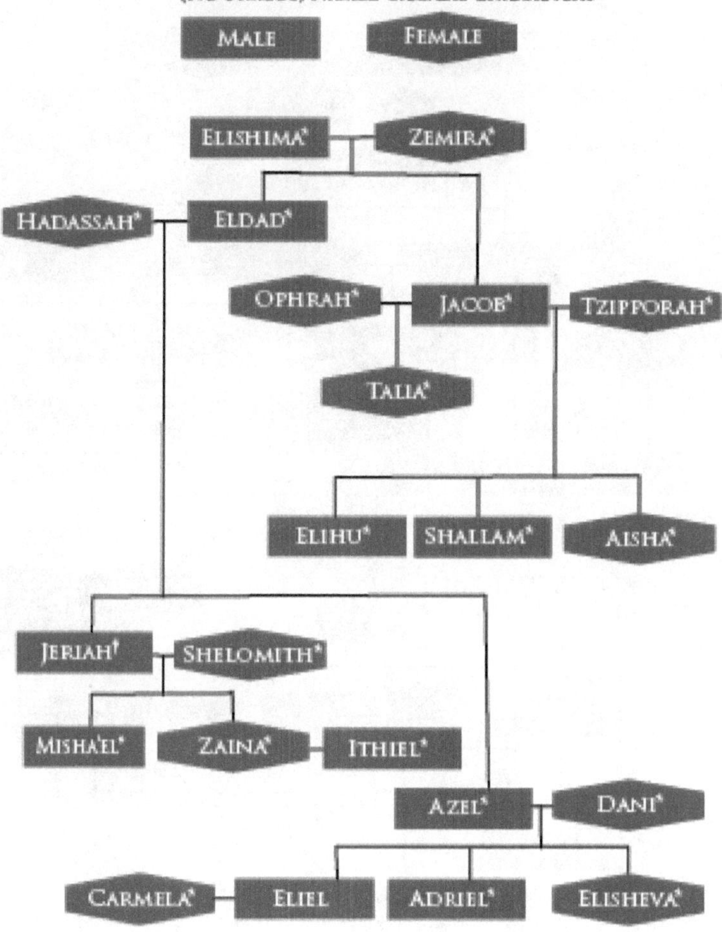

THE FAMILY OF ELDAD OF BENJAMIN
*FICTIONAL CHARACTERS   †UNNAMED BIBLICAL CHARACTERS
(NO SYMBOL) NAMED BIBLICAL CHARACTERS
MALE
FEMALE
ELISHIMA*
ZEMIRA*
HADASSAH*
ELDAD*
OPHRAH*
JACOB*
TZIPPORAH*
TALIA*
ELIHU*
SHALLAM*
AISHA*
JERIAH†
SHELOMITH*
MISHA'EL*
ZAINA*
ITHIEL*
AZEL*
DANI*
CARMELA*
ELIEL
ADRIEL*
ELISHEVA*

The Eternal Kingdom

THE FAMILIES OF THE PRIESTS & LEVITES

*FICTIONAL CHARACTERS   †UNNAMED BIBLICAL CHARACTERS
(NO SYMBOL) NAMED BIBLICAL CHARACTERS

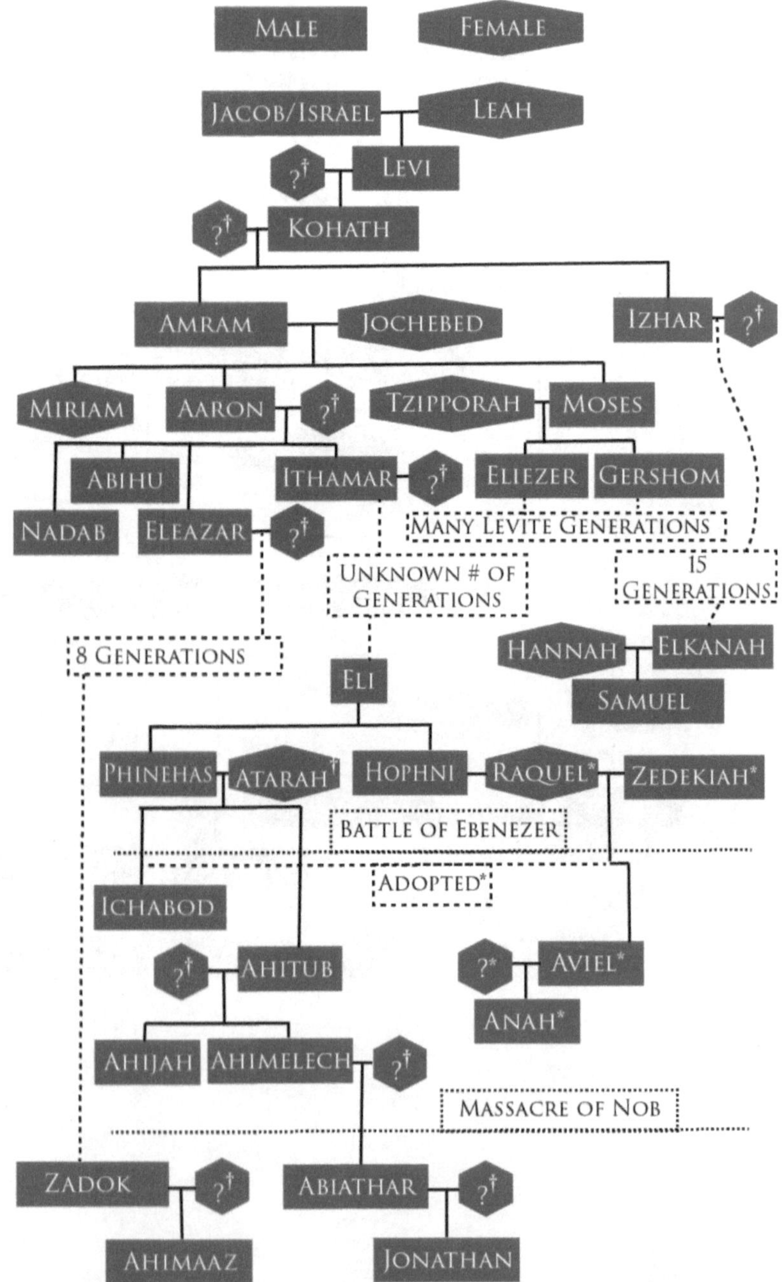

ANCIENT ISRAEL

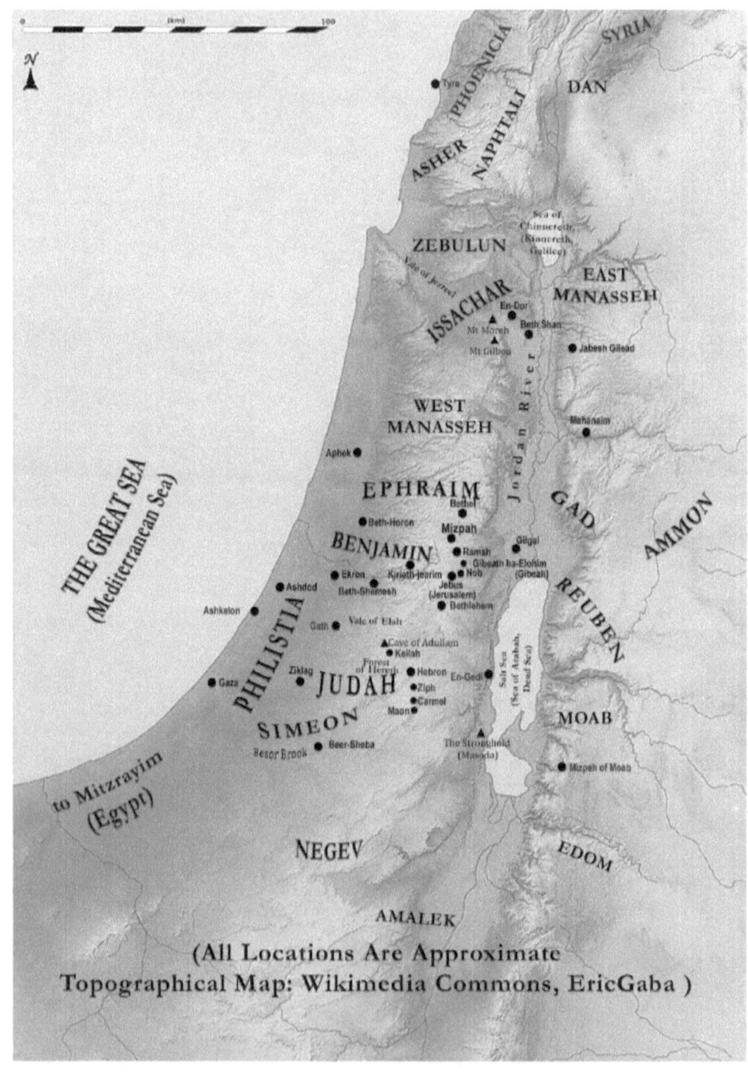

(All Locations Are Approximate
Topographical Map: Wikimedia Commons, EricGaba)

❧ 1 ☙

Your pride and joy, O Israel, lies dead on the hills!

Oh, how the mighty have fallen!

Tell it not in Gath

Or spread the news on the streets of Ashkelon,

Lest the daughters of the Philistines rejoice,

Lest the daughters of the pagans laugh in triumph.

Let no dew or rain fall on Mount Gilboa

Nor its fields grow offerings for God.

For there the shield of the mighty is defiled;

The shield of Saul no longer rubbed with oil.

From the blood of warriors,
*   the bow of Jonathan turned not back,*

And the sword of Saul
*   returned not empty.*

Together in life, together in death,

They were faster than eagles
*   and stronger than lions.*

The Eternal Kingdom

O women of Israel, weep for Saul,

For he dressed you in luxurious scarlet clothing,

In garments decorated with gold.

How the mighty have fallen
In the midst of the battle!

Jonathan lies slain on the hills.

Jonathan, I miss you most!

I loved you like a brother.

You were loyal to me,

More faithful than a wife to her husband.

How the mighty have fallen
and the weapons of war perished!

David set down his lyre and looked at the ground in front of him. The more than 600 outcasts who had followed him in exile and had just listened to his lament adopted the same posture.

David knew without being told that the others were struggling to understand why he was elaborately lamenting the death of King Saul; the unstable monarch who had been trying to kill them all for nine years.

He could only hope they would someday understand that his unwavering loyalty to King Saul, the anointed of Yahweh, was what would command loyalty to his own crown when one day he would possess it.

David heard a rustling nearby and he looked up, to see his nephew and right-hand man, Joab, rise from his seat on the ground and leave the assembly.

Abigail, David's third wife, had prepared food, which she placed before David when he arrived at the tent they shared since the destruction of their Philistine town of Ziklag.

It was well after dark when he sat on a pillow and eagerly dug into the meal. Ahinoam then stepped forward. She was the second wife he had married after Saul's daughter, Michal, had been taken from him.

"David, I have news."

"Oh? What news?"

She sat down at the table, causing him to pause with anticipation.

"I am to have a child."

David stopped in mid-mouthful and looked at her wide-eyed.

"I am to be a father?!"

"Yes," Ahinoam answered. "I hope I can give you a son."

David rose slightly and embraced her.

"It will be if Yahweh wills it. God be praised! When will the child be born?"

"Likely the Fall."

"By then we will have a home. Perhaps I can bring with me a firstborn heir to the throne!"

Ahinoam beamed.

❦ 2 ❧

Each time the wagon jerked and jostled on the stony road, five-year-old Mephibosheth whimpered. He lay on his back, his legs limp and useless. His mother, Mara, had now taken a good look at his injuries and pinched his legs at intervals and asked, "Do you feel that?" She now realized he had no feeling from the waist down.

There would be no way her son would ever walk again.

Her grief overwhelmed her, but she kept her eyes on the road ahead. Soon she would see her parents.

The news of the battlefield death of her loving husband, Jonathan, had been so devastating, followed immediately by the need to flee the hordes of Philistines, which were rumored to be headed toward them in Israel's capital of Gibeah in the land of Benjamin.

She had kept it together to prepare for the trip, but then, Mephibosheth's nanny had fallen with him; fallen *on* him, really. The nanny was also in the wagon and had been crying off and on since they had left. Mara laid a hand on her shoulder.

"Dorit, it's not your fault."

Mara's words just caused a fresh cascade of tears as Dorit, the nanny, looked at her and then buried her face in her hands. Mara's own tears started again, and she lay down beside Mephibosheth, putting her arms around him.

"We're here," Ziba said, as he pulled the reins to stop the donkey pulling the wagon. Mara heard her husband's servant, and she raised up to see they were indeed at her parents' house, near Gilgal just west of the Jordan River.

Her father appeared at the door of the humble, mud-brick house and ran out toward the wagon. He appeared alarmed by the unexpected arrival of his daughter and the others.

"What is wrong?" Eliphaz asked.

Mara could only weep as she jumped down from the wagon and rushed to her father, throwing her arms around his neck.

"The battle went very badly," Ziba said, knowing this barely began to answer Eliphaz' question.

"Jonathan was killed!" Mara said, finally finding her voice.

Her father looked from her to Ziba once again.

"The king, too."

Ziba answered the unspoken question and Eliphaz' face went from questioning to dismay.

"King Saul dead?" Eliphaz said incredulously.

"Father, you and mother must come with us," Mara said. "The Philistines will be coming."

Just then, Mara's mother, Chedva, came out of the house, pulling a shawl over her gray head, having heard the commotion outside.

"Where is my Mephi?" she asked smiling, unaware of all that had already been told, much less the bad news yet to be revealed.

"Grandmother!" Mephibosheth called from the wagon.

"Come here, Mephi!"

When he did not come, Chedva looked at her daughter, whose eyes filled with tears again.

Chedva ran to the wagon and took in Mephibosheth's condition at a glance.

"Oh! My baby boy!" she cried, and she picked him up to carry him into the house.

"Sir," Ziba said, drawing Eliphaz' attention away from his disfigured grandson. "Mara is right; you and her mother should come with us. The Philistines will be coming. Saul's two other sons were killed as well. No one will stop them."

The Eternal Kingdom

Eliphaz looked at his daughter.

"Yes, father. The king's cousin, Abner, is finding a place for us beyond the Jordan River where we will be safe; in Mahanaim. Please come with us!"

Eliphaz' face fell in sadness as the enormity of the tragedy which had befallen the nation and his family began to sink in.

"But this is our home. It has been the home of my family for six generations. I cannot leave."

"But you will be in danger," Mara insisted.

"No, child. The Philistines will not concern themselves with an old couple in a small, out-of-the-way village on the outskirts of the tribe of Benjamin. We are safe here. And if not, Yahweh's will be done. If you feel you will be safer with the tribes across the river, then you should go," Eliphaz continued, "but your mother and I will stay near the graves of our fathers. And near your brothers' and sisters' families."

Mara knew better than to waste her breath trying to convince her father, so she just hugged him tighter.

"But come, stay with us tonight," Eliphaz urged. "You cannot get across the river before dark. And where would you stay even if you could? On the road with lions and thieves?"

Mara looked at Ziba and Dorit and nodded. They jumped down from the wagon and Ziba began unhitching the donkey for the night.

❧ 3 ❧

A hot wind was blowing across the foothills at the base of the mountain. A man stood surveying the valley below where many thousands had died. Though the bodies were gone, and the armies had departed a couple of weeks before, the scars of battle remained.

The sand blew in a whirlwind, stinging his face, so he shielded himself with the hood of the mohair cloak he wore, but he kept looking out as he tried to imagine how and where his brother had died. He had travelled many miles to the north from where he lived with his family to see the battlefield that had taken his only brother.

It seemed no one of his fellow Hebrews could fill in the gaps in the thin bits of information he had been able to acquire, and few had returned from the battle at all.

So, he had turned to the Philistines among whom he lived, because the victors would know what had happened. The men of Gath told and retold their stories of triumph, which he bore because it enabled him to piece together the truth.

Israel's king had been found dead, but there was confusion about how he died. The Amalekite camp follower who brought the king's crown to David, expecting to be rewarded, claimed to have killed him. He told the story one way, but others told a different story.

The Philistines the man talked to said King Saul had died by Philistine arrows with his armor bearer by his side. Still others said he died by his own hand.

It was the armor bearer who concerned the man, and he had concealed his grief from the gloating Philistines until he had pieced together the nature of his brother's demise.

Suddenly he was aware of a presence behind him. He spun around and, like lightning, his hand extended, brandishing his dagger. What he saw caused him to gasp and clutch his chest, releasing an involuntary cry of surprise.

Before him, in the swirling, blowing dust was a young man who looked like his brother had looked years ago.

But his brother, the king's armor bearer, was dead; that was the one fact he knew for sure.

He squinted at the figure before him and calmed down, reasoning that it was not his brother; it couldn't be.

"Uncle Azel?"

When the other man spoke, it sounded like his brother, Jeriah, as well, but when he called him "uncle," Azel realized who it was. He relaxed and lowered his dagger.

"Misha'el?"

Azel's nephew ran toward him then, and they embraced and wept.

"Why are you here?" Misha'el asked.

"I suppose same as you, to see the place Jeriah died."

Misha'el swallowed hard before responding.

"I heard father died by the king's side."

"I would expect no less. Loyalty was his strongest virtue."

"And that which got him killed!"

Azel put his arm on his grieving nephew's shoulder once again and they stood looking at the field in silence for a while.

Before them were trees stripped of their leaves where the hail of arrows and spears and riders swinging swords. The weeks since had restored some of their foliage, but it was still obvious the land had suffered horrible trauma.

The matériel of war which was salvageable had been removed from the field days ago, but there were enough broken chariot wheels, arrowheads and spear staffs to make it obvious that a great struggle had scarred the land.

"How is your mother?" Azel asked, breaking the silence. He hadn't seen Shelomith for nine years.

"She grieves still, and her spirit seems broken."

"I don't doubt it. What of your sister?"

"We are living with Zaina's husband's family in Mizpah."

"'Zaina's husband?' Little Zaina is married?"

"How long were you gone?" Misha'el laughed. "She is not little anymore. She pretty much runs things in the house."

"I suppose we *were* gone a long while; nearly nine years, since Dani and I left Gibeah. I didn't really recognize you, just now. How old are you? Twenty-three?"

Misha'el nodded.

"I thought I was seeing the ghost of your father!" Azel continued. "You look so much like him."

They both laughed, and then grew pensive.

"Why did you leave?" Misha'el asked.

"Your father never explained it to you?"

"I don't think he ever understood himself, really."

"My greatest regret is that the struggle of these years came between us, and now I can never say 'goodbye.'"

"And you dwell among the Philistines!"

"Not for much longer."

"Will David now take the throne?"

"The way may not be open to him. The Philistines occupy the land and Saul still has heirs. Besides, David does nothing without seeking Yahweh's will. It's sometimes frustrating, waiting to hear from the Lord when the path seems so clear."

"But isn't that why you are with him? He seeks the Lord?"

"That's certainly one reason."

Misha'el looked down at the sandy, rocky soil at their feet.

"Will you return home to Mizpah, now that Saul is dead?"

"That will depend on how God leads and how the prophets and priests advise David." Azel then changed the subject.

"You are smithing?"

"Yes. Since we are back in Mizpah, I'm working with our cousins in the family forge," Misha'el answered.

"You are the fifth generation to forge bronze in that shop. Does Uncle Jacob still work?"

"He believes he does, but mostly he just sits on a stool and complains that we are doing it wrong."

They had another hearty laugh before Misha'el added, "He's not in good health."

"And Ophrah?" Azel asked, referring to Jacob's first wife.

"Dead four years ago."

"And my cousin, Talia?"

"Married to a cattle herder from the tribe of Manasseh, across the Jordan. No one has seen her in years."

"Tzipporah still lives, though?"

"Yes."

Azel nodded. His uncle Jacob's favored wife had been much younger, so she should survive Jacob by many years.

"And her sons, Elihu and Shallam, have taken wives and started families. But what of your children, my first cousins."

"Eliel is grown, and a warrior. He will soon take a wife, I expect. Adriel is soon to be declared a man, and Dani will shortly bear a third child."

"You are blessed!"

"Yes, indeed" Azel agreed. "What about you? Have you taken a wife?"

"No, not yet."

"Don't worry, you'll find the right woman. There's nothing like having a wife who supports you in serving Yahweh," Azel told him. "I'm glad you are keeping the forge burning."

"Yes, we are fortunate to have a family home to return to. Those whose ancestral home was Gibeah can't go back."

"The Philistines are there?" Azel guessed.

"Yes. The rumor is they made sure to turn the king's court and his family home to rubble," Misha'el said, bitterly. "There is no kingdom of Israel anymore, to their way of thinking."

"I suppose not."

❦ 4 ❦

"We're going home!"

The words spoken by her father were most welcome, although to Sela they had uncertain meaning. When her father, Zamir, had fled and joined David's refugees, she had been just six years old, so most of her life had been spent camping and wandering from place to place.

Her mother had died while giving her life, so Sela had never known what it was to have a normal home and family. Her father had worked hard to raise her as best he could. She did not know why he had never married again. Perhaps he still bore the grief of loss.

"David is allowing us all to return to our homes until he hears from the Lord," Zamir explained.

For not quite a year and a half, she and her father had had a real home in Ziklag, but then the Amalekites destroyed it. They had been back in Ziklag for the last three weeks, but were camping again, outside the rubble of the town.

Sela's father was of the tribe of Judah and his ancestral home was Hebron, the center of tribal government. He had been in line to serve as elder, when someone betrayed him, accusing him of treason to King Saul, who had always been able to see treachery, whether any existed or not.

So, he had fled with his daughter to join David and the other outcasts at the Cave of Adullam. From there, they had gone with them to all the places where they had hidden over the course of nine long years.

At 16, Sela was old enough now to understand that the death of King Saul meant they no longer had to hide, so her father was taking her home to Hebron, a place she barely remembered.

She didn't know how to feel about it, but then she hadn't been able to feel much of anything after the horror of being abducted in the middle of the night, along with all the women and children of Ziklag. The Amalekites had been cruel, but through God's providence, not one of the women and children was seriously harmed, much less killed, before her father, with all David's men, rescued her and the others.

She was so grateful to David's wife, Abigail, for looking out for her and trying to protect her until they were rescued.

Now, after the passing of the king, she thought perhaps she could look forward to a new chapter and happier times.

❦ 5 ❦

"I only wish you could have been there," King Achish said. "To know our mutual enemy is dead must fill you with relief."

"Yes," David replied, choosing his words carefully. "I and those with me will be able to return to our lives as before."

"And you will have the full protection of the Philistine forces who now occupy Saul's capital and have operational control of virtually the whole of the country."

David managed to force a grim smile to reassure Achish of his continued loyalty. It was a tightrope he had walked for a year and a half since seeking asylum in Philistine Gath. By a miracle of the Lord, he and his men, whom Gath's King Achish had made his personal guard, had been spared the dilemma of fighting Israel alongside the Philistines. King Achish had been fine with David and his men fighting alongside his troops from Gath, but the other four kings had feared treachery, so David's men had been sent home to Ziklag.

"But what of the destiny you were promised?" Achish asked. "You were to be the next king, so your prophets said."

"A poorly kept secret, indeed," David smiled genuinely.

"You can be my vassal," Achish said. "We can rule jointly."

"Your offer is most generous, but I must first consult our God. He decides who will rule His people and when."

Achish squinted at David. "I don't know what to think of one who could easily take the throne but waits on the whim of his god. Surely you WANT to be king?"

"To desire what is not the will of God is to desire foolishly."

Achish again looked at him as if not comprehending, then continued. "Anyway, when you are ready, I will support you. Maybe this is your god fulfilling your destiny."

David said nothing but bowed and left the throne room.

The shofar sounded in the marketplace. The men of Mahanaim heard it and began to move in its direction. The call of the ram's horn was not the call to sacrifice, nor the call to war, but the call to assemble to honor a king.

But what king?

As the men crowded into the market in the prominent Israelite city east of the Jordan River, noisy bargaining ceased. Abner, the cousin of the late King Saul and his prime minister, stepped forward and spoke loudly so all could hear.

"Men of Israel! Listen to me. I am Abner, who stood by King Saul's side. I am here today to proclaim that it is Yahweh's will that the House of Saul be restored in Israel, so His people, worshippers of one God, would again prosper!"

As the men listened, they looked at one another, unsure what might come next.

"The events of this past month devastated our nation and put the very existence of the people whom Moses brought out of Egypt in doubt," Abner continued. "But it cannot be that Yahweh would leave his people without a leader.

"I have called you all here today to make it plain that the House of Saul survives!"

With a flourish, Abner turned and swept his right hand toward forest-green drapes which hung behind him. As he did, the drapes parted and Ish-bosheth, Saul's fourth son, stepped forward. He had inherited some of his father's height and kingly bearing, but he hesitated slightly before coming to the front of the platform.

"See, here is Ish-bosheth, the living son of Saul, heir to the throne and all that God has promised his people," Abner continued. "Can this people live again? Can this kingdom rise? I say, YES!"

The crowd erupted into applause and cheering with some raising fists in the air.

Abner then took a simple crown from his shoulder bag and put it on Ish-bosheth's head. Then taking hold of Ish-bosheth's hand, Abner raised it in a pose of triumph.

The crowd erupted in more applause and cheering, which continued for some time as Abner and Ish-bosheth stood facing them.

Ish-bosheth's mother, Ahinoam, watched the drama from behind the curtain, tears streaming down her face. She had just weeks before lost her husband, King Saul, and their three sons to the throne where her fourth – and now only – son would sit.

Her emotions were strong, but mixed. Sadness and fear mingled with relish in the knowledge that a return to royal life might bring wealth and comforts which she had come to know as queen. Now, as queen mother, would she not again enjoy the luxury of power and affluence?

But at what cost? Already the cost had been too much to bear. She had experienced the benefits of royalty but had had no voice in her destiny. She feared she would have even less say-so now, for she believed her son would likely simply be Abner's puppet.

The crowd was drifting away, now that the ceremony was over. A few were still lifting their voices and their fists with the joy they felt that they would have a king again who might drive away their oppressors.

As others were leaving, two men remained standing before the platform where the king had been crowned. They shared a few words, then went around the platform to the area behind the curtains.

There they saw King Ish-bosheth leaving with a woman they assumed was his mother, accompanied by two big armed men. But they did not follow them. They wanted to talk to Abner.

They found him right away. He stopped as they approached and he looked at them intently, apparently sizing them up.

"General, my brother and I want to offer our services to the new king, I am Ba'anah. This is Rekab."

"I remember you," Abner answered. "You were officers in Abinadab's cohort were you not?"

"That's right. We captained units of 100 each."

"Perhaps there is something you can do. Soldiers are straggling into Mahanaim after the battle. They must be registered and organized into units. Our ranks were decimated, so you can restore them to their former units as much as possible, but the army must largely be rebuilt."

The two brothers looked at one another and Rekab spoke: "Thank you, lord. We can do that. And what would be our rank?"

Abner looked the men up and down again.

"I will make you generals. There may be others of that rank you will find. They must be restored, but I will look to you to organize those of the army which return."

"Yes, lord. We will gladly do this for you, for Israel and for Yahweh."

"Thank you for coming forward. Israel still has many enemies, as well as some who would usurp the throne of the house of Saul. Restoring the army is vital and urgent."

The two men nodded solemnly.

Mara's hand was still on the handle of the earthenware jar she had been filling with water from the well in the marketplace when Abner had stepped out from behind the curtain to crown her brother-in-law as the new king of Israel.

She knew she needed to stand, pick up the jar and take it to her house for the needs of her poor invalid son and their servant, but the crowning ceremony just ended had hit her hard; much harder than she would have expected.

She still wore the black garments of a widow, and still mourned the death of her beloved Jonathan in the battle so many miles away. To see her relatively young brother-in-law accept the crown that should have been Jonathan's kept her from moving from the place she had been sitting for several minutes now.

Her husband had been so strong and noble; such a good-hearted man, so often at odds with his volatile father. He would have made such a great king! But it was not to be. Her sorrow after the battle had been compounded by the tragedy of the crippling of her son, who might have reigned after Jonathan, if things had been different.

But everything had changed. Now she, who had been the future queen, was just one more woman, sitting by the well, drawing water for her family. The future held little promise for her. She might have wept had not the tears already been wrung out of her.

She finally broke away from her dark thoughts and rose to her feet. Picking up the water jar, she began the walk back to the home Abner had found for her. She was grateful for his provision, but she was dependent on him now, and there was nothing to be done about it.

❧ 7 ❧

Zamir slapped the rump of the stubborn donkey, trying to push him to move faster. His news was urgent and he was eager to share it, though he didn't know what the response would be. He and his daughter, Sela, had cut short their visit to their ancestral home of Hebron and were now hurrying back to Philistine Ziklag.

Fortunately, the road was downhill, so they were making good time, though Zamir's impatience kept him from appreciating it.

Finally, the ruins of Ziklag were in view, along with the camp of David's men and their families outside the ruins. Zamir realized some of the families would be away visiting their homes after nine years of exile, just as he and Sela had done, but his message was primarily for David.

"You can go and be refreshed," Zamir told Sela as they entered the camp. "I must find David."

"Yes, father, but come and tell me what he says," Sela said.

"Of course, my dear," Zamir smiled at her as she led the donkey away to their campsite.

Now free of the plodding donkey, Zamir hurried to the center of the camp where the command tent was located.

"I have important news!" he shouted to those in the tent. "I must tell David. Where is he?"

"He is at his tent with his wives," Abashai, David's nephew, replied, as others looked at Zamir expectantly.

"The news affects us all," Zamir said, his voice conveying the urgency he felt.

Abashai pointed to Shammah, one of David's leading young men. "Go, bring David and any others of leadership you find, especially my brothers."

Abashai then turned to Zamir and pointed to a clay pitcher on the table.

"Here is water. You must be thirsty. Refresh yourself while we wait."

Asahel, Abashai's younger brother, was out on a foraging mission, but Shammah was able to find David and Joab, the oldest of David's nephews, plus Benaiah, who had been the first to join David at the cave when David's exile had begun. Together they hurried toward the tent.

By the time they reached it, others had gathered, including Eliam, son of the elder Ahithophel, Abiathar, the priest, and the prophet, Gad.

"What is your news?" David asked Zamir.

"Abner has crowned Ish-bosheth in Mahanaim and declared him king over all Israel!" Zamir exclaimed.

"When did this happen?" David asked.

"Perhaps a week ago," Zamir answered, "but moreover, while surviving soldiers from the battle have fled across the Jordan, many men of Judah who fought for Saul have returned home and have not sworn allegiance to Ish-bosheth. I met some of them in Hebron."

"Why would Abner do that?" asked Joab. "He must know Samuel anointed you – what – 15 years ago now?"

"He wants to see the House of Saul continue," David answered. Shammah thought he could detect weariness in the voice of the rightful, future king.

Abner had not chosen Mahanaim at random. It had significance because it had been named by Israel – formerly Jacob – himself. The name meant "the camp of God," a name which carried both military and nationalist significance.

"What is the mind of the elders in Judah?" David asked, looking around for an answer from anyone who had information.

The Eternal Kingdom

"Those in Hebron are tired of being ruled by Benjamin," Zamir said.

"My father would support you," Eliam commented. His father was an elder at Gihon in Judah.

"After 40 years under the rule of Saul, I would think many are ready for another," Joab commented.

"It is your time," said the prophet.

David considered their words for a moment before speaking again.

"We should inquire of the Lord. Abiathar?"

The young priest stepped forward. He had the ephod with him, although he wasn't wearing the breastplate. It was simply wrapped in a fringed cloth. He immediately took it out of the cloth and held it up.

"Good." David said, "Ask 'Shall I go up to the cities of Judah?'"

Abiathar closed his eyes for a moment and then opened them, looking expectantly at the precious stones embedded on the ancient breastplate. The others in the room barely breathed, waiting for the answer.

"The Lord says, 'Go up.'" Abiathar said, finally.

"Where should I go?"

Abiathar again awaited the answer in the stones, which soon came.

"To Hebron."

The men in the tent cheered and some bowed to David, whom they realized would at last be king. Hebron was the center of life for the tribe of Judah. Going there meant he would certainly be able to rule.

Shammah was among those who bowed, although his joy at the prospect of David finally having a throne was tempered by the knowledge that David would continue to be seen as a rival to the House of Saul.

What will that mean?

❧ 8 ❧

"I should be used to this," Dani thought as she strained to push when ordered to by the midwife.

This was hers and her husband Azel's third child, so she assumed she would breeze through labor like a pro. There was just one problem.

She was older.

Labor always wearied a woman, but Dani was now almost 40 and she hadn't been aware of how different birthing a baby would be from when she was in her teens when Eliel was born.

"Push! Push!" the midwife urged.

She pushed through the pain of yet another contraction, but she was so tired she feared she might black out.

She was thankful for the privacy of the borrowed home. All the homes in Ziklag had been burned and had collapsed except one that had survived enough to be repaired quickly. It was in that house that she squatted now, holding onto a post to stay upright while the midwife worked to bring the new life into the world.

She wished Azel was here, but both he and Eliel had gone on a foraging trip with other men. At the last minute, they had decided to take Adriel with them, because he was soon to be declared a man of thirteen.

"Push!" cried the midwife again.

And again, Dani pushed as another contraction gripped her. Finally, she felt the rush of birth and the familiar relief of knowing she had reached the end of the process.

She listened for the baby's first cry as she sank to the packed-dirt floor, which was covered with colorful carpet.

The Eternal Kingdom

The midwife held the baby and gave it a sharp smack on its backside. Still Dani listened.

Finally, the expected crying started, and there could have been no more beautiful music to Dani. She looked and saw the midwife holding her child, still covered in the fluids of the womb.

"You have a daughter," the midwife told her.

Dani smiled and closed her eyes. "Thank Yahweh," she whispered.

The midwife laid the tiny girl on Dani's breast, and she positioned the baby where she could find the life-giving nipple as newborn babies just seemed to know to do.

"What will you call her?" the midwife asked.

"My husband and I agreed if it was a girl, we would call her 'Elisheva,' at least until we have seen her personality."

"That is a good name," the midwife answered. "Do you need anything?"

"Perhaps just some water. My husband and sons will return soon."

It was about three hours before the foraging party arrived back at Ziklag. Azel and his two sons bore a bounty of wild fruit and herbs they had been able to gather in the countryside, along with small game, like birds and rabbits. They had accompanied Asahel and others of his division, like Adino and Eleazar.

Adriel had been thrilled to accompany the men; his first time on such an outing.

When they came to the camp outside Ziklag, they were met with urgent news.

"We are moving!" a man told the group.

"What? Where?" Asahel asked.

"To Hebron!"

"All right, but why?" Azel had been expecting this news, now that King Saul was dead, they would be free to live anywhere in the open.

"Abner has crowned Ish-bosheth king of all Israel, but Judah has not pledged its loyalty."

Azel looked at the other men for their reactions on hearing this news.

"Will David then be king of Judah in Hebron?" Asahel asked.

"It is Yahweh's will, according to the priest and the ephod. It remains to be seen what the elders will say."

"Go to your tents," Asahel told the foraging party. "We must prepare to move."

The messenger then spoke again, "Azel, your wife went into labor earlier today. You should go to her."

"Eliel, take this," Azel said, giving his shoulder bag which bulged with foraged vegetation to Eliel. "Take everything to the common store. I'm going to see about your mother. Come, Adriel."

Dani had returned to their tent with Elisheva where she lay on the sleeping mat she shared with Azel. She had been just looking at her daughter for several hours now, periodically feeding her until her tiny stomach was full of the life-giving mother's milk.

Azel appeared in a rush, but slowed and grew quiet when he saw mother and child. He knelt beside them and looked at the face of his third child.

"I'm sorry I wasn't here!" Azel exclaimed.

"Say 'shalom' to Elisheva," Dani said.

"A girl? Praise Yahweh!"

Azel then lay down carefully and quietly facing his wife and their new baby and they both simply watched the baby sleep for the next hour.

❦ 9 ❧

Eliel entered the central marketplace of Ziklag to deliver the vegetables they had foraged to the common store so they could be distributed as needed. He left the leather shoulder bag with the women who were there and began the trip to the family tent outside the town, intent on seeing his new brother or sister.

But as he passed the well, he saw a young woman drawing water and he had no choice but to stop.

"Do you need help?" he asked.

"No, thank you," the young woman answered. "My father taught me to draw and carry water from childhood."

"Of course," Eliel said as they began to walk along together. "My name is Eliel."

"I know who you are," she said, averting her eyes briefly. "I am Sela, daughter of Zamir of Hebron."

"Ah, yes, I know your father. I am the son of Azel of Mizpah of Benjamin, although my mother was from Judah."

"Where will you go, now that the king is dead?"

Eliel paused before answering.

"I don't know. My father serves David, and he may go wherever David goes."

"The word is that will be Hebron, where I'm from."

Eliel thought he saw Sela blush and she averted her eyes again. He smiled.

"Perhaps I will see you again on the journey," Eliel began. "Perhaps your father would let me speak to you again?"

"Perhaps," Sela said, a smile brightening her lovely face, which caused Eliel to feel his own face warm.

❧ 10 ☙

The towers of Hebron could be seen before the band of men topped the hill to the west of the city.

Hebron was the center of life for the large, powerful Israelite tribe of Judah, David's own tribe.

David rode a donkey at the head of the entourage, with his nephew Joab at his side. Behind them on foot were Joab's brothers, Abishai and Asahel. All three were commanders of units in David's 600 men.

Behind them, also walking, were Adino, Shammah and Eleazar. They were beginning to be known as "The Three," because they were fast friends and had distinguished themselves in battle. Their youth and strength made them the most promising of all David's mighty men.

Finally, walking alone, was the prophet Gad, who had joined their band of outcasts in the desert by the Salt Sea.

As they entered the city, they were met by a couple of elders who sat at the gate where they heard grievances and judged between those who came before them.

"I wish to speak with the elders of the tribe," David began. "I am David."

"We know who you are, and have been expecting you," one of the older men said. "Make your way into the city to find lodging and we will convene a meeting tomorrow at this same time."

"That will be good," David answered. He and the others then rode further into the city to find lodging and food.

The next day, David and his men went to the city gate, which was not just an opening in the wall, but a series of four towers on the corners of a rectangle which projected both outward and inward from the casemate wall. This afforded increased security and was ideal for defense.

Inside the walls on either side of the gate were rooms, which served as courtrooms and meeting rooms for the elders.

On this day, because of the importance of the occasion, elders from other towns were present. David knew a few: Ahithophel was father to one of his men and there were others he knew by name and reputation. He had often sent them gifts of supplies gained in his raids on Philistine cities.

When all were seated, the head elder of the tribe, a man with a deeply lined face and white hair, spoke as the others listened respectfully.

"Today we gather to hear from our native son, David, who has been a hero and commander of the armies of Israel. What we do here will likely have far-reaching consequences. David, what do you have to tell us?

"Thank you for meeting with me today. As you all know, the Lord was with me, enabling me to fell the giant Goliath, the hero of Gath, and Israel won a great battle. What you may not know is, before that, Samuel anointed me with the sacred oil, saying that I would be king after Saul."

Those around the circle nodded and David continued.

"Now King Saul is dead. I have asked of the Lord and He has sent me to you, the elders of my tribe. I have submitted to God's will, and I will submit to your wisdom. Is now the time for me to be king?"

David looked at the faces around the circle. Finally, an elder he didn't know spoke.

"Isn't it true that you live among the Philistines and your men even protect the king of Gath?"

"Temporarily, yes, we lived in exile to preserve the lives of our families from the threat of King Saul. It was never our desire, but it became necessary. Now we want to come home. We no longer want to be aliens among the uncircumcised."

"My son, Eliam, is among David's band," said Ahithophel. "He would not have joined David if he was a traitor."

"But what about the fact that Abner has now crowned Ish-bosheth and declared him king of all Israel?" said another elder David didn't know. "Saul is not without heirs. Besides Ish-bosheth, there are sons of a concubine."

"Ish-bosheth rules from beyond the Jordan," said another. "Will we, the elders of the great tribe of Judah, serve Ish-bosheth and be subservient to him?"

"No!" said several of the men at once.

"So, you would be king only of our tribe, Judah," the head elder said. Then looking around at the others, "Judah has never had a king. Would that fulfill Samuel's anointing?"

"Ultimately, no, but it may be a first step," David answered, as he looked around the room and tried to read faces.

"But that will mean civil war!" one of the men said.

"As king," began the head elder, looking at David, "will you raise an army?"

"No nation can long endure which does not look to its defense. I have men serving me whom I have trained. They can be the nucleus of a new army of Judah. There are many veterans of Judah who were trained under King Saul. They can swell our numbers."

"Abner is a cunning field commander," one of the elders remarked. "We should not underestimate him."

"You are right," David admitted, "but I know his tactics and methods, as I served him for five years, fighting as one of his commanders, before Saul banished me."

"I don't know why we are hesitating," Ahithophel said impatiently. "He has the anointing on him. God rejected the house of Saul almost 20 years ago. I say we confirm the will of God and of Samuel and make David our king!"

"Here is oil!" shouted Gad, the prophet, holding up his horn. The men cheered and stood.

David and his men stood as well.

"Does anyone here have any objection to making David King of Judah?" the head elder asked. He was met with silence. "Then let us have a Judaite king!"

Another, louder cheer went up and Gad came forward. "Kneel," he said to David, and he did.

Gad began pouring the fragrant spiced olive oil from his uncorked horn onto the head of the 30-year-old charismatic hero. David closed his eyes as the oil flowed through his hair and down his face.

"This oil represents God's spirit which will fill him who receives it," Gad said solemnly as he continued pouring. "God's spirit will bring power and judgement, which any king will need.

"I pronounce God's blessing upon you, David, King of Judah, for when Jacob lay dying, he blessed his son Judah, our forefather, with these words: 'The scepter will not depart from Judah, nor a lawgiver from between his feet...'

"May God richly bless you, David, and the kingdom of Judah, and may you one day rule all who worship Yahweh!"

David rose to his feet and the men around him knelt.

"God save the king!" some spoke respectfully.

"Long live King David of Judah!"

The head elder then raised his head.

"I only wish we had thought to fashion a crown!"

David looked at Joab, who did not move at first.

"Oh, yes!" Joab said finally, and he reached into his leather shoulder bag and drew out the crown that had been taken from the body of King Saul by the Amalekite camp follower.

"See! It is King Saul's crown!" Joab exclaimed. "How fitting it was delivered to David by an uncircumcised Amalekite, though his words sealed his doom."

Gad took the crown from Joab and set it on David's head. All the men in the room cheered their approval.

At long last, God's promise has been fulfilled to me, David thought. *At least partially.*

❦ 11 ❦

In time we will move back to Benjamin, Abner told himself. *But for now, we must rebuild the kingdom here.*

Mahanaim was a good city with adequate defenses and big enough to be worthy of a king's capital, but its best feature was the great distance between it and the Philistines on the other side of Jordan.

Abner continued to use his network of spies, now to trace the movements of the Philistines who had forced the house of Saul into exile. As a lifelong companion, bodyguard and viceroy to his cousin Saul, he wasn't about to let his life's work and legacy be lost without a fight.

It appeared the Philistines were already drawing down the occupying forces in Benjamin. Abner supposed they had decided Israel could not mount any resistance to them after their devastating loss in the Battle of Gilboa.

But Abner was determined to rebuild the ruins of his cousin's monarchy. Saul's fourth son was useless, except for the fact that he was male and continued the line of the house of Saul, but without that blood link, there could be no kingdom; no nation.

He had two brothers rebuilding the army; that was key, but Abner was also reviving other mechanisms of government: getting the elders of the tribes on board. It wasn't easy, because each tribe had its own agenda, but Abner could be a politician as easily as he could be a general, and he believed he was keeping their loyalty. It was no small feat to reassure them in the face of the devasting loss of the king and his three strong sons in one afternoon.

A primary focus was the treasury. No kingdom could function without funds, and that meant taxation. His network of revenue agents was largely intact, with only a few being displaced by the occupation. One of his first actions after getting settled in Mahanaim was to send messengers throughout the kingdom assuring the people that the house of Saul would continue. Many of those messengers were his tax collectors, and in most cases, they were able to pick up where they left off, with only a month or so of revenue lost.

With the king crowned, it was time for construction on a new royal court. He had been able to salvage some furnishings and curtains from Saul's court in Gibeah, thanks to Ish-bosheth and his mother, Ahinoam, who gathered them when they fled. Those things would grace the new throne room when it was ready.

❧ 12 ❧

It wasn't a long journey, but David's former outcasts were moving the substantial belongings they had acquired from the Amalekites, along with the flocks and herds that provided meat, milk and skins.

They were now marching to Hebron as the entourage of a king. Their situation could hardly be more different from the last few weeks of camping outside the charred ruins of Ziklag, much less nine years of living in caves and moving from place to place.

Luckily, Azel had a donkey and a cart, so Dani was able to ride, holding little Elisheva tight, surrounded by their belongings. They had considerably more possessions now than they had lost in the sack of Ziklag, but most of the things were new to Dani, having been distributed to her and Azel from the bounty acquired in their victory. She had been so busy with the baby, she had yet to sort through it all.

The bumps in the road made Dani bounce on the pillow lying on wooden floor of the cart and she had to continually let her arms rise and fall to keep the baby reasonably even and lessen the possibility she would be sick.

The road to Hebron from Ziklag was uphill virtually all the way and, when it grew too steep, the contents of the cart rolled to the back, one bundle tumbling over another. Dani had long since given up trying to keep them in place.

"Are you all right?" Azel asked, as he looked over the walls of the cart from where he was walking.

"Yes, 'Sheva and I are fine," Dani answered.

"'Sheva?" Azel asked.

"Yes, I've taken to calling her that as short for Elisheva. Do you like it?"

"I love it," Azel answered, smiling at them.

There was no need to tell him how weary she was from the continual upheaval of the cart on the bumpy road, Dani reasoned. Nothing could be done except to stop, and she didn't want that. She was looking forward to Hebron and the opportunity to have an established home again.

Ahinoam knew that allowing her to ride in a wagon was David's way of deferring to her being about four months pregnant, but the continual bumping and jerking on the road made her feel it might be better to walk.

She looked over the sides of the wagon periodically at the barren country they were passing through. At another time of year, there would likely be grass on these hills, but it was dry now and if shepherds lived nearby their flocks would be hard-pressed to find pasture.

She shifted her weight and leaned back against a bag of something, she knew not what, but it relieved a little of the discomfort she felt in her steadily expanding abdomen.

This would be her first child, but more importantly, it would be David's first and the potential heir to the throne. Ahinoam shifted again, straightening her back to give the child room to grow.

David rode his donkey at the head of the procession. He had fallen silent and his nephews Joab, Abishai and Asahel, had drifted back, apparently sensing David's need to think.

Under the crown on his head, his mind was a jumble of thoughts and his heart roiled with conflicting emotions.

His destiny was in the hands of Yahweh, the anointing having been laid on him 15 years before by Samuel, who had died several years ago.

He had known these things would happen for half his life, but now, with the prophecy meeting partial fulfillment, he wondered what the future would bring.

Would he be up to the task? Would he be wise enough to unite the fractious tribes of Israel? Would the fact that he was to be the first king of the tribe of Judah make it less likely that he would ultimately rule all the tribes?

Because Abner had crowned Ish-bosheth, a clash of the tribes was likely, but David didn't regard Ish-bosheth's reign as legitimate, even though he was indeed a son of Saul.

Abner likely crowned him to satisfy his own lust for power than from belief in Ish-bosheth's ability to lead the nation.

But Judah had never had its own king. What would a monarchy for a single tribe look like? He had been able to observe Achish of Gath closely, but he did not honor Yahweh, so David realized his own reign must be different.

Before his recent trip, David had not travelled this road to Hebron in a long time. He had avoided going there during his exile because it was one of the largest cities of Judah and the loyalties of the large population there would be mixed at best. Some were likely still loyal to the House of Saul.

But Hebron was the center of governance for David's own tribe of Judah, ever since the patriarch Caleb had driven out the original Canaanite inhabitants. Caleb had been one of just two spies who had advised Moses to take the land, when 10 others advised against it. Because of his faithfulness, Moses had given him the city he requested, Hebron.

Caleb's reasons likely included the fact that Abraham had spent much of his life in Hebron. In fact, the only property Abraham ever owned in the land God promised to him was in the environs of Hebron. He was buried there, in the Cave of Machpelah, along with his wife Sarah, his son Isaac and grandson Jacob, whom God himself renamed "Israel."

David's mind was awash with the memories of his own life and these heroic stories of his youth.

Will my life be remembered like the patriarchs? Will I live up to their heroism? Can I be as faithful to Yahweh as they?

❦ 13 ❦

The elders of Hebron welcomed them with open hearts and homes, giving them their very beds until David's loyal men and their families could arrange housing of their own.

It quickly became apparent that new family homes would need to be built to accommodate the sudden increase in population of Judah's capital. Some of the single men would have to camp outside the city until construction could be completed, but they were accustomed to that. They went to work willingly, working with the craftsmen of Hebron to meet the need.

The first priority was the construction of a house for the king himself, his wives and the children who would be coming, as well as those who would serve the royal family. The head elder of Hebron graciously turned over his house as the royal palace, and the house next to it was acquired as well. The walls of the two compounds were quickly reconfigured by stonecutters to make one large complex. The smaller of the two was designated as the house of women.

Abigail had already made several trips from wagons parked outside their newly united compound into the house where she and Ahinoam, David's senior wife, would live. She was carrying armful after armful of clothing and household items for their new home in Hebron.

David had assigned a couple of young men to help, but there was a great deal to bring in, because of the tremendous wealth they had acquired in the raid on the Amalekites, which had saved Abigail and the other women and children.

Ahinoam, David's other wife, met Abigail in the doorway as Abigail carried another armful of supplies into the house.

"I'm sorry I've not been more help," Ahinoam said, her hand on her belly. She was in the second trimester of her pregnancy.

"Don't worry about it," Abigail answered. "Stay in the house and arrange things as they come in. I'll take care of getting things from the wagon.

Abigail understood, though she had never been pregnant herself. She had failed to give her insufferable, late husband offspring, but she hoped she could honor David with progeny. She knew she would need help and allowances to be made for her then, just like Ahinoam did now.

Abigail had experience running a large household. Her late husband had been a wealthy sheep herder, with multiple wives and many shepherds in his employ. Abigail had been the steadying factor that countered her husband's willfulness, so without being asked, she fell naturally into organizing the king's house and managing the women who would serve his household.

Their time in Hebron was already shaping up to be a very different experience from their years in exile, when Saul was intent on killing David and they couldn't stay in one place very long.

14

Eliel looked around at the marketplace, which was crowded with nearly everyone who lived in Hebron. He didn't think he had ever seen such a large gathering.

He was standing with his family, his father on his right, and to his right, his brother Adriel. Eliel's mother, like all the women, was at their new home in Hebron, caring for Eliel's baby sister, Elisheva.

A hush fell on the crowd as the elders of Hebron and other cities of the tribe filed out onto the raised platform. Then came the nephews of the King: Joab, Abishai and Eliel's commander, Asahel.

Finally, the king himself strode to the front of the platform. Spontaneously, applause broke out, until King David raised his hand. The crowd obediently became silent, waiting expectantly for what he would say.

Eliel looked around again and saw faces raised, anticipating the message that was coming.

"Thank you for coming, my fellow members of the tribe of Judah," David began. "I wanted everyone who could be here to witness this ceremony."

Eliel could see that the other people in the crowd were like him, not knowing what the ceremony was about, but that only kept their attention on the stage.

"Defense is key to the survival and success of any nation. While our tribe has been served well by its elders," David continued, sweeping a hand behind him to honor the elders standing there, "we now have a kingdom of Judah. As such it is important to establish a fighting force for the defense of our people. To that end, today I will announce the men who will command and lead our armed forces."

Eliel shifted from one foot to another, intent on hearing what would come next.

"We are here to begin organizing our defense force," King David continued. "My commander-in-chief will be my nephew, son of my sister, Joab."

Joab took a step forward. Eliel joined the polite applause. This appointment simply made official what was already true in practice, so it surprised no one.

Next David announced that Joab's brothers, Abishai and Asahel, Eliel's commander, would be commanders of 1,000. Again, this was no surprise and was met with applause.

Now will come new information, Eliel thought.

"Next, I would like to announce the commander of my personal guard," David continued. "This man has been with me since the beginning of my exile, when many standing here had to hide in caves and dense forests to avoid the threatening of King Saul. Benaiah, join us on the platform."

The assembly applauded as Benaiah, of whom the story was often told, had killed a lion with his bare hands and a simple dagger on a rare snowy day. He was tall and broad-shouldered and Eliel thought he was an excellent choice to serve as commander of David's personal guard.

David shook Benaiah's hand warmly as he arrived by his side on the platform.

"These four men will be my top generals," David announced, which was met with another round of applause.

"Now, I am announcing a special category. These men have distinguished themselves in many situations as able to carry out special missions, as well as showing great valor in battle." David paused, scanning the crowd before continuing. "Josheb-basshebeth the Tahchemonite, whom we call Adino, because who wants to always say, 'Josheb-basshebeth?'"

The crowd laughed loudly, but quickly quieted to hear the other names, though Eliel already knew who they would be.

"And Shammah, son of Agee, and Eleazar, son of Dodo, join us on the platform."

The three young men were already standing together, so they slapped one another's shoulders and mounted the stairs two at a time and stood beside Benaiah. There was applause again, which Eliel joined with enthusiasm for his friends.

"These have already been called 'The Three' by many of you, for they are a great team and are rarely separated," David continued. "Today I make that official. 'The Three' will by my champions in battle and will carry out missions of special urgency."

The crowd applauded again, and then David continued.

"I have one more category to assign. There are men who served faithfully through my exile and have shown their courage and skill many times. I have selected 30 names from the 600 men who joined me in exile for nine years. These will be an elite force; the tip of the spear, so to speak.

"As I call your names, come forward and stand in front of the platform, facing the crowd. These men whose names I am about to call will the known as 'The Thirty.'"

The king then took a piece of papyrus from under his cloak, unrolled it and began reading.

Eliel knew all the names as they were read. Eliam, the son of Ahithophel, elder of Gilo, was called, then Eliel was surprised to hear his own name.

"Eliel, son of Azel," King David said, then continued with his list.

Eliel turned to his father, who embraced him warmly. Then Eliel went to join the growing group of men standing before the platform facing the crowd. David's original 600 were there, plus the men of Judah who had served under Saul, and citizens of Hebron.

David continued calling names until 30 men stood before the platform.

"This will be my elite force," David said when he had reached the end of the list. The crowd broke out in applause and cheering which continued for some time.

Eliel smiled broadly and looked up and down the line at his fellow members of "The Thirty." Then he looked at his father and he stopped smiling. Azel's name had not been called, which surprised Eliel. He had been serving David since they were together in Saul's army. Why wasn't he included in the elite force?

Azel was applauding, so proud of his son's inclusion in the king's elite "The Thirty," when someone touched his shoulder. He turned to see a young man David often used as a courier.

"The king wishes to speak to you after the ceremony," the young man told Azel.

"To me?"

"Yes, follow me."

"All right," Azel then turned to Adriel. "Adriel, go find your brother." Thirteen-year-old Adriel nodded and hurried to join Eliel near the platform.

Azel did as he was told, following the messenger through the cheering crowd, around the side of the platform behind the backdrop. The elders were filing through the opening wearing broad smiles of satisfaction and talking excitedly to one another.

"Wait here," the messenger said, and he left and stood at the bottom of the stairs. Azel nodded in greeting to some of the elders as they fanned out from the base of the stairs.

Finally, the king appeared, descending the stairs, followed by his nephews. The messenger spoke to the king, who looked in Azel's direction and smiled. King David walked toward Azel and Azel bowed when the king reached him.

"Stand tall, my friend," the king said. "I wanted to tell you why I didn't include you in 'The Thirty.'"

"You owe me no explanation," Azel said.

"Oh, but I do need to explain," the king answered. "You have served me faithfully for many years, and I appreciate you very much. That is why I have a special place for you."

"A special place?"

"Yes, your days as a warrior will soon be over, Azel. I have bigger responsibilities for you."

Azel cocked his head to one side as the king continued.

"I need you to serve me as an envoy – a diplomat. Your heritage in both the tribes of Benjamin and Judah make you ideally suited to represent me in relating to the other tribes."

"My king, I am not worthy."

"I can think of no one better qualified," the king replied. "I have no doubt that you understand me and will be well suited to represent me in the negotiations which will be necessary in the future."

"I am deeply honored," Azel began. "I will do my best to serve you well. May I ask a question?"

"Certainly."

"Does this mean you intend to be king of all the tribes?"

"I believe all the worshippers of Yahweh should be united," David responded. "God's promise to Abraham was that his descendants would be a great nation. I want to do my part to help make that a reality."

David then flashed the winsome smile that caused so many to follow him loyally. Azel returned his smile.

❦ 15 ❧

"A messenger has brought word that David has been crowned king of Judah in Hebron!" Abner said, as he rushed into the rustic throne room of Ish-bosheth. The king looked up and seemed to shrink before Abner's eyes.

"What would have me do?"

"There must be a response!" Abner asserted.

"What kind of response?

"A strong response that will assert your authority. This is a threat to your throne!"

Ish-bosheth looked confused for a moment before saying: "What would be wrong with having a kingdom of Judah and a kingdom of Israel?"

"Because we are one people! Born out of slavery. A nation birthed and nurtured by Yahweh. A great nation promised to Abraham; one people descended from one father. Your father ruled all the tribes including Judah. His son should too."

"It will mean war," Ish-bosheth whispered.

"It was always to be so."

"You knew this when you crowned me?"

"It was inevitable."

Ish-bosheth looked down before speaking again.

"Do you have a plan for defense?"

"No."

"No?!"

"I have a plan of attack."

Ish-bosheth went white.

"Don't worry," Abner said. "You don't have to go. I have everything under control."

Abner left Ish-bosheth's rustic throne room sneering under his breath.

What a worthless fool of a boy!

Abner had not forgotten that Ish-bosheth was now about 41 years of age, but he had none of the maturity Jonathan and his brothers had displayed when much younger. Abner still mourned the loss of his nephews, not so much for their deaths as for their absence at this critical time. Anyone of Saul's older sons would have been a better king than Ish-bosheth.

As Abner made his way to his home, where his wife would be preparing the evening meal, he encountered Saul's other widow, the concubine Rizpah, carrying water in a clay jar atop her head. She was still dressed in the black wool of a widow, though her relatively young face was as beautiful as ever. Armoni, the older of her two sons, was with her.

"Shalom," Abner greeted them.

"Shalom, cousin," fifteen-year-old Armoni answered, though Abner's attention was on Rizpah. They passed him without further comment, but he turned to watch her walking away, the rhythm of her hips discernible beneath the heavy, loose-fitting, black tunic.

He watched until they turned a corner and she was gone.

❦ 16 ❦

It took some time, but finally the royal household was settled into their new home. Repairs and upgrades had been made to the two houses in the newly united compound, and everyone finally felt they could breathe.

To mark the milestone, King David declared there would be a communal meal for just the royal family. A large room in the big house had been designated the dining room and that's where they would all gather.

Abigail was excited as she and Ahinoam prepared for the first official meal of the new kingdom. She knew that as time went on, more people would be added to the group privileged to eat at the "king's table," but this first meal was just for family.

Though she was often involved in the planning of meals for the household, Abigail had let others organize this event. The king had hired cooks and servers as part of the building out of his administration. There would undoubtedly be times when the dining room would host foreign princes and ambassadors, with all their attendants, but Abigail was glad to have this opportunity for her and Ahinoam to have David all to themselves.

At the appointed time, she and Ahinoam made their way to the main house in the evening twilight, where they climbed the steps and were met by soldiers standing guard on either side of the double entry doors. The men recognized David's wives and stepped aside to let them enter.

Inside the vestibule, once the doors closed behind them, the only light was from torches held by sconces on the side walls. Abigail could already smell the food as they stepped through the second set of double doors into a hallway which, to the left would go to the throne room and to the right, to the dining room and beyond that, the stairs which led to the king's bed chamber.

Entering the dining room, Abigail and Ahinoam noticed some things that were new.

"Oh look!" said Ahinoam. "Aren't these drapes beautiful?"

"They certainly are," Abigail responded. "And look at the tapestry on the wall!"

The room was lit by oil lamps and more torch sconces, which caused the room to feel warm and comfortable to the point of luxury.

A young girl appeared with a pitcher.

"Please have a seat," she said, pointing to the low table at the head of the room. They could see that there was a place setting across for them that would naturally be the king's. Abigail had to help Ahinoam, who was eight months pregnant now, lower herself almost to the floor, where they sat upon shiny, cool pillows on the rug-covered floor.

The girl poured wine into the cups in front of Abigail and Ahinoam, then poured wine into the cup before the king's place setting.

Presently the king appeared, coming to each of his wives in turn, bending over to kiss them.

"Welcome, my loves," David said. "Let us enjoy this respite from our busy-ness!"

He sat across them on pillows of his own and spoke to the young server. "We are ready."

She bowed slightly and hurried off to the kitchen, Abigail assumed.

"How are you doing, Ahinoam?" the king asked. "Everything all right with the pregnancy?"

"Yes, I am doing well. I just tire easily." Ahinoam glanced at Abigail. "Uh, how do you want us to address you, now that you are king?"

David laughed a little, then answered, "You have always called me by my name. Now will be no different for you."

David then smiled the infectious smile that made everyone who knew him fall in love with him and said, "Of course there are others around here who must address me as 'your majesty!'" and he laughed.

Abigail smiled, though she didn't want to laugh with him, still unsure how far to push things. Things *were* different now that David was king. It could hardly be otherwise.

Then the servers appeared, laden with multiple fragrant dishes which they immediately began serving the royal family.

"Where did you get beef?!" Abigail asked as a bronze platter of roasted meat was set before her. Her late husband had been a prominent sheepherder not too far away from Hebron, and she knew there were no cattle farms nearby.

"My first foray into trading with foreign lands. I plan to expand this practice to bring variety and ensure that a local famine won't cause problems for our citizens."

"You are really thinking of the larger picture, aren't you?" Abigail said as more of a comment than a question. She had been an administrator herself and she could perceive the level of planning and execution that went into something like getting a rare commodity like beef imported.

"There are a great many things to think about in building a kingdom that serves all the people. The meat on our table is a very small start."

There could be little doubt. Abigail's time of month had come and gone, and she had not bled like every month since she became a woman.

Seemingly, each hour her emotions ran up to a mountaintop of joy and then fell to a despairing valley. To give the king another child would be her honor, and if hers was a son and the child borne by Ahinoam was a daughter, then she would be mother to the heir of the throne.

She did not dwell on that thought, because she was determined to be just as excited for Ahinoam as she would be for her own child.

Another indication she was with child, was that food refused to stay in her stomach. She had to spend hours in bed until mid-morning when she stabilized.

When David called Abigail to his chamber that night, he began showering her with loving kisses, his strong arms around her, but she stopped him.

"David, my love, I have news."

"News? Can it wait?"

"No. I am with child."

"You too?!" David said, drawing back to look her in the face. He wore a bright smile. "I am to be a father again?!"

"Yes," Abigail said, also smiling.

"How the Lord is blessing me! When will the child be born?"

"I suppose in the Fall."

"Praise Yahweh! Do you need anything?"

"No, I am well taken care of. We are settled and I just have to rest a while each day. I'm sure the sickness will not last much longer."

"Don't hesitate to ask for anything you need."

They lay back on the king's bed and just looked at the ceiling for a while, until he fell asleep. Then she escaped his embrace to return to the house of women.

~❦ 17 ❦~

Word came that Abner and the army of the northern tribes had crossed the Jordan and returned to the land of Benjamin, apparently marching to Gibeon. The city was now under the control of Israel, after Saul displaced the Canaanites who had lived there since before Abraham came to Canaan.

It was possible for Abner to return to Benjamin now because the Philistines had withdrawn. They apparently reasoned that, since the inhabitants of Saul's capital had fled and all evidence of the monarchy of Saul was gone, there was no longer any reason to incur the expense of an occupation.

David called the men of Hebron together. Azel and Eliel stood with the other military officers before David's throne, listening to the new king.

"As you all know, Yahweh told Samuel to anoint me as king, but Saul's son, Ish-bosheth, and Abner, his right hand, do not recognize this. They see the crown on my head as a threat.

"Therefore, they have marched to Gibeon and word has come that they intend to challenge the throne of Judah. We will answer their call. Make your preparations, gather your weapons and tomorrow we will march to Gibeon. We may only engage in diplomacy, but be prepared to fight."

The 600 who had been with David in exile marched from Hebron on the road to the north., supplemented by other men of Judah who had served in the army of Saul. That had swollen their number to almost 1200.

"Benaiah," David called to one of his unit commanders, as both rode along on donkeys. "Please continue to lead the men on the road. I and my nephews need to make a quick side trip. We will catch up."

"Yes, Lord," Benaiah said.

David and his nephews, Joab, Abashai and Asahel turned their donkeys to the east and shortly entered Bethlehem, their ancestral home. David rode ahead of the others, wearing a purple robe and the crown of King Saul.

David went to his parents' house, while the other three went to their widowed mother's house nearby.

"David!" said his father, Jesse, when opened the front door.

"Father!" said David as he embraced the elderly man. "I trust the king of Moab honored his promise to me?"

"He provided for us as if we were royalty. And I guess now you can reward him royally! We have to call you king now! Samuel was right after all."

Just then David's mother came from the upstairs bedroom. "David!"

"Mother, I have missed you so!"

"Tell us about Hebron."

"We work to create the mechanisms of a kingdom where there was none. We will be at it for a while."

"What brings you here now?" Jesse asked.

"Abner has set up Saul's fourth son as king of the northern tribes. He is in Gibeon and challenges us to meet him."

"Doesn't he know Samuel anointed you so long ago?"

"He likely knows but is only concerned with his power."

"Does he intend war?" Jesse asked the obvious question.

"That remains to be seen. I'll talk if he wishes, but I am taking my soldiers, as Abner rides at the head of his army."

"May Yahweh be with you, my son."

"Thank you, father. Unfortunately, I need to leave, lest the army leave me behind, but I wanted to see you."

"We are so glad you did," said his mother.

"You must be careful. Abner is a viper," Zeruiah said as her three strong sons stood before her. "He may strike any time."

"Yes mother, we will be careful," Abashai answered.

"Abner is getting old," Asahel assured her. "He cannot hold on too much longer, and Ish-bosheth is weak."

"Ah, but even the weak can be dangerous when cornered," Zeriuah answered. "Is my brother with you?"

"David is with grandmother and grandfather," Joab answered. "We must be going. The army marches on."

"So good to see you; it's been so long since Moab."

"It's good that you are back, mother," Joab said. "I don't think the pretender who occupies Saul's throne will be a threat to any of us. And now we must be going." He gave his mother a kiss on the cheek and Abashai did the same. When Asahel went to her, she spoke before he could kiss her.

"Asahel, you may feel Abner is old, but he will always be dangerous. Be careful."

"Of course, mother," Asahel kissed her. "Goodbye now."

And he followed his brothers out the door, where they mounted their donkeys and rode swiftly away.

A few miles further north, the hill on which the city of Jebus was located became visible. David had grown up just a few miles south of here, in Bethlehem, but he didn't know a lot about the city. It was one of the cities Israel had failed to take in Joshua's conquest. Israelites usually didn't go there.

David looked up to view the formidable walls of the city. Deep valleys ran on the eastern and western sides of the city, coming together at the southern tip, making approaching it very difficult for any army interested in conquest.

That's one of the reasons Joshua couldn't take it, David thought, but he didn't say anything to anyone.

"We just crossed into the land of Benjamin," Joab said.

"So we have," David said, looking up at the walls again.

What a great location, though.

❦ 18 ❦

The men of Judah, more than thousand of them, arrived at dusk at a place their scouts had identified as a good place to make camp.

On the way they had passed Gibeah, with its deserted houses and blackened ruins of what had been the royal court of Saul.

It was a valley where the ground was flat, and the men were able to stake out places for their bedrolls. A few tents were erected for the commanders with a large command tent in the middle of the encampment.

After the sun went down, David's men settled down around a hundred campfires. Some roasted meat they brought with them. Others made last-minute preparations for the battle which they would likely fight tomorrow, rubbing olive oil into the leather of their shields, retying bowstrings or replacing the laces on sandals. Azel and his son, Eliel, found themselves at a campfire with Zamir of Hebron. Eliel purposely sat next to Zamir.

"Will there be a battle tomorrow?" asked one of the men, as he gnawed on some dried goat meat. "The king didn't really say."

"If these were Philistines or Amorites there would certainly be a battle," Azel said, "but since they are fellow Hebrews, there may only be diplomacy."

"What diplomacy can there be?" Zamir said. "We all know God rejected Saul and chose another."

"Not everyone sees it that way, I guess," said another man.

"We need to be ready for whatever happens." Azel said.

"If Abner brought soldiers, I don't know how much diplomacy he is planning," another man said.

"To fight would mean we are in a civil war. The men from the northern tribes are descendants of Abraham, Isaac and Jacob just like we are," Zamir commented.

"How can Abner continue to support Ish-bosheth as king when it is common knowledge that Samuel anointed David?" Eliel asked.

"Some men let ambition overcome submission to God," Zamir answered. "But it is usually a man's undoing."

Eliel bolstered his courage and spoke directly, but in subdued tones, to Zamir. The others at the fire didn't notice; they continued talking politics and war.

"Sir, I wanted to ask you something," Eliel began.

"Oh? What is it?"

"I met Sela the other day…"

"Ah!" Zamir said with a knowing look.

"She seems like a very nice young woman. I wanted to ask your permission to speak to her again."

Azel's attention was now drawn away from the others talking around the fire, and he and Zamir locked eyes.

"Son, your father and I have seen many adventures together, and I've watched you grow up, while we all were in exile with David. I'd be happy for you to get to know my daughter. Just know she is very precious to me."

"Thank you, sir. I understand," Eliel smiled.

Zamir slapped Eliel on the shoulder.

"Now, does anyone have any wine? I may need a little help getting to sleep tonight," Zamir said loudly, and those around the fire laughed. A couple of the men produced clay jars.

Eliel laid back on his bedroll. It would be difficult for him to get to sleep tonight, he felt sure.

❦ 19 ❦

Early in the morning, David and his men rose and, after a quick breakfast, marched to the city of Gibeon.

Zamir could see them while they were still a good way off; Abner's men sat beyond the pool. He estimated their number at about a thousand. He knew most of them would be Benjamites. While the tribe was the smallest in Israel, the men of Benjamin were fierce fighters. It made Zamir catch his breath for a moment, until he remembered that David's men survived the threatening of a Benjamite king for nine years.

"Sit on this side of the pool," came the order from Zamir's commander, Asahel, one of David's nephews. Azel and his son Eliel obeyed and found a place to sit facing the pool.

"See that city on the high hill to the north?"

"Yes, father," Eliel replied.

"That's Mizpah, where you and I were both born."

"I remember it, I think," Eliel said. "We should go and visit our relatives sometime."

"Yes, perhaps someday we can."

There was no conflict in Azel's mind that he still looked at Mizpah in Benjamin as his home, though he now marched with a Judaite king. After all, Azel's mother had been from Judah and so was his wife, Eliel's mother. They were both partly Benjamite and partly Judaite.

The pool of Gibeon was a remarkable engineering achievement, being a broad, round hole, dug out of solid limestone and going down perhaps 50 cubits into the earth. Stairs carved into the walls allowed the people of the city to descend to the depth where they could draw water.

The men faced one another from opposite sides of the pool, looking warily at one another from 30 cubits apart. Then Abner called out, "David, will you speak with me?"

David looked at Abner then turned to Joab at his side.

"You should go, Joab. You are the same rank as Abner. He doesn't yet respect me as king. Ish-bosheth isn't here, so I should not be the one to speak to him."

Joab looked at him through narrowed eyes, but he went forward, threading his way through the seated men. Before going around the pool to meet Abner, he motioned for Adino, Shammah and Eleazar, "The Three," to walk with him. They walked halfway around the pool then stopped.

Abner apparently realized what they were doing, for he motioned for his generals, Ba'anah and Rekab, to accompany him as he went to meet them.

David watched from a distance as the men stood facing each other, not able to hear what they were saying.

It wasn't long before Joab and "The Three" turned and walked back to report what had been said.

Joab walked up to David. "He wants 12 of our men to 'play' with 12 of theirs. Swords, to the death."

"Summon the commanders." David understood. His first experience war had been proxy combat.

Joab turned to "the Three."

"Find my brothers and Benaiah. Bring them to me."

Soon the men returned with Abashai, Asahel and Benaiah.

"Instead of a battle, Abner's proposal is for proxy combat," Joab explained to his commanders. "Twelve of ours against 12 of theirs; fighting with swords, to the death. Both sides will agree to the outcome. Let us each find three volunteers."

The three commanders, Abashai, Asahel and Benaiah, nodded grimly and left to return to their units.

❧ 20 ❧

"I will go!"

It was Eliel who jumped to his feet and volunteered first after Asahel explained to his men what would happen. Two other young men rose and volunteered as well. Azel looked on, worried, but said nothing.

"Good," Asahel said. "Come with me."

"Wait!"

Eliel turned to see who had cried out. It was Zamir.

"Let me go in your place," Zamir said to Eliel.

"What? No, why would I do that?"

"I insist," Zamir said forcefully. "I don't want my future son-in-law maimed before he can even propose!"

"But Lord, you are Sela's guardian, her sole support. You should not be the one!"

"Eliel, I am doing this. As your future father-in-law, I order you to stand aside! You will fight another day."

Zamir brushed past him and hurried to join Asahel and the others as Eliel stood with his mouth agape.

"Besides, I have a plan!" Zamir said, pulling his beard with his left hand, then turned away.

Scores of men had to move from where they had been sitting to make room for the two dozen men who now faced off beside the pool. They each pulled their tunics from behind through their legs and tucked the hems into their belts, so their legs would be free and nimble.

Joab and Abner paired them off, so each stood facing the other, a sword in each of their right hands and knees bent, ready for action.

Abner called loudly, "And... FIGHT!"

"Hurrahs" went up on both sides as the men of Benjamin and the men of Judah each cheered on their proxies.

The 12 pairs of men at first feinted and thrusted and dodged as each got the feel of his opponent. Each pair knew one of them would not survive.

Zamir danced around in a circle, facing the muscular, bearded man of Benjamin before him. He thrust out his sword a couple of times to get a read on the man's reflexes. Their swords clanged together as they swung and parried, varying offensive and defensive postures in a dangerous dance.

Suddenly his opponent lunged and Zamir grabbed for his sword hand with his left, but missed. The sword sliced deep into his upper arm. Zamir knew he could wait no longer to activate his plan. With blood dripping down his left arm, he reached out toward the man's face, grabbing his beard.

The man cried out as Zamir jerked his head down. The man tried to pull loose, but Zamir held tightly. Zamir pulled back his sword, intending to bury it deep in the man's abdomen, but the man somehow sensed what he was doing and grabbed Zamir's right wrist, stopping his thrust. Zamir continued holding the man's beard, but he raised his head in spite of the strong hold Zamir had on his beard.

Zamir was surprised the man could lift his head, and his opponent took advantage. Letting go of Zamir's sword hand, the furious Benjamite grabbed a handful of Zamir's beard.

Zamir cried out at the pain of having his own beard pulled, but he recovered and, his right hand now free, he thrust his sword into the man's throat.

But the Benjamite mirrored Zamir's movement, driving his own sword deep into Zamir's abdomen.

They fell together as one, unable to move again.

Suddenly, the cheering stopped. Joab couldn't believe his eyes. All but two pairs of men had fallen – both members of each of 10 pairs lay on the ground – none had risen again.

Then one of the remaining duos fell; both fell together like the others, each struggling desperately, holding the beard of his opponent with one hand while thrusting with the other.

Finally, the last pair, bloodied by repeated cuts and nicks, also grabbed one another's beards and dealt simultaneous, fatal blows with their swords and fell together to the ground.

All are dead! Nothing is settled! Joab realized.

There was shocked silence for a few seconds. Then men on both sides jumped to their feet, shouting and brandishing swords and spears. The shouts became one loud roar, and the men closest began running around the pool to the other side. There was a great clash of iron on bronze on leather-covered shields and shouts of anger became cries of pain.

No order had been given to charge and fight, but every man there knew that 24 men had died for nothing. Nothing was settled, so 2,000 angry men would settle it now.

Eliel ran to where Zamir had fallen. He rolled him over and saw the sword still embedded in his abdomen and his tunic drenched in blood. He was certain Zamir was dead.

He wiped his tears, then steeled himself to join the battle.

"Charge!" Joab called belatedly. A ram's horn sounded, and David's men surged forward. Hundreds swarmed around the pool to meet their brothers who had become their enemies.

Soon the Benjamites realized they were being surrounded and some of them began to run. The Benjamite officers tried to keep them in the fight, but many were already scattering.

❧ 21 ❧

"Hold the line!"

Abner was determined to inspire the men of Israel's northern tribes to stand firm and fight, but David's Judaites were coming too fast. He pulled the reins to turn his donkey to survey the field. The battle was not going well.

Then the donkey shuddered and fell with him. An arrow had struck the poor animal in the neck and must have severed a vital artery, for the faithful mount lay shaking and quiet, great volumes of blood coming from the wound.

Abner saw he would now have to fight on foot. With great difficulty, he pulled his right leg out from under the dying mount. Some of his men were fleeing the field, but Abner rose and called, "Men of Israel, stand and fight!"

As he said it, a Judaite charged toward him with sword raised. Abner jabbed at him with his spear, striking him in the chest. The man fell and did not rise again.

He turned to face another and used the spear staff to parry a sickle sword swung at his head. He stabbed the man in the neck with the bronze-clad butt of his spear and the man fell.

Abner looked forward and saw a number of David's men rushing toward him and realized all was lost. He turned to run after his men, most of whom had already fled.

King David's nephew, Asahel, slashed the neck of a soldier from a northern tribe, then turned to see Abner fleeing. He immediately gave chase, calculating the angle he would need to run to intersect the line being travelled by the older man.

Asahel knew if he caught and killed Abner, the fighting would end, and his uncle David could take the throne, but he was surprised at how fast Abner could run at his age.

❧

Azel finally overcame a man with whom he had been locked in desperate struggle and looked up to see Asahel pursuing Abner.

"Asahel, I'm coming!" Azel shouted. He began running to join his young commander, but along the way had to deal with a lone man who chose to stand and fight. He deftly avoided his shield to land a sword blow on the side of the man's head, opening a bloody gash. The man fell, but Azel didn't stop to see if he was dead. Instead, he struggled to catch up with Asahel, as always, for few could run like him.

Abner sensed he was being pursued. He quickly stole a look back and thought he recognized his pursuer.

"Is that you Asahel?" he wheezed.

"It is!" Asahel's voice was strong.

It is only a matter of time until he catches up.

Abner's chest heaved and his breath came in painful, hot bursts. He didn't know how long he could continue this pace.

"Turn aside... to the right... or left; take on a younger man... and strip him of his weapons!" Abner gasped.

There was no response from Asahel.

He is getting closer.

"Stop chasing me!" Abner pleaded. "Why should I... strike you down? How could I... face your brother, Joab?"

Asahel didn't answer, so Abner grasped his spear with both hands and suddenly stopped cold, leaning back, planting his feet and holding the spear's bronze-clad butt behind him.

Asahel's face showed surprise as the relatively dull butt of the spear sliced through his midsection. He could not stop, so the spear impaled him, going all the way through his torso. His speed continued to carry him forward, so Abner let go of the spear as Asahel tumbled to the ground.

Abner saw that Asahel lay still, his tunic drenched in a spreading circle of crimson. Then Abner saw David's men in

58

pursuit, so he ran again, leaving his spear. He was relieved to see the men stopped where Asahel lay, so he could slow enough to catch his breath, though he kept moving.

Azel was close when Asahel fell.

"Asahel!" he cried, bending over him. "My God!"

Asahel was still and his eyes were closed. Azel cradled his head in one hand and put his other hand on Asahel's chest, then in front of his nose, but there was no sign of life.

Several other men arrived and stood over them with grim looks on their faces. Suddenly Asahel's older brother, Joab, burst through the group and knelt beside Azel.

"Asahel! Asahel! Oh no! What happened?"

"Abner struck him, general," Azel answered, awaiting the King's right-hand-man's reaction. "His spirit is gone."

Joab said nothing, but his face darkened as he looked down at his brother. Then he stood and spoke in a loud voice: "Pursue them to the ends of the earth!"

The men obeyed the order and began running after the fleeing Israelites, but Joab caught Azel's arm.

"Help me put my brother onto my donkey. Then could you take him to the rear? I must continue to lead the men."

"Yes, Lord," Azel nodded, and he held the body while Joab pulled Abner's spear out of his midsection. The body fell limp in Azel's arms when the spear was out. Then Azel and Joab lifted Asahel's body and laid it over the back of the donkey.

"I'll take care of him."

"Thank you."

Joab looked at his brother sadly, then left on the run after the men of Judah pursuing Abner's army.

Azel looked at the body of his friend and commander whom he had served with for 10 years. With a sigh, he took hold of the leather reins and jerked forward, so that the donkey began slowly walking back toward Gibeon.

❧ 22 ❧

Ba'anah, one of Abner's generals, was pushing his donkey as hard as he could. The animal was running, just as the men of the northern tribes were running, sensing danger, but Ba'anah was not fleeing in fear; he intended to get ahead of the retreating men and stop them so they could make a stand.

Ahead he saw a hill which looked like good ground from which to make a stand. He was on pace to reach it before the bulk of the retreating men did.

As soon as he was ahead of them, he stopped and turned the donkey to face them.

"Men of Israel! Stop! Do not fear the Judaites. You are of the house of Saul! Stand and fight. Let us mount this hill and stand as a wall, lest they take our land."

That stopped most of the men. Ba'anah's brother and fellow general, Rekab, arrived then on his own donkey and he also worked to rally their troops and lead them to the top of the hill.

Men continued to straggle to the spot where Ba'anah had decided to make a stand. Finally, Abner arrived.

"General, we feared for your safety. We didn't know where you were."

Abner collapsed on the ground, heaving, struggling to get his breath.

"They are coming," he said when he finally was able to speak. "Let us make our stand."

The hill was called "Ammah" by the locals, and beyond it was the wilderness of Gibeon. It would soon be sunset and there could be no fighting in the dark.

The first of David's men appeared, and Abner saw they were marching in ranks. They had taken time to reform and were now before them as disciplined troops. Joab marched before the first rank and David rode a donkey beside him. Abner knew he had to do something.

"Joab! Must the sword continue to devour always?" he shouted into the dim light of pre-darkness. "This is bound to end in bitterness. Tell your people to turn aside from pursuing their brothers."

For a moment there was silence, then a shofar sounded and the Judaites stopped marching.

Joab looked at King David.

"Let's finish them right here!" Joab fumed, slapping the flat of his sword against his shield.

David took hold of Joab's arm.

"Abner did not plan this battle. It was a spontaneous response after 12 lives on each side were lost needlessly," David said, trying to calm Joab down. "I loved Asahel too, but Abner is right; we are brothers."

Joab scowled and uttered a low growl as he struggled with what his uncle had said. Finally, he raised his head, cupped his hands around his mouth and shouted, "As Yahweh lives, if you had not said this, it would have been morning before we abandoned the pursuit of our brothers. We will go in peace, and you may also."

Then Joab gave the order to return to Hebron and David's army turned and started back toward the land of Judah.

"Is it a trick?" Rekab asked Abner.

"I would put nothing past Joab. I was forced to kill his brother today."

Rekab looked at Ba'anah, his brother. No one needed to tell them how strong the bond between brothers was, or how certain Joab's retribution would be – someday.

"We must make our way across the Jordan," Abner said.

"Tonight?" Ba'anah questioned.

"We dare not stay another moment. Joab may have a change of heart."

"I'll give the order," Ba'anah said.

It took all night, but the army of the northern tribes moved rapidly eastward across the territory of Benjamin and forded the Jordan River below Gilgal in the hours of early morning. By nightfall the next day they were back in Mahanaim, spent but safe.

When they called the roll, they found that 360 of their number were missing. Abner knew instinctively that not all were dead on the field. Many had simply not stopped running.

Still, it was a devastating loss.

❧ 23 ❧

"Sela?"

"Yes?" she said as she answered the door.

Abigail cleared her throat, though she didn't need to. It was just to put off what she must say to the poor girl.

"At the battle," Abigail began, and Sela's young face showed that she feared what was coming. "Your father – he won't be coming home."

Sela sank to the floor. Tears came in a torrent and a low moan came from deep in her chest. Abigail came inside to comfort her. They were in the big room of the house where her family had always lived in Hebron.

Abigail put her arms around the girl and stayed for a long time as Sela grieved.

"What will I do?" Sela sobbed when she was finally able to speak. Abigail drew back and looked at her sadly. She never knew her mother, and now her father would not return.

"Come live with us," Abigail said. "We have room. It's kind of a madhouse, with Ahinoam's baby coming, and soon I'll have a baby of my own, but you'd be welcome."

"To live in the king's house?" Sela looked up at Abigail with wide eyes. "Are you sure it would be all right?"

"I manage the house and I make sure everyone has what they need. What is one more? And you will be able to help."

"Oh, yes! I can help with the chores, the cooking, whatever you need me to do!"

Eliel went to Zamir's house as soon as he was able after returning from the battle. He was surprised to find it empty and abandoned.

"Where has the girl gone who lived here?" he asked a neighbor. The man merely shrugged, as if to say, "I don't know and I don't care."

Eliel asked further until a woman in the market was able to tell him that Sela was now a ward of the king and living in the king's wives' house.

"I must go and get her," he told his mother when he arrived home. Dani, with baby Elisheva on her hip, returned a serious look.

"Son, you can't just take her out of the house. She now belongs to the king. Are you prepared to pay the bride price required by a king?"

"But she hasn't been there long," Azel protested.

"It doesn't matter. Her status has changed. Did she know you wanted to marry her?"

"No."

"How about this? I will approach Abigail to find out more and explain the situation. It may be that the king will be amenable to giving her to one of his Mighty Men," she answered her son with a proud smile.

"Thank you."

"But remember," Dani continued, caressing her oldest son's black hair. "King David is her guardian now and that complicates matters."

"Yes, mother," Eliel said.

A couple of days later, Dani kept her promise. While Adriel watched baby Sheva, she went to the king's compound and requested to speak with Abigail, for she knew Abigail was chief of the women's house.

The soldier who stood at the gate was not one of the men Dani knew from their time in exile, but one of the men of Judah who had joined David after he became king. He took her request through the gate and told her to wait outside. She hadn't waited long when Abigail came to the gate.

"Dani! Come in," Abigail said, and she led the way into the walled compound.

"Here, sit," Abigail said, pointing to a wooden bench alongside the wall.

"Thank you. And thank you for seeing me."

"What can I do for you?"

"It is for my son, Eliel, one of David's 30 mighty men," Dani began, "He had met Zamir's daughter, Sela. After Zamir was killed, he hoped to ask Sela to marry him, but with all that's happened, we didn't know what to do. We are just getting settled in Hebron and don't have much for a bride price."

Abigail looked down and then spoke softly.

"I am so sorry, Dani. I didn't know any of that. When she was orphaned, I invited her to live with us.

"Her status has since changed again, however. Night before last, David went in to her. She's his concubine now."

Dani blinked in surprise. *So soon?*

"Oh, of course... I understand," Dani said, rising to go.

"I'm sorry... If I had known..."

"You couldn't have known," Dani mumbled as she turned to go out the gate into the street.

When Dani told Eliel what she had learned from Abigail, his face grew red, and he ran out of the house to the door of the forge. There he took up a hammer and a scrap of bronze and began mercilessly and aimlessly pounding it.

The noise brought his father, who looked at him from behind for a moment before speaking.

"What are you doing?"

Eliel jerked around to face Azel, and he threw the hammer and bronze to the packed-earth floor. The hammer bounced and clanged into some plates which had been hung to cool.

"What would make you do that?" Azel asked, apparently displeased at the abuse of his tools.

"My life is over!" Eliel shouted.

"It doesn't seem like you are dead."

"But I have no reason to live!"

Azel sighed.

"My son, whatever you have suffered, I assure you, your life will continue."

"Not as I wish it would!"

"What happened?"

"Sela has been taken into the house of the king! Into the women's house, as the king's concubine!"

Azel did not immediately answer on hearing this news.

"And my life will never be the same," Eliel continued.

"Well, that is indeed disappointing. Did she know you wanted to marry her?"

"No," Eliel admitted.

"So, the king likely took her into his household to protect and provide for her."

"I would have provided for her!"

"Yes, I do not doubt you would have made a good husband. Unfortunately, no one knew of your intentions, except for her father, and he can no longer pass that news along."

Eliel didn't respond, so Azel continued.

"If she has indeed been made the king's concubine, she is no longer available to you. You are young enough to find another you can love. Best to put her out of your mind."

Eliel struck the anvil with his fist and uttered a low, grieving moan.

Azel went over and put his arms around Eliel.

"You are strong; one of the king's mighty men. You will find fathers eager to give their daughters to you."

Eliel hung his head, but he no longer shouted desperate, grieving nonsense.

Azel stayed with him, and they continued talking as the sun sank below the western horizon and the forge was illuminated only by the orange light of the furnace.

❧ 24 ❧

"I have a delivery of leeks and onions and lentils for the king," said a merchant who had appeared at the door of the house of women, holding a wooden box full of produce.

"Abigail!" called Sela, who had answered the door. "Food delivery!"

Abigail came downstairs to the main room of the house.

"Come with me," she said to the merchant, "Those need to go to the main house."

"I was told I could be paid on delivery,"

"Yes, that will be done at the main house as well."

Abigail led the man to the King's house. She nodded to the soldier on the portico, and he opened the door for them. The merchant, having never been inside a king's house looked about, taking in everything, as Abigail continued down a corridor.

"The kitchen is this way," Abigail said to fill the silence.

"It's a large house."

"Yes, this house serves as the king's throne room and headquarters as well as a place for entertaining."

The merchant seemed in awe.

Finally, they reached the kitchen, at the back of the house. The fragrance of a variety of fruits and spices filled the air, as a couple of cooks stood preparing food at a counter.

"Put everything here," Abigail said indicating a large wooden table at the center of the room.

"It will take me several trips to my wagon, but I need to be paid," the merchant said.

"Yes, while you go and get the next load, I will fetch the clerk who handles payments and bring him here."

The merchant didn't move immediately, and Abigail wondered if he didn't trust her, or even the king, but finally he did retrace his steps for another box of his crop.

By the time he returned bearing the second batch, Abigail had brought Jehoshaphat, the recently hired royal secretary, who managed the king's treasury. The merchant set the box on the table with the other one.

"You are Zerah?" Jehoshaphat asked as he looked at his papyrus ledger. "I have your bill at seven bars of silver."

"Seven?!" said Zerah, the merchant, loudly. "I said 10!"

Jehoshaphat looked at Abigail, then turned to the merchant.

"Seven is what you said when we ordered the food. Seven is what you will receive."

"You will give me 10 or I will take it all back!"

Jehoshaphat sighed and lowered his ledger. "Fine, the king will find another vendor who will honor his word."

The merchant sputtered and stewed for a moment before finally saying, "I cannot take it back. It may spoil before I can sell it elsewhere. I'll take the seven bars."

Jehoshaphat opened a leather bag attached to his belt and counted out seven small silver bars on the table.

"I keep careful records," Jehoshaphat said. "See that you do the same. You have more to bring in, right?"

The merchant scowled, "Yes."

"All right, see to it and I'll be here to count it all when you've finished."

The merchant left to retrieve the last of the produce from his wagon.

"Did he not remember?" Abigail asked.

"More likely he thought he could get more from the king by simply demanding it," Jehoshaphat smiled, "but my records don't lie, even if he does."

Abigail returned the smile.

Since they had moved to Hebron, Azel and Eliel had worked to make the home they acquired livable for the family. Adriel helped and together they had begun constructing a forge as soon as the living quarters were serviceable.

It was time for Adriel to begin his apprenticeship, so completing the forge had been vital. It was made more important by the fact that, while Azel and Eliel could supervise, their duties in the rapidly expanding army of Judah kept them away much of the time, so it had not been spoken yet, but Azel knew it would fall to Adriel to be in charge of the forge earlier than would ordinarily be the case.

As soon as the forge had been ready, they became busy. Because of Azel's proximity to King David and his nephews, the fledgling kingdom turned to them for a variety of needs. The army needed weapons, but also the royal family needed all kinds of bronze items, like bowls, spoons and cooking knives.

This meant that Adriel had received a crash course in the family trade, having an opportunity to work on a variety of projects. There was little need to promote their services, because they had all the work they could handle.

❧ 25 ❧

"Are you almost ready?"

Abigail's question hung in the air while Ahinoam wearily gathered herself and stood.

"I'll get the baby!" Sela said, and she quickly went to the crib and lifted the newborn, wrapped in blankets, and hurried to Ahinoam.

The birth of Ahinoam's baby had been without incident; the midwife enabling a safe and efficient birth, although because it was her first baby, the process took several hours.

Abigail had been there, and she knew her time would be coming soon. She was glad to be able to observe Ahinoam's birth experience as a preview of her own.

"Yes, I'm ready," Ahinoam answered finally. "I'm just so tired."

"We'll be with you to uphold you," Abigail said.

"Some help you'll be!" Ahinoam laughed, pointing to Abigail's expanding belly with its own promise of new life.

"Thank you, Sela," Ahinoam said, as she took the baby in her arms.

"Today is a big day," Abigail said with a smile. "It isn't everyday you get to present a king with his firstborn son!"

"No, it isn't. I suppose we'd better go," Ahinoam said, taking a deep breath and beginning to walk as Abigail and Sela followed.

All three wore their best jewel-encrusted tunics and colorful cloaks, with fragrant perfume in their hair, for this was to be a momentous occasion.

The throne room was already crowded with the top echelons of King David's government. His top generals were there, elders of the tribe and the courtiers who stood before the king advising and serving him in whatever he needed.

As Ahinoam, Abigail and Sela arrived, Benaiah met them dressed in his finest soldier's tunic and sword. He smiled and waved a hand to send them forward, then followed behind as their escort.

There were a great many people in the street, hoping to catch a glimpse of the infant prince, but most would not be able to see over the wall into the compound.

Ahinoam led the little procession, holding the baby securely in her arms. They entered the king's house through the double doors into the hallway and on to the throne room. The crowd parted to let them pass, men and women smiling as they gazed upon the crown prince for the first time.

At last, they stood before the king, sitting on his throne, attired in his royal-colored best. Ahinoam realized she hadn't stopped smiling since leaving the house of women. Then she remembered to bow. By the time she rose upright, David was up off his throne and taking her in his arms. He kissed her warmly, then kissed the baby.

The people applauded. Next, the king turned to make the official announcement: "Welcome my newborn son, Amnon, heir to the throne!"

The people standing around the walls of the relatively small room applauded again, some shouting their approval.

David led Ahinoam to a chair, which had been placed beside his throne and invited her to sit. She was very glad for the opportunity.

David then carefully took the baby from her and, with both hands, raised him above his head. Ahinoam thought she saw the boy smile, but maybe she only wished it. This was just such a grand moment she could not stop smiling herself.

The Eternal Kingdom

"Yahweh has blessed me beyond measure; to have a son who can succeed me! Let us all praise the Lord!" David then held Amnon close for a moment before handing him back to Ahinoam. She took him and cradled him in her arms.

"Let us now enjoy the feast that has been prepared for this occasion," David said.

The people began moving to the dining room. It took a while for everyone to find a place, sitting next to low tables as a steward directed them. The higher the rank, the closer they were seated to the head table.

The king, Ahinoam, Abigail, Sela and the king's closest advisors sat at the head table facing the others and servants worked to quickly serve large quantities of food and drink.

As Ahinoam took in the scene and basked in the attention she and her baby were receiving, she was thankful that she had not birthed this child during their nine years of exile, when they had no permanent home. Now they were settled, and she could raise her baby in a civilized fashion.

David filled a cup with wine and set it in front of her.

"Thank you for giving me a beautiful son!" he said, smiling.

"I'm honored to be your wife and be able to bless you."

He squeezed her hand and said, "And now, eat; the finest food our kingdom can provide."

"Thank you!"

"Your majesty," said the young maiden who had just filled the king's cup with wine. He couldn't help continuing to look at her. Her cheeks were naturally ruddy and her dark eyes reflected the light of the lamps on the table like silver.

"What is your name?"

"Haggith," she replied looking down.

"Thank you for your excellent service," David said.

She is so very beautiful!

Then he returned his attention to Ahinoam and his firstborn son.

❧ 26 ❧

"The king summons you."

"Now?"

"Yes," Benaiah answered.

Azel wondered what could be so urgent, but he laid down his hammer on the anvil and began washing the sweat off his arms.

"I will come right away," Azel told Benaiah.

Benaiah nodded and turned to leave the forge.

Azel was ushered into the room King David used for audiences, the largest room in what had been the head elder's home, where a number of men were always gathered. Benaiah had already returned and was standing on the king's right. A man Azel didn't know stood before the king, airing some grievance, he supposed.

It was a relatively simple room, with few of the ornate furnishings and architectural niceties of King Achish's throne room in Gath; no pillars with gilt capitals or polished stone floors. Instead, David's confidence and command of every situation alone demanded that those before him show him proper deference.

The one standing before the king completed his business, bowed and backed away.

"Azel, come," King David, smiling. Azel stepped forward.

"Your grace."

"I have an assignment for you," the king began. "It will not be without danger, so I advise you to take companions. Your strong, young son would be a good start. Perhaps his squad should go as well."

"All right," Azel said, wondering how much danger was ahead. "What is it you want me to do?"

"Because you are the son of a Benjamite, you may not be suspected if you travel to the north," David said, not needing to explain that the lands of the northern tribes were enemy territory during their civil war.

"I need you to go to Geshur," the king continued.

Azel cocked one eyebrow but said nothing. Geshur was a kingdom of nomadic people, some of whom had migrated south to live among Judaites, but their homeland was far to the north. They lived east of the Sea of Kinnereth in Bashan, not far from Syria, on the high plateau populated by cattle farmers. The king was right about danger; it was also a few miles north of Mahanaim, Ish-bosheth's capital.

"I want you to be my special envoy to King Talmai in Bethsaida. I wish to seal an alliance."

The young king motioned to a scribe sitting at a table nearby, who automatically handed him a slim scroll of papyrus. David then held it out to Azel.

"Take this with you and read it in his presence. I want to emphasize to you that my hope is that this alliance will show Ish-bosheth the futility of opposing me."

"Yes, my king," Azel replied.

"If anyone questions you, say you are from Mizpah, which is true, for you were born there, and you are merchants on a journey. Have your companions disguise themselves so they are not recognized as soldiers. I have arranged for several donkey loads of expensive gifts to accompany you, for the king and to support your cover story as merchants. Benaiah will show you where they will be tomorrow. Please begin your journey then."

"As you wish, your grace."

"And remember, this mission could be the means of ending our civil war and saving many lives."

Azel bowed and backed away with the scroll in his hand.

Azel first went immediately with Benaiah to see where he would be readying the donkeys with their burdens. Then he hurried to the camp of the army, where he found Eliel.

"Son, I am now an envoy of the king and I need an escort."

"Where are we going?"

"To Geshur."

Eliel's eyes widened. Neither father nor son needed to say it would be a hazardous journey.

"Have your squad accompany us. We must present ourselves as merchants from Mizpah so, while you must take weapons, you must not be recognizable as soldiers."

"When do we leave?"

"At first light tomorrow."

"I will let them know."

"How long will you be gone?"

"I can't say exactly. Geshur is not that far away, but since we are dealing with a transaction between kings, there may be ceremonies and protocols that must be observed. I'll have a detail of soldiers accompanying me, so it should be fine."

Dani's face didn't show that she was satisfied with Azel's answer, but she helped him and Eliel finish packing, making sure to include dates and salted, dried mutton, for the trip.

They were finally ready and Azel and Eliel led their donkeys out of the compound gate into the street. Dani, with little Elisheva on her hip, came and kissed them both as Adriel stood nearby.

"Be careful," she said.

"Always," Azel answered. "We'll be back soon; before you know it."

Azel and Eliel mounted their donkeys and began riding to meet the other soldiers who would accompany them.

❧ 27 ❧

Benaiah had done what the king said he would, so when
Azel, Eliel and the others arrived, the donkeys were where he
had said they would be and were loaded with gifts. There
were also donkeys there for the men to ride on their journey.

Each of the men wore normal clothing in neutral colors so
as not to draw attention, with their military garb tucked
inside their leather shoulder bags. They also hid their
weapons among the stuff borne by the donkeys, which they
would only reveal if necessary.

Azel did a cursory examination of the burden borne by the
donkey he would lead on the journey and saw that there was
fine Philistine pottery, jars of wine and olive oil, and several
household articles of gold and silver. There were also
supplies for their journey and even things they could barter
on their journey.

He looked at the other donkeys, knowing they carried
similar items of value, and marveled at the change in fortune
for David now that he was king.

This is the level at which kings negotiate.

Azel was experienced in bargaining in the marketplace for
small items, both as buyer and seller, but he marveled at such
a collection of riches in one place.

"Let's be going," Azel said as he and the others mounted.

Azel had not needed to think long about the route they
would take. Geshur was north of Israel's northern most tribe
east of the Jordan and the capital, Bethsaida, was on the
northern shore of the Lake of Kinnereth, just to the east of
where the river emptied into the lake. At another time they

might have gone east and forded the Jordan at Gilgal and then gone north through the territory of Gad and the eastern half of Manasseh, but that would take them through – or at least very near – Mahanaim, Ish-bosheth's capital. That route would also take them to Jabesh-Gilead, which was known to be loyal to the House of Saul.

Instead, they would take the mountain road north through Benjamin and Ephraim, then cross the Jordan north of the lake.

That would make more sense anyway, since they were posing as merchants from Mizpah in the heart of Benjamin. It would allow him and his son the opportunity to visit their uncle and cousins.

"We will be stopping in Mizpah for the night," Azel announced as they passed Gibeon, the site of the battle which had initiated the civil war.

"We are going into the city?" one of Eliel's fellow soldiers asked, and the others awaited the answer, concern showing on their faces.

"We have family there. They will give us lodging," Azel assured them. "And if you are merchants from Mizpah, you should have at least been there once."

When they arrived at Mizpah, they entered the gate into the city and the large group of travelers with their pack animals naturally attracted attention in the marketplace, with many eyes following them as they rode by. Azel steadfastly refused to interact with any of the townspeople as he led his men along the familiar streets to the walls of the family compound built by his great grandfather.

When they arrived, he rapped on the wooden gate and waited for a response.

Soon, the gate opened.

"Misha'el!"

"Uncle Azel!" Misha'el exclaimed as he stepped out of the gate. "And - are you Eliel?" Misha'el marveled.

"It's been a long time, cousin," Eliel said.

Misha'el rushed over and grasped Eliel's hand in greeting.

"Welcome! And who are your companions?"

"May we stay the night? If we can come inside, we will answer all your questions," Azel told him.

Misha'el cocked his head a bit at that, but said, "Yes, don't remain in the street any longer. We will get water for your animals.

Not wanting to be a burden, Azel provided food and wine from their provisions for the evening meal. It was a large gathering, for not only was Uncle Jacob's family present, including his two sons Elihu and Shallum, with their wives and children, but Azel's brother Jeriah's son, Misha'el, his mother, the widow Shelomith, and her daughter, Zaina, and her husband and children joined them as well. There was no room large enough to accommodate the two extended families and the visitors, so they improvised a table in the courtyard and Tzipporah, Jacob's wife, brought loaf after loaf of pita from the oven in the corner of the courtyard.

Azel greeted his sister-in-law, Shelomith, warmly when she arrived from Zaina's husband's home where she lived.

"Dani would love to see you," Azel told Shelomith. "She misses you very much."

"I have missed her for many years," Shelomith answered. "But even more now. The years brought sorrow to our family."

She no longer wore the black garments of a widow, Azel noted, but she was more subdued than he remembered.

Uncle Jacob, brother of Eldad, Azel's father, was the patriarch of the family now. He was very old and appeared to not really understand what was happening. He only ate a little and said even less as the younger family members talked and laughed.

Azel realized Eliel could barely remember his second cousins, Jacob's sons, and their families, so he was glad they could get reacquainted.

The men of Eliel's squad sat eating and talking by themselves, since they didn't know anyone.

"What brings you to Mizpah, Uncle Azel, besides the opportunity to bask in our company?" Misha'el laughed.

Azel looked around at the gathering, hoping no one there was an enthusiastic supporter of Ish-bosheth.

"We are on a trip to deliver goods for barter far to the north," Azel said, hoping it would be enough to deflect further questioning.

"You are a merchant now?"

"We still forge bronze, but I have other duties as well."

Misha'el looked around at the men who were accompanying his uncle and cousin.

"And you have quite an entourage."

"It's a long journey, and our cargo is valuable," Azel said. "There is safety in numbers."

Misha'el's eyes narrowed.

"There are indeed bandits on the road. Please be careful."

❦ 28 ❦

The next morning, after saying their goodbyes, the party headed out again, continuing north into the territory of the tribe of Ephraim. The men had broken up into small groups as they rode along, each carrying on its own conversation. Eliel rode with his father.

"What does the scroll say?"

Azel looked over at him surprised. He hadn't thought to read it, he had been so absorbed with the journey.

"I haven't read it. I guess I didn't think it was my place."

"But didn't the king tell you to read it to King Talmai?"

"Yes, of course," Azel said, and he reached into his leather shoulder bag and withdrew the papyrus document.

"I guess I should know what it says before I stand before the king."

Eliel smiled and nodded.

Azel scanned the document before selecting the parts to read aloud.

"'To the mighty and wise Talmai, King of Geshur, from David, King of Judah...' is how it begins," Azel said. "'Please accept these gifts brought by my messengers to seal our commitment as we have agreed...'" Azel looked up from the document. "Wait, there is already an agreement? I thought we were initiating the alliance."

Eliel shrugged and Azel kept reading.

"I am happy to accept your generous offer of your daughter's hand in marriage to seal our bond. Please have her come to me accompanied by my escort...'"

Azel looked up and again looked over at his son. "Does 'my escort' mean us?"

"It must."

"So, we are bearing the bride price?! And we will have another companion on the way home?"

"It would appear so."

The donkeys burdened with the fine gifts for the King of Geshur moved slowly on the mountain road and sometimes balked on the inclines, so the party had to stop for the night again, this time nowhere near a town, so as not to draw attention to themselves.

They required most of the next day to round the northern shore of the small inland sea, then cross the Jordan River above the sea. Bethsaida was just a little past the river's ford on the north bank of the sea.

Azel and the others had never been here and, with the sun low in the western sky, the walls of the city appeared kissed by gold. There were fishing boats in the lake, their white sails billowing in the golden light.

"We are envoys sent to meet with King Talmai," Azel said when they were stopped at the gate by soldiers. "We bring greetings from King David of Judah."

The soldiers looked at one another and the ranking soldier gave an order in a Canaanite tongue not too different from Hebrew, so Azel could tell he had sent the soldier to get confirmation from the palace.

"Dismount, men," Azel said as he climbed down from his own donkey. "It may be a while."

The weary men were glad to be able to stand on firm ground for a while, and several of them found dried figs or mutton from their bags to fill their stomachs while they passed the time.

It was nearly dark when they were ushered into the city by the soldiers who had met them at the gate, the king having confirmed they were expected.

"Tomorrow you will have your audience with the king," the soldier in charge of the guards at the gate assured them. "I'll take you to your quarters in the palace."

Azel wondered how they would ensure their valuable stuff would be protected, but he needn't have worried; the king's guard ushered them into luxurious accommodations inside the formidable walls of the king's palace, complete with secure stables for the animals.

As he settled into the comfort of the quarters he was given, he wondered how the transaction of the riches in the donkeys' saddlebags would be exchanged for the daughter of the king. He knew this was common practice – kings establishing an alliance by the giving of a daughter in marriage – but he had never been involved in the process.

As he drifted off to sleep, he decided King Talmai would know how he wanted to handle it. Azel must just give him due honor.

29

The next morning, the men took the opportunity of the king's accommodations to wash the dirt of their journey away and put on their military dress garments for the audience with the king.

Each man carried a heavy burden to lay before the king, which was only a fraction of everything they had brought with them, but it would be a symbolic offering until the rest could be transferred to the Geshurite monarch.

When the time came, members of the king's guard led them to the throne room, where they were ushered in and Azel immediately felt the curious eyes of Geshur's noblemen taking measure of them.

Then they stood before the king. King Talmai was in his forties, Azel guessed, as he had the beginnings of gray at his temples. Azel thought what he would not say: this king's palace was not as opulent as the one in Gath, but at this moment, he was focused on the important task he had been assigned by his own king.

The king smiled and spread his arms to welcome the envoys from the new kingdom to his south.

Azel stepped forward.

"Welcome to Geshur," King Talmai began. "I have heard great things about your king. David is indeed a great man; a warrior and leader of men."

"We are flattered, your majesty," Azel responded, bowing.

"When King David made the overture of alliance, I was glad. Each of us has enemies uncomfortably close."

Azel nodded, understanding that he meant Syria immediately to the north of Geshur, but unsure if he referred to Ish-bosheth or the Philistines as David's enemy.

"We have brought gifts with which to seal our agreement," Azel said, stretching out his arms, and on cue, his men brought their burdens forward and set them before the king. "There is much more than we could carry before you. We have left it with your steward," Azel said. Then he drew the papyrus scroll from his leather bag.

"My king has commanded me to read this document in your presence."

Azel then proceeded to read the single page of papyrus as the king listened politely, but Azel could see that nothing in the document surprised him.

"Thank you for that message and for the king's generosity." Talmai said when Azel was done. "Please give the message to my scribe for recording."

Azel's eye was caught by a man off to the side with his hand out. He gave him the scroll.

"Now, let me introduce you to my little jewel, my daughter, Maacah." Talmai raised his hand and a courtier obeyed the unspoken command, opening a side door. Through it came a young woman, dressed in the most ornate and luxurious tunic and cloak Azel had ever seen. As she entered the throne room a fragrant cloud of perfume accompanied her. Her nose and mouth were veiled and her head was covered, allowing only dark eyes to be seen. Strings of jewels sparkled from around her neck and sown to her garments.

The effect is most enthralling, Azel thought, having never seen clothing quite so extravagant.

"My daughter will seal our compact by becoming David's wife. You and your men will now be her guardians and surety on the journey to Hebron," Talmai said. He lowered his eyes and his voice as he continued. "I know I don't need to tell you how serious this responsibility is."

"No, your majesty. We can guarantee that no harm will come to your daughter."

What was not mentioned by Talmai was that quite an entourage was to accompany his daughter. It turned out she would ride in a wheeled, covered sedan with colorful, sheer curtains, pulled by two donkeys. Inside the wagon, two young handmaidens rode with her.

But that was not all; a detachment of soldiers rode with them as well.

Talmai is taking nothing for granted, Azel thought.

The extra people were not a problem however, for they were very well supplied. The donkeys which had borne the riches comprising King David's bride price, were loaded again with provisions for the journey from King Talmai's storehouses. Azel was glad, for he hadn't known how he would provide adequately for a princess on her way to marry a king.

"Is this how you imagined this trip?" Eliel asked his father as they rode along slow enough to match the wagon and the loaded donkeys.

"Not at all," Azel said. "Not at all."

They had been riding for some time, and were somewhere north of the ruins of Shiloh, when they were startled by the appearance of several men with weapons drawn. Azel looked around and saw that they were surrounded by perhaps 20 armed men, who came out from behind rocks and trees. They looked dirty and bedraggled, but that might only make them desperate – and dangerous.

"Stop and hand over your valuables!" ordered the man standing directly in front of Azel's donkey, brandishing a spear. Azel stole a look at Eliel, whose hand was already on the pommel of his sword under his cloak. Azel hoped the others were stealthily accessing their weapons as well.

"Who makes these demands!" Azel shouted. "Ours is an official mission."

"If you don't hand over your stuff, you'll be dead and then it won't matter who we are," the rough man said.

"What is the meaning of this?! Why have we stopped!"

It was Maacah, the king's daughter, sticking her head out of the wagon's curtains.

Oh dear, Azel thought. *What now?*

"What have we here?" asked the leader of the bandits.

"Would you risk the anger of King Talmai of Geshur?" Azel said quickly.

"So, we have a queen?" the ringleader said looking at his fellow bandits, smiling broadly. "She must be traveling with great wealth!"

"I am not a queen – yet," Maacah said loudly. "I am a princess; daughter of the king of Geshur and betrothed to King David of Judah. If anything should happen to me, you risk his wrath as well!"

The leader's smile froze. "David?"

"The longer you stay here, impeding my progress, the more likely it is you will incur the wrath of TWO kings and the armies of TWO COUNTRIES!"

The leader's face went white at that, and he turned to his men, and said, "Let them go. There will be other travelers on the road." The men disappeared into the trees and rocks just as quickly as they had appeared, and Azel and his group were left alone.

Azel looked back at Maacah, who returned his look for a moment with what appeared to Azel to be the slightest of self-assured smiles. She then disappeared behind the curtains of her wagon. Azel looked over at Eliel, who gave him a bemused smile and a shrug.

"Forward," Azel called loudly, and the procession continued southward.

❦ 30 ❦

There were soldiers on the walls of Hebron who saw the procession approaching and relayed word to David's throne, so that by the time Azel led the soldiers and the luxurious sedan carrying the princess through the city gate, there were people on either side of the street, watching curiously. Maacah obliged them by throwing back the colorful curtains, revealing her and her maids. She waved to them and they waved back tentatively.

Azel and Eliel, riding at the head of the entourage, guided them to the king's house, where word of their arrival had preceded them and members of the king's personal guard, three on each side stood with spears crossed above the entrance of the gate, forming an impromptu archway for the princess to pass under.

Some of the soldiers from Geshur helped Maacah down from the wagon and went with her to the entrance of the compound, with the highest-ranking soldier leading the way.

Azel dismounted and fell in beside the officer ahead of the princess, so he could make the introductions.

Awaiting them inside the gate was the king, wearing his crown and a purple cloak, a smile on his face. Beside him was Benaiah, commander of his personal guard and his two wives, Ahinoam and Abigail.

"His majesty, King David," Azel began, "May I present Princess Maacah of Geshur."

Maacah, who had removed her veil, appeared none the worse for wear from the journey, her face radiant with a beautiful smile as she bowed before David.

He also bowed and took her hand in his. "Welcome, Maacah. I'm so glad to meet you. I know you must be weary after your journey."

"It is my privilege to become your wife to seal your alliance with my father," she said dipping her head again. "Your men have taken very good care of me, so that I am hardly weary at all."

"Come and I will show you to your quarters. We have prepared space for you. Ours is a new kingdom and I fear it will not be as grand as that to which you are accustomed. We are daily working to improve things."

"I do not expect special treatment. I am your servant."

Azel knew that even though she spoke of being a servant, this addition to the house of women was a momentous thing. His two other wives, while being very capable and strong, had not been princesses.

David led the way and Ahinoam and Abigail accompanied them as they went to the house of women.

Meanwhile, the officer from Geshur gave an order to his men to fetch the considerable baggage that they had brought on the pack mules from Geshur.

Azel hoped there would be room for it all.

Because she was a princess, and because David was now a king, the marriage ceremony for Maacah was very different from the rustic vows spoken in the wilderness by Ahinoam and Abigail.

Abiathar the priest, the last of the house of Eli, officiated. Once he had given his blessing, those in attendance went inside where food was provided, served by maidens, some of whom were concubines of the king like Sela.

Later, after the guests had departed, David took Maacah to his bed chamber, where she indeed became his wife.

In the kitchen, the royal tableware was washed and put away. Some of the staff had already left, but Haggith was still finishing with some of the bronze platters which needed drying. She brushed a lock of her shiny, deep black hair from her face and kept wiping the platter.

It is such a privilege to work in the royal house, she thought, even though there were some in her village who considered such work beneath her. She was the daughter of an elder after all, but it was a small village in the south of Judah, almost to Beer-sheva.

To Haggith, any service was noble. She would do anything for the king. He was one of those men who inspired loyalty in many people, both men and women.

He is so dashing and brave and strong!

King Ish-bosheth roared in anger before wadding up and throwing the papyrus at the messenger who stood before him, causing him to flinch and back away.

"How dare David make an alliance with the kingdom of Geshur so close to our capital!" Ish-bosheth shouted. "Abner, how could he?"

Abner was standing off to one side and didn't immediately respond. The development of David's alliance with King Talmai of Geshur had blindsided him. He kicked himself for not seeing it coming.

David had always been a brilliant battlefield tactician. Now he was showing his skill in international relations. By forming this alliance, David had effectively boxed in Abner – and King Ish-bosheth – between the two kingdoms. They were at war with Judah to the south; would they now have to defend their northern border as well?

King Talmai's capital of Bethsaida was no more than 65 miles from Mahanaim; within easy striking distance of Abner's – and Ish-bosheth's – capital.

"It's not ideal," Abner said finally, "but we have no quarrel with Geshur. Perhaps I should make a trip to Bethsaida to shore up relations."

"See that you do!" Ish-bosheth said, with uncharacteristic decisiveness.

Abner scowled but, with the messenger present, didn't respond to the weak-willed king he had installed.

Abigail did her best to welcome Maacah into the house of women, but she and Ahinoam admitted to one another they didn't know how to treat a princess.

While it was obvious to Abigail that the accommodations of the women's house were more rustic than that to which she was accustomed, Maacah didn't complain, even with sideways comments. Abigail supposed she knew she was doing her duty by being in Hebron, married to a man she didn't know and about whom she had known little.

It took some time, but eventually they all grew comfortable around each other. Maacah seemed sincere when she made over Abigail's obviously eight-month-pregnant belly.

There were cultural differences as well as differences of station, since Maacah was not a Hebrew. It was true that the Geshurites, though based to the north of the tribe of Reuben, had also found places to settle within Judah, so Maacah was not a complete stranger to Hebrew culture and religion.

For Abigail, another wife meant more to manage, with responsibilities to be parceled out among the women and, as they grew, their children. They did have maids which aided them, but even though they were the wives and concubines of a king, their days were not spent in idleness.

Abigail wondered how many other wives and concubines would be added. Would each political alliance add a resident to their house?

❧ 31 ❧

Adriel was becoming accustomed to working in the forge, often alone, as it turned out. Eliel spent most of his time with the army, where he commanded a squad, and his father, Azel, was occupied more and more with matters of the royal court.

They had just returned from a trip together, but being back did not mean they would all be at home. The king was taking more and more of Azel's time, so he saw his father in the evening, when he wasn't off on some diplomatic mission.

Adriel, now 14, could feel his body toughening as he performed the hot, difficult work of bending metal to his will. Soon he hoped to be as strong as his father and his brother.

As he withdrew red-hot bronze from the forge and plunged it in water to set its shape, his mother appeared.

"Adriel," Dani began, "will you stop for supper soon?"

"Yes, mother. I have just a little more to do and I can stop."

"Let me see what you are working on."

He drew the tongs from the water and held up the bright bronze platter, which reflected the light from the forge beautifully, both because it was wet and because of its smooth, mirror-like surface.

"It's beautiful, son. You have a real talent for making beautiful things."

"Thank you, mother. I just wish I was a good as father at selling our wares."

"Don't worry, you will improve with experience. Your work is so beautiful, it may very well sell itself."

"That would be fine with me," Adriel laughed. "I much prefer the forge to the marketplace."

Dani put her arm around her young son, who was now as tall as she, but not as tall as he likely would be.

"Come to supper when you are ready. 'Sheva is hungry."

"Ha! When is she not?" he laughed. "I'll be there right away."

Dani left and Adriel turned his attention to his project, intending to make quick work of it so he could go enjoy his mother's wonderful cooking.

He very much enjoyed the stability they had now in Hebron. He could barely remember their home in Gibeah, eleven years ago now. For most of his life they were on the run. Except for a year and a half in Ziklag, they had never known where they would be sleeping any given moment.

I hope we don't move again for a long time.

❦ 32 ❦

"A-a-a-augh!"

Abigail's cry went from a groan to a scream as the midwife called, "Push! Push!"

She didn't know how much longer she could push. The contractions had been coming for hours now, but it seemed she was no closer to birthing the baby.

She fell back when the contraction released, breathing hard, knowing that another would be coming soon, as they had been coming closer and closer together.

Ahinoam held her hand as Abigail endured each contraction. The midwife was showing her own signs of weariness, even as she assured Abigail that first babies often took their time coming.

The expected next contraction came and Abigail's grip on Ahinoam's hand turned to iron again. Ahinoam dabbed Abigail's forehead with a cloth, vainly wiping away the perspiration which would only be replaced by more in moments.

Abigail's cries could be heard all over the house and the other women tried to go about their business, though their faces showed their concern.

Sela finally could take no more and she went to the door of Abigail's bedroom and looked inside. She had good reason to be interested, for her own belly was swelling with another potential child of the king.

She had known she was pregnant for some time, but had only recently told Abigail, who had been her protector ever since they had been taken from Ziklag by the Amalekites.

She didn't know a lot about birthing a baby, but it seemed to her that the process had been going on for an abnormally long time. As she looked in the door, she didn't see much of a difference since the last time she had peeked.

Then, suddenly, things changed. Ahinoam shrieked and stood, looking down at Abigail and the midwife stood as well. She went to Abigail's head and shouted, "Water! We need water!"

Sela wasted no time but ran to the house's water supply, which was kept in several large clay jars. She hurriedly dipped a smaller clay pot of water from the supply and ran it back to the room.

Ahinoam met her at the door.

"Thank you, Sela!" she said, turning to take the water to the midwife.

The midwife took a handful of water and threw it in Abigail's face. Abigail stirred and the midwife threw more water and Abigail finally moaned and opened her eyes.

"You must stay alert," the midwife said. "I sense that the baby is turned and that's why it's having trouble."

Ahinoam looked alarmed. Sela knew that her delivery had been a breeze, but she also knew that women died in childbirth, and she was suddenly gripped by fear.

God help her!

As Sela watched, the midwife reached inside Abigail's pelvis, her hand rotating, as if turning clay on a wheel. Sela realized she was attempting to reposition the baby. She looked at Abigail and saw she might be about to faint.

Ahinoam saw it too, so she threw another handful of water in Abigail's face.

Sela prayed silently that Yahweh would cause the baby to come soon and that Abigail would be all right. Her labor had already been going about 12 hours and it was now getting dark outside.

❦

After another six hours, the baby finally passed through the birth canal. Ahinoam's concentration had been on Abigail, but now she turned her attention to the baby, which she could see was a boy. The midwife held him upside down to drain fluid from his windpipe and gave him a sharp smack on his bottom, but he didn't cry.

Ahinoam looked at the midwife and then over at Sela, whose sleepless eyes were wide. Once again, the midwife slapped the baby's backside and finally, he cried.

It was a soft, weak sound, but it was the sound of life.

Ahinoam looked at Abigail and saw she was smiling but was too weak to lift her head.

"Look, Abigail," Ahinoam said. "You have a son!"

In the weeks that followed, Sela stepped up to help Abigail, taking on some of the duties she was responsible for. She ran the household, so Abigail's attention to her new baby left an unanticipated vacuum.

So many things you don't miss until they are gone, Sela thought, as she carried out the task of placing a food order for the king's table, guided by Abgail's instructions.

Sela was determined to relieve Abigail as much as possible so she could focus on the baby, whom she had named "Daniel." He was taking much of her time as she nursed him, because he seemed weak and was sick more often than seemed normal to Sela.

33

"Pound it harder!"

Adriel clenched his teeth and tried to obey his father's command. Azel's arms were hardened by years in the forge, but Adriel did not yet possess that kind of strength; not like his father or his older brother for that matter.

He gripped the handle of the hammer and pounded for all he was worth.

"That's better," Azel said, "but you must also be purposeful. You must know where to strike the metal so it bends to the shape you want for it."

Adriel frowned. There was so much to remember. Strike the hot metal harder, but be sure to strike in the right place. Make sure the metal is hot enough, but not so hot that you pound through it.

Will I ever learn?

As if sensing his thoughts, his father added, "In time, it will become second nature. You won't have to think about it. That's the way it is with learning any skill. At first there is so much to think about and learn to do, but then one day you will realize you worked all day and didn't have to think about what you were doing. It will be part of you."

"I look forward to that day," Adriel said, wiping sweat from his forehead to keep the salty perspiration from flowing down into his eyes.

"Son, the responsibility of the forge will fall to you sooner than it usually would. The king wants me to be one of his emissaries and Eliel is one of the king's Mighty Men. We will help when we are able, but there will be times when you will be the one in charge of seeing that the work gets done.

Adriel hadn't thought of that. Though he was 14, it seemed he had been officially declared a man only a few months ago at his thirteenth birthday. With his father and brother having such important responsibilities, he would often be the man of the house; provider and protector of his mother and little sister.

He gripped the hammer once again and clenched his muscles, striking the glowing metal once again with greater power and accuracy.

While her husband and son were in the forge, Dani nursed little Elisheva and thought about how she would arrange the house. She lacked much that was needed to outfit the new household, they had lost so much to the destruction of the Amalekites at Ziklag.

They had recovered some of it and much more when Azel and the rest of David's men had rescued her and Adriel, along with all the women and children of David's band and the residents of other Philistine towns as well.

With Azel's new position as advisor to and envoy for the king, they needed a home fitting for their new status. She was enjoying the project.

❦ 34 ❦

The days and weeks passed rapidly, with much to be done to build a kingdom where none had been. So, when Maacah asked to see the king, it didn't happen immediately.

When Benaiah finally came and said David was asking for her, Maacah was glad she could finally share her joyous news.

She followed Benaiah through the double doors into the main house and down the short hallway to the double doors which led to the throne room.

Once inside, she could see that there were many people present. Advisors and officers of the army and more.

"Please sit here," Benaiah said, "He will call you."

Maacah just nodded and sat where she was told. She was thankful she didn't have to wait too long.

"Maacah, wife to the king," called out a royal clerk.

Maacah walked forward, not the least intimidated by the men watching her, no doubt wondering about her business.

"My dear, to what do I owe the pleasure of your appearance before me today?" asked King David.

"I have news which I hope you will find agreeable. I have learned that I am to have a child."

"A child! What a blessing!" the king said as he rose from the throne and came down the steps to embrace her.

"I pray I may give you a son," Maacah said.

"The child will be cherished, whoever it is," David smiled as he kissed her on the forehead.

"Thank you, your grace."

"Men! Rejoice with me. I am to be a father once more!"

The men standing around the room applauded.

Maacah smiled up into the face of the father on her child.

❦ 35 ❦

Mara's back hurt. She had just brought a pot of water from the well in Mahanaim's marketplace, carrying it on her head. It was a task she performed twice a day, but she was also responsible for caring for her poor, crippled son, Mephibosheth. Lifting him was getting more difficult by the day as he grew.

Being sister-in-law to King Ish-bosheth should have made her life easier, but she had very little help. Her nanny had abandoned her some time ago and the kingdom couldn't afford to hire additional help.

Ziba was faithful, though. He had been her husband Jonathan's servant, and he continued to be of help to her, but his time was split between her and her son, Ahinoam, the king's mother, and Rizpah, concubine to the late King Saul.

She opened the gate into the family compound which Abner had arranged for them and started toward the small home allotted to her and Mephibosheth.

Then she stopped, because she heard loud arguing coming from the king's quarters.

"Just what would you have me do?!"

Abner glared at his kinsman, Shimei, who had accused him of dereliction because the war with Judah was not going well.

"Can you not unite the tribes to fight?" Shimei asked. "Your generals limp along with mostly Benjamites, when there are ten other tribes who should stand by your side!"

Abner knew that Shimei had been a courtier of Saul when he was very young and still nursed an exaggerated sense of self-importance. Still in his thirties, he always wore clothes that were beyond his means and made a pest of himself cozying up to power. Abner tolerated him because he was both his and his cousin Saul's relative.

"If it was that easy, don't you think I would have done it?" Abner growled. "The tribes each go their own way with their own agendas. It's akin to trying to force goats to stand in a queue. I need help, but the king is worthless. He does not project authority or command allegiance."

"Ish-bosheth has always been the least of Saul's sons," Shimei admitted. "If only Jonathan was still with us. He was a charismatic leader indeed."

"Why don't YOU represent me – and the king – to the other tribes?" Abner asked, only now thinking of it.

"Uh, I suppose I could."

Abner smiled inwardly, knowing that his kinsman might shrink from real responsibility.

Maybe that will shut him up.

While Mara was listening, the king's two generals, Rekab and Ba'anah, had entered the courtyard as well and had heard most of the exchange. Mara hurried away, not wanting to get caught eavesdropping, but the generals weren't interested in her. They climbed the steps to the king's quarters and knocked.

Mara didn't wait to see what would happen next.

❧ 36 ❧

Tonight's meal was ordinary. It was just the royal family.

David sat at the head table as usual, surrounded by his wives and his two nephews, Joab and Abishai. Often others dined at the king's table: diplomats from far-away lands, elders of the tribes, officials being honored.

But tonight, it was just family. David looked around at each of them. He loved each of them in their own way.

Ahinoam ate slowly, pausing periodically to nurse little Amnon. He was growing aware of his surroundings, able to sit up and "talk," or what a six-month-old could do.

Abigail sat beside her on a pillow. Sela had volunteered to watch Daniel so she could attend without worrying with him.

Beside her sat Maacah, who had also just revealed she was also pregnant. The royal family was growing rapidly.

The maidens entered the dining room, bringing another course and refilling the wine cups.

"Thank you, Haggith," he said, when she refilled his cup.

"Your majesty."

The girl smiled and blushed as she said it and David smiled back. He already knew her father, an elder of the tribe.

I must get to know her better, he thought.

No one was more surprised than Haggith when David asked her to become his fourth wife; fifth if you counted Michal, Saul's daughter, who had been taken from him.

Her mother and father were also surprised and honored. He was an elder in the tribe of Judah, but their village was small and far to the south of Hebron, almost to Beer-sheva.

The Eternal Kingdom

When Haggith had gone to the city of Hebron to serve in the royal household, they had never dreamed of this.

Haggith's mother and her circle of friends worked to prepare the dress that Haggith would wear on the day she would wed the king. Haggith could see their envious looks at her mother, even as they celebrated the family's good fortune.

Haggith had returned home to prepare for the wedding, set for just 10 days from now. It was not much time to weave the linen and cut and sew a dress fit for wedding a king, then festoon it with jewels, to make the best impression possible.

She tried to imagine the life she would have as one of the royal wives, being served instead of serving; lying in the arms of the handsome king, instead of demurely pouring his wine.

To be a royal princess was something she had not even spent time dreaming of. She was counting the days, even as she busied herself with many chores in preparation.

To Haggith, her wedding day seemed like a dream.

Going from being a servant girl to the wife of a king was more than she would ever have hoped. After the ceremony and the feast after, the king took her to his chamber where they became intimately known to one another.

She was overwhelmed with all that had happened, and it was early the next morning when Benaiah accompanied her from the king's chamber to the women's house.

"Welcome, dear," Abigail said with a smile. "Your things have already been delivered and are in your room, ready for you to arrange them to your liking. Later we can talk about the chores you would like to have assigned to you."

"Thank you," Haggith said, realizing she had only begun to learn what new things to which she would need to adjust.

"Let me show you your room and you can begin getting settled, then we'll call when the food is ready."

Haggith nodded and followed Abigail up the stairs.

❧ 37 ❧

The sun was coming up at the palace of Gath. King Achish strolled through the garden before going to his throne.

The monarch's white hair shone when the rising sun caught it. His bones creaked as he walked on the polished stone floors as he entered the throne room.

His recording scribe, already there, bowed upon seeing the king. Achish wordlessly dipped his head. The scribe continued arranging papyrus on his desk as the king went to the throne, preparing for the day's duties.

Achish was unsettled because ordinarily at this time of year he would be out with the army, but the political situation in Israel required that he hold off.

He had promised David he would not interfere with his new kingdom of Judah as along as he was at war with the northern tribes of Israel. Time would tell how that would turn out, but Achish assumed David would make quick work of the weak son of Saul, Ish-bosheth.

Achish knew David was always several steps ahead of his enemies. How else could he have escaped capture by the wily Saul for seven years before seeking sanctuary in Gath?

Since becoming king in Hebron, David had maintained ties to Ziklag, the city Achish had given him, which wasn't a concern to Achish. He had actually sent workmen to help David's men rebuild after its destruction.

For now, he would need to be patient; as hard as that was.

Haggith was still basking in the glow of being the wife of the king and a royal family member rather than a servant, when she heard surprising news.

"Haggith, you may have to share your room," Abigail told her. David is planning to marry again."

"What? Who?"

"A woman of the tribe of Manasseh on the other side of the Jordan River. I don't know her name yet."

Haggith considered this and decided it would be best to be agreeable. "I can easily accommodate another in my room."

"I'm sorry to spring this on you so soon after your own marriage, but I have to manage these developments as they come. David is staking out territory near the house of Saul."

"Don't give it another thought. When will she arrive?"

"I don't know yet; probably in the next couple of weeks.

"I will begin arranging my things to make room."

Abitail felt scared, but her parents were excited for her to be marrying the dashing King David. Her father was an elder in a town near to Ish-bosheth's capital in Mahanaim.

At age 16, she was scared for several reasons. First, she had never been on the other side of the Jordan River. Her father and brother had travelled to Gibeon to worship at the Lord's Tent, but as a girl, she was not expected to go.

Second, Ish-bosheth's kingdom was in a civil war with the Judah, and her marriage to David could provoke Ish-bosheth, or worse, Abner. Abner was the true power behind the throne; even she knew that, even though she was a girl and no one talked to her about politics.

Third, she feared getting married enough, but marrying a king was overwhelming. Her mother joyfully made preparations, with which she helped, but a cloud remained.

The days were going by too rapidly, and she knew she would soon make the journey to Hebron to be the wife of a man twice her age whom she had never met and did not love.

❧ 38 ☙

After jabbing the bronze-clad butt of his spear into the soft ground so it would stand upright, Adino sat down on the dirt, then lay back, exhausted. He was back in camp after yet another battle with the forces of the northern tribes.

The war had continued for over a year. David's army of Judah had again been victorious. How much longer could this war continue, when the northern tribes failed at every turn?

If David's 30 "Mighty Men" were the tip of the spear, "the Three," which Adino led, was its sharpened point.

"General, you are needed in the command tent."

Adino, whose given name was Josheb-bassabeth, looked at the messenger, who had already left, presumably to deliver the same message to others.

With some effort, he roused and sat up, then planted one muscular hand on the earth to support him as he rose to once again answer the call of duty.

Adino entered the large command tent which was always erected in the center of camp and saw that many of the other officers were already there.

Among them were members of "The Thirty" Mighty Men, each of whom commanded their own units.

Joab, commander of David's armies, was impatient to begin so, after Adino's arrival, he started his presentation.

"The time has come for us to finish the job we began at Gibeon. King Ish-bosheth and the House of Saul have designated us as their enemy and Abner has not relented despite repeated losses.

"I believe this next battle will finish their ability to fight. I will lead our force to Gilgal, which has been the gathering place for Israel's armies for generations. It was Saul's staging ground for training and equipping his forces. Abner will not be able to let our presence there stand. He will attack. Here is how we will trap them and end this war."

Adino listened as Joab continued laying out the details of a plan that was genius in its simplicity and was certain to be successful. He could see the fingerprints of the king on the plan. Since Joab was the king's nephew, they were usually in sync concerning strategy.

"We march to Gilgal the day-after-tomorrow at first light," Joab concluded. "Any questions?"

None were required. Adino knew the mission was clear.

Eliel and his unit marched with the unit led by Eliam. They held similar rank among "The Thirty" and so they commanded elite fighters; men who were veterans, some of whom had served with David since the days of exile in Ziklag. These men had no illusions about the danger they would face, but they had ultimate confidence in their commanders.

They were marching loosely, not in rigid ranks. Eliel figured Gilgal was about 50 miles from Hebron north and east toward the Jordan River. It would take a day to travel half the distance. Then they would continue through the night, so their arrival would be unlikely to be found out by Abner.

"Have you made this trek before?" Uriah asked, having fallen in beside Eliel at the head of his unit.

"Never exactly like this," Eliel answered. "We criss-crossed this country many times during our exile, when Saul was determined to kill us all, but we stayed away from places Saul was likely to be, like Gilgal."

"I'm glad Abner will have a march of his own, once word reaches him we have arrived on his doorstep."

"Yes, the rest will do us good," Eliel smiled.

❦ 39 ❦

"General, the army of David is in Gilgal."

The messenger spoke fearfully. Abner was uncertain if his fear was because of anticipation of his reaction to the news or the messenger's own foreboding about the formidable force David would inevitably put into the field.

"They are there now?"

"Yes, general."

"Have you informed General Ba'anah?"

"No, I came straight to you."

"Alright, go and find General Ba'anah and tell him to inform the men we will march at daybreak, then have him and his brother, General Rekab, come to the throne room."

The messenger bowed and left Abner and Ish-bosheth alone. Ish-bosheth's face was ashen.

"Will they invade across the river?" the king asked, unable to completely still the tremor in his voice.

"Who can say? We will be ready in any event. It may be that they intend to draw us across the river. I will send scouts to bring word of their exact position."

Abner looked at the king, who stared vacantly. There could hardly be more difference between him and the warrior who sat on the throne of Judah. Ish-bosheth's only value was that he was the last living son of Saul, other than the children of Saul's concubine. Abner would make all the decisions. He was alone in that, and he felt that loneliness acutely now.

The camp was well established since the army of Judah had arrived in Gilgal two days ago. Adino had just left the command tent with orders for his cohort, which consisted of perhaps 1,000 men.

"Gather the officers," he said to his second in command. The man returned a look that said he knew they would soon be moving. He left to spread the word.

It only took a few minutes for the 10 commanders of 100 to appear in the center of the section of the encampment.

"Men, our scouts have indicated that news of our presence in Gilgal has reached King Ish-bosheth. Their army is on the march. We have been tasked with defending the route from the North. We will march in two hours. Relay this to your men."

Adino saw that the officers didn't immediately move to carry out the order.

"You are dismissed."

"Begging your pardon, sir," one of the men said, looking sideways at the others. "Aren't they most likely to come across the Jordan from the East?"

Adino scanned the faces of the men before him and saw the same question in each of their eyes.

"We have our orders. If you're concerned about being left out of the fight, remember there are other places to cross the Jordan. Besides, when the battle is joined, if there is no fighting where we are, our task will be reinforce the main body to prevent Abner and his army from crossing the river again. We must be ready for a fast march to the East."

"Yes, sir," the man answered.

Adino saw that this answer satisfied them. The men turned on their heels, each to inform his unit of the plan.

Eliel led his men forward under the command of Eleazar, a member of "The Three," along with Shammah and Adino. They had been ordered to the East along with Shammah's men to meet Abner's force which they expected to cross the river. They would be ready with more than 2,000 men.

Joab's reasoning had been that Abner would want to cross the Jordan at Gilgal because it was in the territory of Benjamin. Accordingly, he was positioning the bulk of his forces there, but Eliel knew that Adino had taken 1,000 men to the North as well, in the unlikely event that Abner crossed the river to the North and came at Gilgal over land.

It was downhill as they marched toward the river. A trumpet sounded, and the men stopped. Messengers came back through the ranks giving the word of their next moves.

"Take your unit south and take the position at that crest above the river," one messenger said to Eliel, pointing to a promontory that dropped off quickly toward the river.

Eliel nodded to him as he continued on to other units.

"Men, we are to array on that crest which is above the river," Eliel shouted to the men in his command. "We will be able to observe them crossing the river from there."

Eliel's men positioned themselves on the crest in a double line where they were able to see the river. Eliel realized his unit was the very end of the right flank of the battle line. He went to the men at the right-most end of his unit of 100.

"You men! We are the right flank of the battle line. Position two squads to face south, in case they have crossed below us."

Eliel knew it would be unlikely Abner would have taken his army from far to the North in Mahanaim and crossed south of Gilgal. It would add a day to their march. Still, it was wise to be prepared for anything.

Eliel returned to the center of his unit's battle line and looked toward the river. The Jordan cut a deep valley into the earth, and it was hot at this elevation. Eliel had to wipe sweat from his eyes from time to time. They couldn't really see much of the river from here, because dense trees and undergrowth lined its banks.

Now they would simply wait. Some of the men sat on the ground in their ranks and set about checking their weapons.

❦ 40 ❦

"They're coming!"

The word of a scout rang out as he ran down the battle line from the left flank to the right.

Eliel's unit was therefore the last to get the word. His men roused from where they had been sitting without being ordered to do so. Eliel squinted into the haze before them. He thought he detected movement among the trees on the riverbank. There had been no order yet, and so he waited.

Gradually, Eliel saw men emerge from the dense growth at the river and hastily form a battle line.

It would begin soon.

"Steady, men. Steady," he called out.

Joab sat on his donkey at the center of the battle line, among troops commanded by his brother, Abishai, watching Abner's force get across the river and into formation. He could have ordered his men to charge and engage them before they all got across the river, which would have given them a great advantage. The reason he didn't was that these men were all descendants of Israel like his own men. They would have a fair fight.

After a half hour of watching Abner's force take their positions, Joab spotted Abner himself, riding a donkey, accompanied by one of his generals.

His face flushed red as he saw the man who had killed his brother.

Someday I will have satisfaction.

Joab decided they had waited long enough.

"Forward!" he shouted. A trumpet sounded near him and others answered, each father away that the last. Joab spurred his donkey forward and the battle line of the army of Judah started marching down the slope toward the river to meet the army of Israel.

Adino's 1,000 men were north of the main body, awaiting an attack no one expected, but was a possibility they also couldn't afford to ignore.

They found a place in a clearing where they could sit under the trees while they waited, but could see anyone emerge from the thicket on the other side while they were still some distance away.

Adino had already designated a messenger to relay the word that Abner had come from the North in the unlikely event that is what actually happened.

Then another messenger came with word that Abner had indeed crossed at Gilgal and Joab and the main force was engaging them there.

"Men, the battle is joined to the South. We must go and join our brothers."

The men rose from the places they had been sitting, gathered their equipment and began forming ranks for the march south.

Adino mounted his donkey which had been contentedly munching the soft grass which was plentiful in the fertile valley. He kicked to start the animal moving, but it stepped in a hole and went down to its knees. Adino fell to the ground, a stone bruising his ribs.

His second-in-command, Zerah, ran over. "Are you all right?"

"I'm fine, but I'm not so sure about my mount," Adino said, getting up on one knee to examine the animal. "You take the men to join the main body. I'll be along soon enough."

"Yes, sir."

The officer left on his own donkey to get to the head of the column which had already begun their march, the unit officers having given the order to join the fight.

Adino's donkey was lying on its side. Its breathing was labored and accompanied by wheezing. He examined the front legs of the faithful animal and found that one of them was obviously broken. Adino knew there was only one thing to do.

He took his spear and drove the sharpened bronze deep into the donkey's skull to end its suffering.

Adino looked down at his mount which had served him for some time. It was a shame, but it couldn't be helped.

Adino felt no urgency to rejoin his men. They would be late to the battle, and while they would certainly be important reinforcements, Adino had no doubt that Joab would meet the attack with such fury that there would be no doubt of the outcome. Perhaps this really would be the day that the civil war would end.

He picked up his helmet, which had come off when he fell, and cinched its strap under his chin. He then took his shield which had hung from the donkey's saddle and slipped his arm through its straps. He made a mental note to return after the battle and retrieve the saddle, for it had value.

He turned to go after his men, who had already quickly marched south to join the main force. He rested his spear on his shoulder and began walking.

What was that?

His ear had picked up something; a rustling like footsteps in the distance, but not in the direction his men were marching. It was to the north.

Suddenly he felt urgency as he looked in the direction of the sound. Now it sounded like many men walking.

He looked at the direction his men had marched. The last rank had already disappeared around the bend in the road. He turned back to the north to see three men come through the undergrowth, heavily armed. They saw him and two of them hurled spears in his direction. He sidestepped them, then charged them with a shout, his spearpoint well forward.

The men were drawing their swords. Adino's spear caught one high in his chest and he fell back, blood flowing fast. With no time to spare, Adino jerked back to regain control of his spear and ran the bronze-tipped butt of the spear into the midsection of the second man. He cried out and fell also.

With no time to spare, Adino spun around to run the point of his spear through the neck of the third man, who dropped like a stone.

Breathing hard, Adino had no time to think, for there were five more emerging from the thicket with weapons forward.

"I tell you there is fighting back there!"

A soldier in Adino's cohort was arguing with another.

"That's not possible. The fight is ahead of us."

"I know what I heard. We need to tell the commander."

"You do it. It will be on you."

The man whose sharp ears had heard the struggle behind them went to his squad leader.

"Sir, I heard the sound of fighting behind us."

"I really doubt that," the squad leader argued. "Our mission is now to reinforce the main body."

"Please, we should check. General Adino is still there."

The squad leader's confidence was shaken a bit when he was reminded of that. "I will inform General Zerah," declared the squad leader.

He ran ahead and caught up with the general on his donkey.

"Sir, one of my men thought he heard the sound of fighting behind us, where General Adino is."

"What?! That's not possible," Zerah answered.

"That's what I said, but he was insistent. Should we check it out?"

Zerah thought for a moment.

"General Adino has not caught up with us?"

"No, sir."

"Take your squad and return to where we were positioned. If there is indeed something happening there, send one of your men to tell me."

"Yes, sir!"

❦ 41 ❦

Adino was fighting for his life. He had now killed or disabled a dozen fighters, but more were coming all the time. He used his shield both for defense and as a blunt weapon which he smashed in many faces, even while he jabbed and parried with both ends of his spear. Then he used the spear staff to stop swords from reaching him, constantly moving, barely escaping injury and death over and over.

He saw out the corner of his eye that some of the men were not coming at him but were going down the road his own men had taken and they would reach his rearguard before long. He killed two more and then sprinted away to try to get ahead of those going down the road. He jabbed the legs of one man, taking him out of the fight, then thrust his bloody spear between the shoulder blades of one of the leaders. He fell and the soldier behind him fell on top of him, allowing Adino to run him through as well.

There was no time to reflect, for there must have been a hundred soldiers running toward him now. He moved like lightning to escape the blows intended to end him, while lashing out with first the sharp, bronze point of his spear and the metallic butt in turn, sometimes even using it as a club.

His small shield was taking a beating and might not last much longer. He even more urgently struck every soldier that came near. He moved backward as they came, not running away, but holding them as he slowly reduced their numbers.

But there always seemed to be more.

The rearguard squad was hurrying back to where they had been positioned; where they had left the general, who had promised to catch up. Now they could all hear it: the unmistakable sounds of metal on metal, metal on wooden shields and the choked cries of wounded and dying men.

They began running faster, unsure what they would find. When they rounded the bend and came out of the trees into the clearing the squad leader couldn't believe what he saw.

There before them was their General, Adino, with what must be hundreds of bodies stretching away from him. He was covered in blood and sweat, dancing and thrusting with his spear, backing up as he did, holding his own against a whole cohort of Abner's troops.

"Go tell General Zerah to turn the men around," the squad leader told the man closest to him. "We have a second front."

The man saluted and went back the way they had come. With a loud shout, the rest of men ran to join the fight.

"The enemy attacked from the North and General Adino alone holds them back!" The man breathlessly said when he caught up with General Zerah. "We must join the fight!"

Zerah's eyes were wide as understanding dawned.

"Turn back! General Adino is in distress behind us!"

The men turned and ran, ranks broken, the rearguard becoming the front line as they retraced their steps.

"Where is everybody?" Adino demanded, as he continued defending himself and killing as many as he could.

"They are coming," the squad leader answered as he held up his shield and slashed at two men with his sword.

Adino was winded, but he could not rest, for men kept coming through the trees, no matter how many he killed.

The squad who had returned fought valiantly until finally the main body of Adino's command rounded the corner and surged through the troops sent by Abner. The tide turned and Abner's men began running back the way they came, with Adino's fresh troops able to pursue and kill many of them.

❦ 42 ❦

"Report!"

Joab's voice reverberated off the metallic weapons and armor of the officers gathered after the battle. He scanned the circle and saw they were all covered in dust and smeared with blood and terribly fatigued, but the mood was buoyant.

General Shammah reported first.

"Our high ground position gave us an advantage. Abner's troops were against the river. They had no place to go." Shammah had commanded the left flank of the main body.

"Losses?" Joab probed.

"18 killed and 57 wounded from my cohort."

"Abishai?" Joab looked at his brother, who had commanded the ranks in the middle of the battle line.

"We had 26 killed and 83 wounded, but we pushed back and held the land," Abishai answered. "Abner's troops were forced back across the river."

"Eleazar?"

"On the right flank, we planned for an attack from the south that did not come, so we were able to curl around and crush their left. Our killed numbered 14 and wounded 32."

"And now, let us hear from Adino," Joab continued, "who was positioned to fend off what we didn't believe was likely, but materialized anyway: an attack from the North."

Adino stepped forward, appearing barely able to put one foot in front of the other.

"General, our cohort was tasked with ensuring our rear and left flank was protected in case Abner crossed the river to the North and came south instead of crossing at Gilgal like we expected," Adino stopped to catch his breath.

"As it turned out, he divided his army and came at us from both directions, but my cohort routed them."

For a moment it appeared Adino was finished.

"Begging your pardon, general," Zerah interrupted. "My commander is much too modest. When we received word that the battle was joined at the river, we began moving to reinforce the main body according to the plan, but General Adino's donkey was injured, so he remained behind, promising to join us right away, but he was set upon by the cohort Abner sent across the river to the North.

"For quite some time, he held them alone; killing no less than 500 of the enemy, with just his spear!"

A mummer of amazement went around the circle.

"It was closer to 800!" one of Adino's officers asserted.

"You give me too much credit," Adino said. "You brought the cohort back and that was what won the victory."

"General Joab," Zerah continued. "I have it on good authority, hundreds were already dead when we arrived."

For a moment, there was stunned silence, then the men began clapping. Joab surveyed the room with a grim smile.

"We have seen acts of heroism before, but this is truly amazing. Someone pass a jar of wine and give Adino the first cup. He's earned it!

On the other side of the Jordan river, there was no command tent and no reporting. Abner and what was left of his army struggled to put as much distance as possible between them and the disastrous battlefield. It was a chaotic retreat, if it could even be called that.

They had essentially run for their lives. Abner didn't even try to get his troops to march with any discipline.

I'm too old for this, was his only thought.

Had this been the last gasp of the House of Saul?

❧ 43 ❧

Rizpah's sons were old enough they didn't require much of her time, but the work of the household kept her plenty busy. Her oldest, Armoni, was 15 now, and his brother, was 13, so both had been declared men. His brother's name was Mephibosheth, a name he shared with the son of Jonathan, their half-brother. They had taken up the trade of the family, tending flocks of sheep and goats, plus raising donkeys, so they were away much of the time.

Since the death of their father, King Saul, Rizpah's status had changed dramatically. Whereas, she had always just been Saul's concubine and therefore had fewer rights and privileges than Ahinoam, Saul's wife and mother of his six children, Rizpah still enjoyed a good life as a member of the royal household in Mahanaim.

The family compound Abner had found for them was nice enough and they had plenty of room, since Ish-bosheth was the only child of Saul still living with his mother and Rizpah and her sons had their own apartment.

Now, though still technically a member of the royal family, with Saul's son Ish-bosheth installed by Abner as the king of the northern tribes, her status was somewhat reduced. Without the buffer of Saul between her and Ahinoam, she often had thrust upon her the most undesirable household duties. Yes, there were some servant women to take up the slack, but Ahinoam seemed to take satisfaction from saddling Rizpah with drudgery.

Still, she couldn't hold it against Ahinoam; after all, she had lost not just a husband, but three sons on that fateful day in the north.

The Eternal Kingdom

When Saul had been alive, he often favored Rizpah, she being the younger of his women, and she had borne him sons as well, but now he was gone. Now Ahinoam made it clear that she ran the household. Rizpah wondered if Armoni would be considered for the throne, should Ish-bosheth be deposed for some reason. Ish-bosheth was not taking part in military operations like his late older brothers had, so he would not fall in battle as they had. He had no wife or children and no prospects as far as Rizpah knew, so there might yet be a way Armoni could be king after him.

She had mulled these thoughts many times while performing any number of tasks. Today she was mending a garment for Ahinoam, when there was a knock at the door. She laid the garment aside and rose to open the door. Her eyes grew wide when she saw who it was.

"Your majesty?!"

"Shalom," King Ish-bosheth answered. "I wanted to speak to you."

"Of course."

Rizpah watched Ish-bosheth's face. He looked away, like he didn't know how to begin. At 41, he was a little older than her, but he lacked the self-confidence of his late older brothers. Finally, he spoke.

"Rizpah, I have known you for much of my life. I have not taken a wife, but I must think about my future. I must think of someone to carry forward the house of Saul."

He paused. Rizpah wasn't sure what he was trying to say.

"You were my father's concubine. As such, I have inherited the responsibility for your welfare. I have always admired you. I want you to give me an heir."

Rizpah's mouth fell open. She didn't know what to say.

"Come to my bed, Rizpah. You are most beautiful," he said, holding out a hand as invitation.

Rizpah took a step back. "Ish-bosheth – I mean, your majesty – I am hardly worthy of such an honor!"

"Nonsense! You were often bedded by my father, and he was more formidable than I. You are more than worthy to be my concubine – or wife."

What?!

Was he proposing marriage or just wanting her to serve as a brood mare to father an heir?

Conflicting emotions flashed through her heart. She really wasn't interested in Ish-bosheth personally, but, on the other hand, being his wife, concubine, or whatever, might raise her status in the household. Ahinoam would still be queen mother, but perhaps she would be less likely to give her all the undesirable jobs if she was giving the king an heir.

Still, she didn't like the idea of going to bed with Ish-bosheth. She decided to try to fend him off.

"But doesn't the law say it is unlawful for a man to lie with his father's wife?" she said, not knowing if that would work, for she wasn't technically Saul's wife.

"Uh, yes it does," he began. "But doesn't that only apply when the father is alive?"

Rizpah didn't know how to answer that, so she tried a different tack.

"Have you spoken to your mother? What will she think?"

That stopped him, because Rizpah was certain he wouldn't have spoken to Ahinoam. As king, it was true he didn't need to ask permission of either his mother or even of Rizpah. Kings took what they wanted; that was just the way it was, but Rizpah was banking on Ish-bosheth not having the self-confidence to assert his rights.

Her gamble paid off.

"All right, I'll speak to her," Ish-bosheth mumbled, and he turned to go.

Rizpah closed the door in relief. Would he speak to his mother? He seemed to fear her as much as anyone; almost as much as Abner. And if he did, what would Ahinoam say?

❦ 44 ❦

Two of David's wives, Abigail and Ahinoam, were at the doorway into Maacah's room in the house of women. She was in labor and a midwife was working to keep her focused.

Things seemed to be going well as far as Abigail could tell. This was the third time they were going through this; first Ahinoam birthed Amnon, then Abigail had Daniel and now it was Maacah's turn. Their family was growing rapidly.

The midwife spoke: "Push, Maacah! Push!"

And she did. It seemed she had done it before, she was so poised and calm.

Perhaps it is her lot being born a royal, Abigail thought.

After just a few hours, the midwife announced Maacah had a baby girl. It was a quick birth for a first baby, especially after Abigail's own experience.

It was their first girl; David's princess. Maacah announced she would be called "Tamar."

Abigail left Ahinoam to "ooh" and "aah" over the new baby and Sela and other concubines of the king came as well. Abigail was weary from the responsibility of the growing harem, plus caring for her own child.

She was worried about Daniel. He was fussy and seemed to cry a lot. She didn't know what it could mean. She thought maybe she should find an older woman who could give counsel about him.

Perhaps she just worried too much, but Ahinoam's child Amnon didn't seem to be as sickly.

When yet another wife was added to the house of women, Abigail left her orientation to others. She was preoccupied with her son, Daniel, who was more sickly than ever, it seemed.

Eglah was the newest of David's wives. She was older than most of the others at 25, but apparently she was important because of who her father was and what alliance the marriage would cement.

Being older, she was assertive and Abigail thought she could prove to be a problem with the competing personalities that now populated the house.

Abigail had no time to understand this latest alliance and how it fit into David's plans. Her son occupied her every waking moment. He would soon have his first birthday, but he seemed listless and tired, rather than being a bundle of energy like his older brother, Amnon, and his infant sister, Tamar.

❦ 45 ❦

"Are you sure that's what you want?"

"Yes, mother."

Ish-bosheth watched his mother's face for some sign of what her answer would be.

"It seems like you could do better," Ahinoam said. "Why not take one of the maids? They are younger and could give you many children."

"But I have grown to love Rizpah."

Ahinoam looked at his earnest face, at least Ish-bosheth hoped he appeared earnest. It had taken him a couple of weeks to work up the courage to ask his mother if he could take Rizpah, and he was feeling very nervous.

"All right then, will you make her your queen or just your consort?"

Ish-bosheth smiled. "Thank you, mother! I will go tell Rizpah now!"

And he rushed out the door into the night.

The apartment Rizpah shared with her two sons was in the compound where Ish-bosheth lived with his mother, so he didn't have to go far. He looked and saw light coming from the window beside the front door. He was glad she was awake, for it was late and he didn't want to wait until morning to give Rizpah the news.

He had only thought how much he wanted to make love to Rizpah, but his mother's question echoed in his mind.

Would he make her his queen? Why yes!

There could be a ceremony installing her. It would be glorious! The people of Israel would certainly approve.

As he reached the steps which led up to the front door of Rizpah's apartment, the door opened, letting the light from oil lamps spill out into the yard. Ish-bosheth looked up, expecting to see the slender silhouette of Rizpah greet him, but instead a much larger person – a man – stood in the doorway.

It was Abner!

"What are you doing here?!" Ish-bosheth shouted without thinking. "You have slept with Rizpah! How dare you!"

"How dare *I*?" Abner bellowed. "How dare YOU accuse me of sinning in that way? Am I the head of a dead dog from Judah? I have been loyal to the house of Saul your father and to all his relatives and friends. I made you king and established your kingdom, and I can take it away!"

Abner's eyes then narrowed and Ish-bosheth shuddered.

"May God judge me severely if I do not do for David exactly what Yahweh promised him: I will transfer the kingdom from the house of Saul and establish the throne of David over the whole land from Dan to Beer-Sheva!"

Ish-bosheth had to step out of the way as Abner bounded down the stairs and hurried out the front gate.

He was shaking from head to toe after the acrimonious confrontation with Abner. He knew Abner did not make empty threats.

Then he saw the slight figure of Rizpah, silhouetted in the doorway. She pulled her shawl over her head and closed the door, shrouding the courtyard in darkness again. Ish-bosheth did not move for a while.

Would Abner really take the kingdom from him?

Had Abner denied sleeping with Rizpah?

No, he did not deny it.

❦ 46 ❦

Ahithophel stood beside Azel as they together looked at a plan which had been drawn by Joab, who stood on the other side of the table beside the king in a corner of David's throne room.

"You have defeated Abner at every turn," David said to Joab. "This is a good plan. We should be able to hold the territory of Benjamin between Gibeon and the Philistine lands. That will be a good beginning."

"The population there is far from Ish-bosheth's throne across the Jordan," Azel commented. It was his job to relate to the other tribes, especially Benjamin. "The people would likely welcome our presence as a strong buffer between them and the Philistines."

"My thought exactly," David said.

"Our fortification work at Sha'araim will be ready for a garrison soon," Joab put in, referring to the city at the western edge of the valley where David had slain Goliath, the giant. "That would help hold the area."

"Begging your pardon, sire?"

The men turned to see who spoke. It was Benaiah standing at the door.

"What is it?" David answered.

"A messenger."

"Have him wait."

"I think you're going to want to hear this."

David looked at the others and then back at Benaiah.

"Send him in."

Benaiah opened the door and ushered a man in, looking bedraggled from a long journey. Benaiah followed him in with his right hand on the pommel of his sword.

"What is your message?" David asked.

Withdrawing a papyrus scroll from his leather shoulder bag, the man began reading.

"From Abner in Mahanaim: 'To whom does the land belong? Make an agreement with me, and I will do what I can to have all Israel turn to you.'"

"That is the entire message?" David asked.

"Yes. I will take your answer back to Abner."

The four men looked at one another.

"Can it really be that easy?" Azel asked.

"Yahweh never ceases to surprise," David answered. Then he turned to the messenger.

"This is good! Tell Abner I will make an agreement with him, on one condition. He will not see my face unless he brings Saul's daughter Michal when he comes to visit."

The messenger had a blank look on his face. He was obviously not prepared for this response. David picked up a stylus, dipped it in ink and walked over to the messenger. He took the papyrus from the messenger and began writing on its back side.

"Take this message to your master, Ish-bosheth: 'Give me my wife Michal, your sister, whom I acquired for a bride-price of a hundred Philistine foreskins.'"

David finished writing and gave the papyrus back to the messenger. "When this is done, Abner should come see me."

❧ 47 ❧

Thankfully, the Philistines now had a reduced presence in the land of the tribe of Benjamin, so Abner and his small escort of soldiers could move about and not be concerned, as long as they didn't go to Gibeah, Saul's former capital.

They had brought a wagon for Michal to ride in. They were on the way to Gallim, a town of Benjamin, where Michal had been banished by the whim of his cousin, King Saul. He had taken her from David and she had been married to Paltiel for about 12 years.

When Abner and his escort arrived at the home of Paltiel, they could see no one, until the prosperous planter himself emerged from a stable behind the large, ornate house.

Paltiel's face went white when he saw Abner and the weapons of the soldiers. Abner could see that he looked much older than when he last saw him. Then one of Paltiel's grown sons came out of the stable, holding a hay fork.

"By order of King David of Judah, Michal, daughter of Saul, must be returned to him," Abner announced.

"What?!" Paltiel cried. "Lord, I pray you will reconsider!"

"It is not for me to decide. The King has ordered it."

Then Michal came out of the house accompanied by another wife of Paltiel and a couple of children.

"Cousin Abner!" Michal exclaimed. "Why are you here?"

"King David has decreed that, now that your father is dead, you should once again be his wife."

"But I am happy here! Paltiel needs me!"

"The king has spoken. You must come with me. Gather whatever belongings are important to you."

Paltiel took a step forward. "Lord Abner, do not rip my family apart! We are a loving family here. What have we to do with a king in Judah?!"

"Stand aside, Paltiel. We have our orders."

"So, you serve Judah now, you snake!" Paltiel scoffed.

Abner had to make only the slightest motion to the soldiers who accompanied him, and they quickly moved to restrain Paltiel and step between him and Michal. Paltiel's grown son tensed his hands on the hay fork, but a soldier lowered a spear in his direction, and no one moved.

"Michal, you must gather whatever you wish to take with you," Abner said. "Do it quickly!"

Michal and Paltiel looked at one another, tears running down their faces, but they were prevented from approaching one another by the soldiers.

Finally, she entered the house, escorted by a couple of Abner's men.

"Please, lord, if this must be, allow us a proper goodbye!" Paltiel pleaded.

Michal emerged from the house of Paltiel carrying a couple of bundles and a leather shoulder bag, accompanied by the soldiers. She looked at Paltiel sadly for a moment and then turned wordlessly to climb into the wagon.

She was determined not to weep or show any weakness for the benefit of Paltiel, but also to avoid feeding Abner's power fetish. He had sent her to Paltiel in the first place, carrying out her father's decree. She had wept endlessly then but would not give him the satisfaction now.

Abner climbed in from the other side to sit beside her, as if to let her know she couldn't easily jump out and run away.

One of the soldiers swatted the rump of the donkey pulling the wagon and it leaned into the harness, causing the wagon to lurch into motion.

Paltiel began to weep loudly and followed along as the procession left his property. Abner looked back at him, annoyed. Michal knew Abner would likely assume Paltiel would stop following them, but he did not. He continued crying, following just a few cubits behind the wagon.

The broken-hearted man followed for miles, continuing to weep loudly, until they reached Bahurim, near the desolated former Levite town of Nob, when Abner could take no more.

"Stop it!" Abner cried. "Stop following us. Return home to the rest of your family."

Michal turned to look back as Paltiel partly obeyed Abner and stopped pursuing the wagon. He did not immediately turn toward home however, but stood watching them go with tears continuing to flow.

Michal felt sorry for him. She had been forced to marry him 12 years ago and had resisted his overtures until he won her over with his patience and authentic love. His tears only confirmed what she already knew: he really loved her.

But just as she had been taken from David so many years ago, she was now taken from Paltiel to be returned to David. She had truly loved David, but she was older now and knew how capricious men could be, especially kings.

She wondered what it would be like to be with David again. When they married, he was not yet 20. Now he was more mature, and she knew he had fiercely loyal followers who had supported him through his exile from her father.

Why had David asked for her? She had failed, during their brief marriage, to give him a child of either gender, much less a son who could succeed him as king. She had also failed, during the 12 years of marriage to Paltiel, to give him offspring. She had cared for the children of Paltiel's other wife, but remained childless herself.

Time would tell what her life would be like as David's queen. As always, she had little control over her fate.

❧ 48 ❧

Abner and Michal arrived in Hebron with the small detail of soldiers which had accompanied them. Michal had never been to the tribal capital of Judah and, being the daughter of King Saul, she wasn't sure how she would be received.

She need not have been concerned, since, if they recognized anyone, the people in the street stared at Abner, knowing he had crowned the king who was David's rival.

Michal was scarcely noticed.

They stopped in front of an abnormally large compound. It was not opulent and had the look of having been built for some more humble purpose than the palace of a king.

Abner jumped down from the wagon and held his hand up for Michal to take as she climbed down. She felt the impulse to refuse his offer of help, but she realized it was a long way down and she would need his aid, lest she humiliate herself by falling on her face in the dust of the road. She took her father's cousin's hand, reasoning that she had already suffered enough humiliation for one day.

A couple of soldiers took Michal's bags from the wagon and followed Abner and Michal toward the front gate.

A soldier stood there, which was no surprise. When he saw Abner, he dipped his head and stood aside, opening the gate for them. He looked at Michal briefly with only slight curiosity in his eyes, then went back to standing at his post beside the gate.

Michal followed Abner to the steps which led into the main house. She noted some other buildings within the compound, including another complete house.

The Eternal Kingdom

As they topped the stairs they encountered two more soldiers, who also acknowledged Abner without a word and swung open the double doors leading into the house. Abner's soldiers followed with Michal's belongings.

Inside seemed dark after being out in the sun all day, but Michal's eyes gradually adjusted, aided by the firelight from the sconces on the walls. They were in a small entryway with benches on either side and another set of double doors before them.

"Set them down here," Abner directed the soldiers, who set her bags on a bench in the entry way. "You are dismissed. I will let you know our next steps, after I have seen King David."

Then Abner turned to Michal. "Ready?"

She didn't immediately answer, so he continued.

"I'm sorry dear, but David made your presence here a condition of our alliance."

"Your alliance with David? Against my brother?"

"My hands are tied."

"Same as they were when you took me from David?"

Abner looked down.

"I never meant to hurt you. I had to do what your father wanted."

Michal sighed. She was tired after the journey, so she wouldn't finish telling Abner what she thought of him. She just wanted to get it over with.

"Let's do it," she said looking at the double doors.

❧ 49 ❧

David was bent over a table in the middle of the room with Ahithophel, Azel and Benaiah. They were examining a papyrus map, when the doors opened and in walked Abner with Michal.

"Men, leave me now. We will continue this tomorrow," David said. The three men looked Abner and Michal up and down as they left.

"Do you not want me to stay?" Benaiah asked.

"Stay close. I'll call when I need you."

Benaiah looked at Abner a long moment before he left.

"Michal!" David cried and he went to her and threw his arms around her. She did not reciprocate. "It is so good to see you again. Thank you, Abner, for bringing her to me!"

"I live to serve," Abner said, his words sounded hollow, but David did not call attention to his insincerity.

"You must be hungry after your journey," David said to Abner. "We have prepared a banquet to welcome Michal and you, which will be ready soon. Have your men come in and dine."

"Thank you, that would be appreciated. I will go inform the men."

Abner left through the front door of the house.

David took a good look at his former wife who would be his wife again.

"Thank you for coming Michal."

"Did I have a choice?"

David wasn't sure of the best way to answer, so he continued. "I have missed you so much."

"You could have come for me. You never even sent a message."

"For a long time, I didn't know where you were," David answered. "Then my movements were restricted by your father. I had to stay hidden or he surely would have killed me. You understand."

She looked away. He knew she knew how much danger he had been in and why he had to flee, but he sensed that she blamed him anyway.

"Then, with your brother being declared king and you married to another man, I couldn't just come take you."

"But you can now?"

"A lot of things are about to change," David answered cryptically. Then he changed the subject. "I know you have to be exhausted after your trip. We must catch up when you have recovered. I'll have Benaiah take you to your quarters."

"'My quarters'?"

"Yes, there is a place just for you. Benaiah will take you there. You will be able to be refreshed and then return for your banquet.

"Benaiah!" David called and Benaiah came through the double doors.

"Yes?"

"Help Michal with her things and show her to the house."

"Yes, sire," Benaiah said. Then he picked up her bundles and turning to Michal, he said, "Come with me."

Michal looked from David to Benaiah and then back again before following Benaiah out the front door.

The sun was going down as Benaiah led Michal to the house of women. She suddenly had a revelation.

David is wearing my father's crown! How did he obtain it?

She hadn't seen her father or his crown for almost 12 years, so she didn't recognize it at first, but there could be no mistake, David wore Saul's crown. Was she, Saul's daughter, just another symbol of David's right to the throne?

Benaiah knocked on the door before opening it so Michal could step through. Benaiah set her bundles down just inside the door and left, closing the door behind him.

Michal's mouth fell open at what she saw. In the large common room of the house there were six women and three children, all looking back at her. The women were in groups of two or three, as if they had been in conversation. The children were mostly on the floor, playing, and appeared to be from a few months to three years old.

After an awkward moment, one of the women spoke.

"Welcome, Michal. We've been expecting you. I'm Abigail."

Michal looked at her through wide eyes.

"Who ARE all of you?"

"We are David's wives and concubines," Abigail answered. "Meet Ahinoam and her son, Amnon, David's firstborn."

"My mother's name is Ahinoam."

"Uh, yes I know," Ahinoam said, "but I am of Judah." Ahinoam then looked down, as if wishing she hadn't said that last part.

"Ahinoam was David's first wife," Abigail blurted out.

"*I* was David's first wife," Michal asserted.

"Yes, of course," Abigail hurried to say. "I meant she was the first AFTER you."

For a long moment the other women just looked at Michal as she looked back at them.

"And this is my son Daniel, and this is Maacah and her daughter Tamar, and Haggith and her baby, Adonijah, and Abital and Eglah. Then there's Sela, David's first concubine."

Michal thought she might faint as she looked at all of them. It was overwhelming.

Finally, Abigail spoke again. "We have your room ready."

"My room?"

"Yes, we each have a room. Well, some may share, but we have a room just for you. Come, I'll take you to it. It's upstairs. Let me help with these."

Abigail reached down to pick up Michal's bundles. Michal started to say she could manage them herself, but then she saw the value of having the manager of the house carry her things, so she let Abigail pick up her two bundles. Michal then picked up her shoulder bag and followed Abigail up the stairs to the room which would apparently be her home.

The room was dark when they arrived.

"Oh, I'll fetch a lamp," Abigail said, and she hurried back down the stairs.

Michal looked at the darkened room. The small window made her remember the window of the upstairs bedroom she and David had shared and how she had lowered him down on an improvised rope of bed sheets so he could escape the men her father had sent to kill him. That seemed so long ago now. She had not seen David again until today.

Abigail returned with an oil lamp. Its flickering light drove away the shadows and Michal could now see the room for what it was: small and dingy, furnished with just a small bed, a chair and small table. It was nothing at all what she had expected as the wife of a king.

"We hope to have better accommodations soon," Abigail said, setting the lamp on the table. "We are quickly outgrowing our house."

"So, you all stay here? And the king stays – where?"

"In the big house; where the throne room is. He sends for us when he wishes to see one of us."

Michal reeled. She had been foolish to think she could pick back up where she and David had left off almost 15 years ago, when they were teenaged newlyweds. She was reduced to staying in a tiny room in the same house with all David's other wives and concubines.

How I wish I could go back to Paltiel!

❦ 50 ❦

The banquet room was decorated with festive palm fronds and bright, colorful drapes and tablecloths. The tables were laden with all manner of food: lamb roasted with leeks, pomegranates, figs and honey made into a paste and stuffed inside pita pockets, grape-leaves stuffed with spiced rice, plus abundant wine, among other delicacies.

Young women, dressed all in white, glided between the tables, refilling clay cups and replenishing bowls of this food or another.

Michal was seated beside David and Abner was on the other side of the king.

Azel was seated across from them, along with Dani, who was able to come because Adriel was watching Elisheva. Azel had been invited because he was Benjamite and had served in Saul's army.

It had been maybe fifteen years since Azel had seen Michal, when she had hidden from his brother and the rest of Saul's personal guard after she helped David escape. She had been so young and vulnerable then.

While everyone tried to be pleasant, it was clear to Azel that there was a great deal of tension in the air. Michal smiled only rarely while David kept the conversation going, and Abner kept looking over at Benaiah. Azel had the sudden thought that Abner was probably wondering why Joab was not present. Azel was glad that Joab and Abishai had led some men on a raid of a Philistine village earlier that afternoon.

To Azel, it seemed that Abner shouldn't be worried. If anything, he, the king and the others from Judah were in a more precarious position than Abner, since his escort of 20 men was also seated across the room at another table.

Several men of David's personal guard sat at another table with their commander, Benaiah, which served to balance things somewhat.

At yet another table were David's wives and concubines, who had been invited as well, and Azel was certain he discerned some tension there. After all, none of the other wives received quite this reception. Of course, Ahinoam and Abigail became David's wives while they were all on the run, so a banquet was out of the question; they were lucky to eat at all during that time.

Maacah was a different case, since she had been a princess; the daughter of a king. There had been a ceremony when she arrived, but it had been of a different character.

Dani caught Azel's eye, and she looked over toward the wives table and then to the head table where Abner and Michal flanked David. Azel could tell Dani sensed the tension as well.

Azel guessed that in David's mind there was no need for a ceremony other than tonight's celebration, since he and Michal were already married. The ten years she spent with the other man was as if it never happened.

It had been important to the king that Azel be there, since he would be the king's envoy to the other tribes, and that was about to become a high priority because of the alliance Abner had come to seal.

Azel's newfound diplomatic sensibilities caused him to understand that this celebration was likely as much for Abner as for Michal and what he could do in bringing the other tribes around to accept David as king. Azel also discerned that claiming the daughter of Saul as his wife would only help David in his relations with the other tribes. A case could be made that there was a line of succession from

Saul to David, thanks to his renewed union with Saul's daughter.

Presently, there was entertainment. Several musicians, whom the king had recruited for events like this as well as for worship, came to provide music.

This seemed to soothe the tensions in the room somewhat; at least it provided a distraction.

The hour was late when the celebration broke up. Michal left to go to her allotted bed chamber in the house of women without having spoken ten words all evening. The king offered Abner and his men lodging in an inn nearby, but they opted to make camp outside the city walls.

When the city awoke in the morning, the king sent word to offer breakfast to the delegation from Mahanaim, but they were already gone. David dressed for his day on the throne, knowing that there would be no need to plan military operations against the northern tribes. He would be sure to visit them very soon.

He could see that Yahweh had moved to fulfill his promise to him that he would now rule all Israel. He didn't know what had changed for Abner, but he wouldn't question the change in attitude.

David was standing over the map table again, when Joab and Abishai noisily burst into the throne room. Benaiah tensed with his hand on his sword until he saw who it was.

"What is it I hear that Abner was here, and you let him go?" Joab demanded.

"His business here was done," David said.

"What were you thinking? Don't you know he deceived you? He was just here to learn when you go in and out and all about our defenses! Come Abishai!"

King David's volatile nephews stormed out.

The Eternal Kingdom

Abner and his men were just a few miles north of Hebron, near Sirah, having watered their donkeys at the well there and taken some breakfast. They were mounting up to leave when two young men riding donkeys fast and hard came up behind them. Several of Abner's men drew their swords, not knowing what to expect.

"Peace to you!" one of the men called. "I have a message for General Abner!"

Abner looked at the messenger but didn't recognize him.

"What is it?" Abner asked.

"My master, Joab, has returned and requests you to return to Hebron. He has urgent matters to discuss."

Abner looked at the man's face, trying to discern if he was hiding anything, but couldn't see anything but sincerity.

"Joab is my counterpart in Judah," Abner said to the officer in charge of his detail. "It is not surprising that he would need to discuss terms of the transfer of authority."

The officer looked doubtful, so Abner reassured him.

"You saw how David treated us last night. It will be fine. Take your men and go on to your homes."

The officer didn't immediately move.

"I'll be fine, really," Abner insisted.

Finally, the officer gave the order, and the detail rode away, continuing north and west toward the Jordan River.

When Abner arrived back at Hebron, the messengers led him, not to the king's house, but to a building beside the gate they identified as Joab's military headquarters.

Abner dismounted his donkey and was ushered inside by one of the messengers, who told him to sit in the anteroom.

He didn't wait long. Joab appeared from a back room.

"Thank you, for returning, Abner," Joab began. "I'm sorry I was not here when you came. Come with me so we can discuss some urgent issues."

Abner followed Joab into a second room. As soon as they were inside, the door closed. Abner turned to see who had closed it. It was Abishai, the brother of Joab – and Asahel.

"What is this?" Abner asked the two men who were perhaps 40 years younger than him. Suddenly Abishai grabbed Abner's arms and pulled them behind him.

"This is for Asahel!" Joab shouted, as he drew a dagger from his belt and plunged it into Abner's stomach.

Abner cried out and doubled over, then fell to the floor. He had only a moment of surprise and regret before his heart stopped and all went black.

❦ 51 ❦

King David had no idea that Joab had sent messengers to bring Abner back, much less what he and Abishai would do to him, but the treachery could not be hidden long, because too many people knew.

Too many people knew that messengers had been sent. Too many people saw Abner return and go into the rooms by the gate, and too many people realized he never came out.

When word reached the king, he sent Benaiah and a detail of his personal guard to bring Joab and Abishai before him. Azel and other advisors were present when Benaiah and his men returned with David's nephews.

When they were brought in, David was seated on his throne, his crown on his head, to make it instantly clear that he was the authority in the room.

"What have you done?!"

"We have avenged our brother!" Joab said defiantly.

In a rush of memories, David saw the four of them, not that different in age, for they were sons of his much-older sister, playing at soldiering in between times of learning to be shepherds. That was so long ago, and the stakes were so much higher now!

"Don't you know that you may have ruined everything I have been working toward for years?!" David scolded. "Don't you know your crime may have frustrated God's will for the kingdom?!"

Joab and Abishai's faces, still hard with anger and defiance, now softened a bit as confusion filtered through.

"I know he killed Asahel – I loved him too – but Abner was negotiating with the tribes to make me king as only he could!

You have ruined that advantage. You may have turned the tribes against me and may indeed have prevented God's will from being fulfilled!"

Joab and Abishai looked at one another and then looked down at the threads of the embroidered carpet before the throne.

"Here is what you must do," David continued loudly. "You must lead the donkey which will pull the cart bearing Abner's body to the grave we will prepare for him. You will tear your clothing, cast dirt on your heads and weep in mourning for Abner and I will follow behind the bier, weeping.

"If you cannot mourn for Abner," David added, "mourn for the loss of the kingdom, for it may indeed be lost to us all!"

Joab and Abishai did as they were ordered, like the good soldiers they were, though it galled them. Their uncle David, the king, followed the bier, weeping as he had said he would.

They arrived at the burial place, not far from where the patriarchs Abraham, Isaac and Jacob had been buried hundreds of years before. There they interred the one who had been their enemy for so many years; the one who stood beside the unstable king who drove them into exile and threatened their lives.

When it was over, Joab left the funeral ceremony, where the people of Judah joined the king in mourning the death of the general on the other side in their civil war. It was all very maddening.

Just because he is king doesn't mean my uncle is always right, he thought.

Michal left the short funeral with mixed emotions. She had nursed hatred for Abner for many years, yet he was her second cousin and now David's nephews had killed him.

I hate them all.

Azel was leaving the funeral with Eliel, when Benaiah tapped him on the shoulder.

"The king wishes to speak to you," Benaiah said.

"Lead the way," Azel answered, and Benaiah immediately began threading his way through the departing crowd with Azel following.

The king had not left, but was standing before the now-sealed entrance to the cave in which they had buried Abner. Most of the other people had drifted away.

"Azel! Good!" the king said when he saw Azel approaching. "I have a job for you. You have seen the procession and ceremony today; I need you to go to the elders of Benjamin and relay what you've seen."

"I understand," Azel said. "I assume you need me to leave immediately?"

"The sooner, the better. The other tribes must know I had nothing to do with the death of Abner."

"It will be done," Azel promised.

❦ 52 ❦

Azel decided Eliel should accompany him, for it would make the journey safer and would give his firstborn a chance to see his cousins again. The road from Hebron to Mizpah was well-known and they were able to make the trip in a few hours, arriving at his old home in Mizpah near sunset.

Jeriah's firstborn, Misha'el greeted them in his smith's apron and welcomed them.

"This is a surprise!" Misha'el exclaimed. Azel noted again how much he looked like his father had, and that the work of the forge had hardened his shoulders and arms.

"What brings you both to Mizpah this time? Merchanting again?"

"Not this time. I have an urgent message to relay to the elders of Benjamin," Azel replied.

"A message from David?"

"Yes."

"You may not be received cordially, after all that's happened."

"I know. That's why I'm here, to give a first-hand account and dispel any gossip that may be about."

"So, what DID happen?" Misha'el asked. Their other cousins came out of the forge just then, apparently having overheard the way the conversation started.

They all greeted one another before Azel could answer Misha'el's question.

Azel's mind went back to the time more than 10 years ago when Jeriah challenged him concerning his loyalty to David. He knew his nephew's question came from a similar place.

"To answer your question: the death of Abner was the doing of Joab," Azel began. "He killed him to avenge his brother's death at the hand of Abner. I was there, at the battle of Gibeon, not 20 cubits away, when Abner struck him down."

"But that was in a battle," Misha'el pointed out. "People die in battles."

Azel realized the sting of his father's death on Mt. Gilboa was still fresh for the young man nearly two years later.

"Yes, so Joab and Abishai were wrong to take revenge, but David knew nothing of it. In fact, I was also there the night before, when David staged a banquet in honor of Abner and the daughter of Saul, with whom he is reunited. David sent Abner on his way in peace, but Joab brought him back under false pretenses. That's when he and Abishai killed him."

Misha'el considered what Azel had told him.

"Rumors are flying," Misha'el said. "You may have difficulty convincing the elders."

"I know. I will do the best I can as an eyewitness to most of what has taken place."

"Once before, I asked you if David would take the throne by force," Misha'el said. "Will he now?"

"Before his death Abner was negotiating on David's behalf with all the tribes. I don't believe David would take the crown by force. He has had many opportunities to do that already."

Misha'el nodded.

"Well, come and sit at table with us, Tzipporah likely has it hot and ready!"

Azel smiled and they all made their way to the main house where he grew up.

❧ 53 ☙

The next day, Misha'el accompanied Azel and Eliel to meet with the elders. At the evening meal it had been proposed that Azel should not go alone. Misha'el was ideal to accompany Azel, being the son of the man who died by King Saul's side.

They went to the gate complex and found several elders conducting business, hearing disputes and so forth. Azel, Eliel and Misha'el patiently waited their turn.

Finally, after several of the locals had stood before the elders, they recognized Misha'el. He stepped before the bearded men, seated on colorful cushions on wooden benches. Azel was glad there were several elders present. Standing around the edges many other men who had come to ask the elders' judgement had remained to hear what would come next. Azel was glad they were there as well.

"Elders of Benjamin, I am Misha'el, the smith, son of Jeriah, who served King Saul as armor bearer and died by his side in battle. He was the son of Eldad, who was head elder of this city and fought in the Philistine wars before we had a king.

"Today I bring with me another son of Eldad, Azel, who also served in King Saul's army and then in the command of David, who slew the giant. Azel still serves David, and he has important information for this body."

"You bring a traitor before us?!" one of the elders shouted.

"Be quiet! He is our guest," another said.

The gathering devolved into a noisy shouting match. Azel looked at Eliel, wondering if they would do more than shout.

"Silence! Silence!"

The oldest man there, Hezron, a man with white hair and beard, finally made himself heard and got the men to settle down so Misha'el could continue.

"I really believe he has information we all need to hear. This is my uncle Azel."

Azel stood and surveyed the faces before him. Some were still hard after Misha'el revealed he still served David. Other faces were questioning in anticipation of what he would say.

"It brings me great pleasure to again visit my childhood home. I grew to adulthood here in Mizpah. As a boy I played on its heights and on the plain below, learning the ways of war, watching the horizon for approaching Philistines."

Azel hoped the mention of their common enemy would help his cause, but he didn't see evidence of change in the faces before him just yet.

"Recent events have caused great distress, not just in Benjamin, but in Judah. I have been witness to much of what has happened and can give an account on behalf of David, who now is king in Hebron, but ever served Saul loyally, despite the king's suspicions of him.

"Abner's death was a blow to David. He had nothing to do with it. On the night before he was killed, David feted Abner and Michal, the daughter of Saul, whom he gave to David as wife, at a banquet which I and my wife attended. From there Abner intended to go speak to all the tribes to propose uniting under David's authority and protection.

"The next morning, Abner went his way in peace, until Joab called him back under false pretenses and, with the help of his brother, Abishai, surprised and murdered him."

Some of the men turned and muttered to one another at this recounting, so he hastened to add, "David knew nothing of this plot. When he learned what had happened, he immediately planned a funeral ceremony to honor Abner and, for good measure, required Joab and Abishai to lead the procession to the grave, tearing their clothes in mourning."

Azel watched carefully for signs that the elders' faces were softening, but it was difficult to tell. One elder spoke the question that many were probably thinking.

"Saul and Abner were sons of Benjamin, like you are," one elder began. "Why do you serve David, who is of Judah?"

"David was King Saul's champion, and you cheered for him, until Saul turned against him," Azel answered, choosing his words carefully. "I served under David in King Saul's army, but I learned that Samuel, who often led us in worship right here in Mizpah, had anointed David to be the next king of all Israel. That's why I serve him to this day."

Azel could see those assembled were listening intently and thinking about what he was saying, so he continued.

"I was there, when Saul was pursuing David to kill him and Saul entered a cave in En Gedi alone. We were hiding in that cave. David could have easily slit Saul's throat and taken the throne, but he refused. He refused to raise his hand against the Lord's anointed. Such is his respect for the authorities Yahweh has ordained. That means he would never order the death of Abner."

Some of the elders looked at one another, apparently never having heard that story. Then one of them spoke.

"What about Joab? He seems to have no such qualms."

"David knows he must control Joab," Azel answered. "His killing of Abner was revenge for killing his brother, Asahel, in the battle of Gibeon. David does not believe the killing of Abner was an honorable response to a battlefield death."

Some of what Azel said was assuming the best, for he hadn't specifically talked to David about it, everything had happened so quickly.

"What of King Ish-bosheth? What will become of him? Will David slay him?"

"David has loved all of King Saul's children. Jonathan was his best friend. He mourned long for Jonathan. He married

Saul's daughter. Ish-bosheth is David's brother-in-law. He will treat him honorably."

The men looked at one another, but no one had any other questions. Finally, Hezron stood and began speaking. Azel knew this would be the final word.

"We were incensed at hearing of the killing of Abner. He was the strength of our kingdom after the death of Saul. We still believe Joab and his brother bear watching, but we also already heard about the funeral for Abner and David's behavior. We can tell that you were not involved, and we understand that this kind of revenge against the house of Saul has not been David's policy.

"We are still technically at war," the head elder continued. "though without Abner, we may not prevail. Does your master believe that the rift between our tribes can be healed?"

"He does. Samuel, the prophet, anointed him to serve as king over all Israel," Azel answered. "He has ever treated those from all the tribes as brothers, in spite of occasional betrayals and infighting."

The head elder then turned to the other elders. "David was indeed a hero for all Israel. We served Saul, but he was admittedly at times unstable."

Several nodded in agreement. Azel could have stated it more strongly, after spending nine years in exile, fearing for the lives of himself and his family, but he didn't comment.

"Perhaps the time has come for David to finally assume the role Samuel had for him," the head elder concluded.

"I will never accept David as king!" one of them shouted.

"You will not accept the one anointed by Samuel, God's prophet, priest and judge?" the head elder said loudly. "Yahweh spoke to Samuel and he was the judge of our town for many years!"

The other man remained silent.

Azel smiled inside, while maintaining an appropriately solemn expression.

❦ 54 ❦

Azel divided his time between the throne room in Hebron and trips to the northern tribes. Today, he was in Bethel, the main city in the territory of the tribe of Ephraim.

The men of the tribe were proud of their heritage, never allowing one another to forget that this was where Jacob received the name "Israel," which meant "He who wrestles with God." So, they regarded Bethel as the birthplace of the whole country.

This made Azel's job more difficult, because the elders of Ephraim were perhaps even more reluctant to give allegiance to a king in Judah than they had been to acknowledge kings from Benjamin.

Today he would once again meet with the tribal council. He hoped there would be movement. Progress had been slow at previous meetings. Now with Abner gone, and with King Ish-bosheth being so weak, they should have welcomed the protection of King David, but Azel also knew that they had to save face as they moved in David's direction.

Azel's status as a member of tribe of Benjamin both helped and hurt, for some saw him as a traitor, while others saw his loyalty to David as a path they could walk as well.

Azel was on his way to the city gate complex to meet with the elders once again when he was stopped by someone he hadn't met before.

"May I speak to you?" the man said as he lightly touched Azel's arm. "You are King David's representative, right?"

"I am."

"We have not met. I am Hushai, elder of Archi just to the south. I was unable to attend when you have been here before."

"I am Azel, a native of Mizpah in Benjamin."

"Yes, I know. I have wanted to meet you. I strongly believe it would be best for our tribe, indeed all the tribes to align with David. Our king is weak and should have never been installed. It was Abner's vanity which led to his coronation. Now that Abner is gone..."

Hushai didn't finish his thought, but there was no need.

"Will you be joining the council today?" Azel asked.

"Yes, I'm glad circumstances have made that possible today. I am ready to speak in favor of your proposal."

"I'm very glad to hear that. I too, as a Benjamite, believe it to be in the best interest of all the tribes to align with David. I made that choice almost 20 years ago."

"There will still be resistance," Hushai warned. "Time is on your side, though. The elders I have spoken to are slowly coming around to the reality of our circumstance, but they must maintain an appearance of independence."

"I would expect nothing less."

"Anyway, I wanted you to know, I will support you in the meeting. See you there."

"Yes, thank you."

Azel watched the man leave him as if he didn't want to be seen entering the council with him.

So many games have to be played in the political and diplomatic realm!

❦ 55 ❧

For two days, two-year-old Daniel's forehead had been hot to the touch and his mother, Abigail, was really beginning to worry. It wasn't unusual for children to have a fever for a few days – all children did – but Daniel always seemed weaker than the others.

He had hardly been awake for several days. Abigail tried to feed him, but he barely roused. Today she tried again.

"Daniel, darling, please, you must eat something. Daniel?" She felt his forehead once again. It was on fire. She went to get a cloth dipped in water.

When she returned, the boy's mouth was open and he had gripped the blanket with one hand and pulled it over him. Abigail touched the wet cloth to his forehead. Then she touched him with her hand. He was not as hot as before.

Has the fever broken?

"Daniel! Daniel, wake up!"

The boy didn't move. Abigail took his hand in hers. It was cold. She shook his shoulders.

"Daniel!"

Alarmed, she picked up the small, limp frame. His grip on the blanket released and his head fell back.

"Daniel!"

King David sat with his arm around Abigail as they both wept. The boy, Daniel, lay on the bed where he had died.

"You did all you could," the king assured her.

"I don't know…"

"You did. Yahweh cares for him now."

David knew these words would only be comforting later. For now, she would grieve.

❧ 56 ☙

"What are we to do?"

"You are king. You have power," Ish-bosheth's mother told him. "You can command the army yourself."

"But that was Abner's role, and now he's gone!"

Ahinoam frowned. Her fourth son had inherited the crown because the three other sons of King Saul were not alive to take it. How he failed to possess the nobility of Jonathan she did not know.

She watched Ish-bosheth as he barely controlled the fear that made him visibly tremble. What could she say to reassure him?

"You have generals with experience. They fought under your father and Abner. They will command the forces on the ground," she insisted. "You need only give them your wholehearted support."

He looked at her as if he didn't fully understand. The look filled her with dread, for there was only so much she could say to bolster him, when her own fear threatened to break out at any moment.

They had fled the Philistines on the day her husband and three sons had died. Would they need to flee again, this time from the rival her husband had been bent on killing; now that Abner's protection had gone with him to the grave?

"We need to do something."

The two brothers, Rekab and Ba'anah, were huddled in Rekab's house. Both men's wives and children had been asleep for an hour so, in the dark of night, the two generals could speak their minds.

"With Abner gone, it's only a matter of time," Rekab finished his thought.

"David has already brought many of the elders of our tribes to his side, and Abner had talked others into throwing their support behind David," Ba'anah agreed. "How long before all Israel joins David? We need to do something to ingratiate ourselves to him."

The brothers looked at one another. They were very close and often did not require that every sentence be finished.

The path was clear.

The sun was high overhead. Rekab and Ba'anah made their way to the king's home. They encountered a guard at the gate to the compound. He snapped to attention and saluted. The two generals returned the salute as the guard opened the gate for them as he had done for them many times before.

Rekab was nervous, but there was no reason to think the guard would stop them. There was no reason for anyone to think this visit was unusual.

But unusual it was.

Rekab and Ba'anah knew that King Ish-bosheth's routine was to nap during the heat of the day and that was why they chose this hour.

They let themselves into the house without knocking or announcing themselves. The queen mother, Ahinoam, was undoubtedly there, but she would be sleeping also. Servants would also be elsewhere or napping themselves. At least that's what they were counting on.

Rekab motioned to his brother to follow him up the stairs. It was not necessary, since they had rehearsed their every move multiple times, but he felt he needed to show initiative, being the oldest.

They were as quiet as possible, making every effort to avoid scraping their sandals on the mud-brick stairs. The last thing they wanted was for the king to awaken and challenge them. There was no doubt they could overpower him, but it would make things messier if he tried to defend himself.

When they entered the king's bed chamber, he was snoring peacefully in the darkened room.

How can he sleep when our nation's situation is so dire?

Rekab scowled. Abner had commanded his respect, but the king Abner had installed failed to inspire loyalty. With Abner gone, there was only one practical course of action.

Rekab nodded to Ba'anah, who drew a knife from its scabbard in his belt with only the slightest sound. Rekab went to the end of the bed where Ish-bosheth's head was and put one hand on his shoulder to prevent him from moving, while Ba'anah raised the knife.

The knife came down with a flash and sliced deep into the king's stomach. Ish-bosheth's eyes opened wide, but his cry was muffled, for Rekab held one hand over his mouth.

Ba'anah raised the knife again and brought it down on the king's neck this time, opening a prodigious blood flow, quickly soaking the bed clothes. He then used the knife to finish the job of severing head from body.

Rekab held the head up over the body by the hair, with a great volume of blood pouring down from it. Ba'anah wiped the blood from the knife blade on the king's garments and sheathed the knife. He then withdrew a leather bag from inside his shoulder bag. When the blood was down to a trickle, he held the bag open and Rekab dropped the severed head into it.

The generals left as quietly as they had come.

❧ 57 ☙

Ba'anah had put the leather bag inside his shoulder bag, which changed its shape, but the guard didn't notice.

The two brothers hurried away to where they had tied their donkeys already burdened with supplies for a journey.

Their plan was to go south all the way past the Salt Sea to the Arabah, in the nation of Moab, where they would cross to the west, then climb up to the heights of Judah and Hebron. That way they would avoid the common fords of the Jordan, where people would see them and wonder why two of Abner's generals were travelling to Judah.

Ahinoam had been awake for maybe half an hour, when she realized that her son had not risen from his midday nap.

"Ish-bosheth!" she called, but there was no answer.

Did he rise early and go to the throne?

She decided to check his bed chamber first.

She left the large common room of the house and climbed the stairs, again calling his name, but there was no response. She went through the door, again calling out to him. He was there in the still-darkened room.

"Ish-ba'al, why are you not up?"

She went to the window and opened the curtain, letting in a shaft of bright sunlight. She turned to look and what she saw made her scream, then faint and fall to the floor.

"I'm afraid I have bad news."

"Bad news?" Mara looked at Ziba, the servant who had supported her since the death of her husband, Jonathan.

"Ish-bosheth is dead."

Mara's eyes filled with tears. They had fled to Mahanaim east of the Jordan river to escape the Philistines and Abner had made a home for them, but when David became king in Judah, a civil war had ensued. Now Abner was dead and so was her brother-in-law, King Ish-bosheth.

"Mother, where will we go?" asked Mephibosheth. She looked down at her son, who sat on the floor as he did much of the time. Now seven years old, he had been crippled since the day they left Gibeah in the land of Benjamin.

Mara had asked herself that question after their protector, Abner, had been killed. Thankfully, Ziba had an answer.

"I have spoken to Makir in Lo-Debar. He will take us in."

"Oh, blessed be Yahweh!" Mara exclaimed.

"Who is he?" Mephibosheth wanted to know.

"Makir is a wealthy herdsman in Gilead," Mara answered. Everyone knew Makir because he was rich, and his generosity was legendary.

"We can go right away. We will be safe there," Ziba said.

"Yes. Yes, that will be good."

"I will begin making preparations."

"Thank you. I will also begin gathering things for the journey," Mara said.

"So, we are moving?" Mephibosheth asked.

Mara looked at him, knowing he might be remembering the trauma of their move two years earlier.

"Yes, my dear. We may not be safe here."

That seemed to soothe the boy.

≪§ 58 §≫

"Messengers from Ish-bosheth are here," Benaiah announced. David turned from the table where he and advisors, Azel and Ahithophel, stood.

"What is the message?"

"They desire to speak to you directly."

David looked at the others. "Azel, will you hold a spear?"

"Yes, my king," Azel said as he selected a spear from several hanging on the wall.

Ahithophel backed up from the table toward the corner opposite the throne. He was older and had never been a warrior. David went to the throne and sat down, resting his hand on his own spear.

Benaiah went out and presently the door opened. Rekab and Ba'anah walked through, followed by Benaiah with sword drawn and two heavily armed guards.

Rekab and Ba'anah bowed low before the king.

"May you live forever, Oh king." Rekab said.

"What is your message?"

Ba'anah opened the leather bag and held the head of Ish-bosheth up for all to see. Several of the men gasped audibly.

"Here is the head of Ish-bosheth, son of Saul, your enemy, who sought your life. Yahweh has avenged my lord the king this day of Saul and his offspring."

"Did you do this thing?" David demanded.

"Yes, we killed him while he slept," Rekab answered.

"Do you not understand, he is my brother-in-law! As Yahweh lives, when another thought he was bringing me good news by announcing 'Saul is dead,' I seized him and killed him at Ziklag. That was his reward!"

The two brothers looked at one another, eyes wide.

"How much more, when wicked men have murdered a righteous man in his own house on his own bed, will I require his blood at your hand and rid the earth of you!

"Kill them!" David shouted, and Benaiah and the two guards with him immediately thrust their swords and spears into the backs of Rekab and Ba'anah, who dropped the macabre head to the floor.

When the two brothers were lying on the floor and it was clear they were dead, the king spoke again.

"Cut off the hands that severed the head of an innocent man and the feet that brought them here. Hang their bodies by the pool in the center of the city! Then prepare the head of Ish-bosheth for burial. We will put it in Abner's tomb!"

The shocking news of the manner of Ish-bosheth's death had quickly spread in Judah. It couldn't be contained.

One of the last to hear of the assassination of King Ish-bosheth was his sister, Michal. The news didn't come from King David, however. She heard it in the streets of Hebron.

She had ventured out of the walls of the royal palace complex to make tentative connections with people of the city. To some it was scandalous that a woman would be seen out in the city unaccompanied by a man, but she no longer cared what anyone thought.

She was surprised that the news of the death of her last full brother affected her so little. Only she and her sister, Merab, remained of her mother's children. But it seemed she had no more tears to devote to this news. There had already been so much sorrow in her life.

❦ 59 ❧

"You're pregnant AGAIN?"

Haggith's eyes were wide as she looked at Maacah, who had just announced to several of David's wives that she would have another child of David. She had already birthed her daughter, Tamar, but Haggith had yet to deliver an heir to the throne.

"Perhaps this time I can give the king a son," Maacah responded.

Haggith's eyes met Abigail's, where she saw weary sadness. After many months she still mourned for Daniel.

Haggith had looked forward to being called to the king's bed chamber. After they had made love and she returned to her room in the women's house, she had felt that she might finally bear a child for the king.

Now, two months later, she knew it was true. She would give the king a child. She hoped it would be a son, though he would not be the firstborn; Ahinoam and her son, Amnon, had that honor, and Maacah would give birth soon so, if Haggith was fortunate enough to give the king a son, he might only be third in the line of succession.

But as they had seen with the death of Abigail's son, Daniel, children did not always live to adulthood.

She shook off the thought. She did not want to wish ill of the children of the others, but the temptation was great.

The next month, Maacah gave birth to a beautiful baby boy, whom the king had said should be named "Absalom" which meant "father of peace."

Haggith had to admit the baby was the cutest she had ever seen, which caused jealousy to well up within her. She tamped it down, reminding herself that it would be her turn in just a few months.

Abigail was by her side when Haggith went into labor. Though Haggith was glad her baby was finally coming, she discovered she was fearful of this new experience. She had attended and even aided in the births of the other wives and concubines of the king, but this was her first time going through it herself. She was suddenly keenly aware that not all women survived childbirth.

After several seemingly interminable hours of labor, Haggith pushed for all she was worth and finally heard the small voice of her baby's crying. She lay back exhausted, but managed to raise her head to see the baby in the arms of the midwife.

"You have a son," the midwife told her with a smile. "What will you call him?"

"Adonijah," Haggith answered. It was David's choice to give him the name which meant "the Lord is Yahweh."

❦ 60 ❦

"You have the ear of the king. He listens to you. You could make him act."

Joab's accusatory words hung in the air. Azel didn't like being between the king and his nephew.

"Has your influence with the king evaporated? You are still his kin and commander of the army," Azel responded.

"He has not called on me for counsel since the incident with Abner."

Azel thought it was a bit rich of Joab to call it "the incident" when it was his knife which had ended Abner's life.

"Is military action the best course, though," Azel questioned, knowing that military action was the only course of action that would occur to the general.

"Are we just to sit and wait? My uncle repeatedly fails to take the initiative. He has done it over and over. It has been decades since Samuel anointed him to be king over all Israel."

"He waits for Yahweh to move before he moves."

"How do we know that's true?"

"He consults prophets and the ephod."

Joab scoffed and turned away.

As he stalked off, Azel wondered if Joab had respect for Yahweh's prophets and priests at all.

Azel had made several trips to the northern tribes during the past few weeks after Abner and Ish-bosheth were murdered. So far there had been little movement. Having grown up in Benjamin, Azel was all too aware of the rivalry the other tribes felt toward Judah

With its much larger territory and population than any of the other individual tribes, Judah had more resources, though together the other tribes appeared more formidable, because of their combined territory.

Yet they had failed in the civil war just past, because there was no comparison between David and Ish-bosheth as rival kings, but also because the training given to Judah's warriors under Joab was superior and Judah had warriors like The Three who could hold their own even alone on the battlefield.

Azel knew there were also rivalries among the northern tribes that prevented them from having a solid alliance. Unity was elusive even though they all shared rivalry with Judah.

Joab was right about one thing: if David wanted to, he could take the other tribes with a military invasion. There would be little real resistance, but would that be the way David would want to rule, as a conqueror?

For several days King David's house had been a beehive of activity. The throne room had been decorated with new drapes and all clutter had been removed. Every wooden surface had been re-oiled and polished and the bronze, silver and gold trim had been burnished until it shone in the light of the sconces. There was an air of expectancy everywhere.

In the kitchen, the royal cooks were busy, preparing what promised to be the greatest feast ever staged by the fledgling kingdom. Staple foodstuffs were stockpiled for last-minute cooking and baking and exotic fruits had been acquired from distant lands to make the event second to none.

Abigail was in charge of purchasing for the event. The king had told her to spare no expense, so she was intent on making this an event no one would forget.

Planning had begun after messengers arrived saying that envoys from the northern tribes had asked for an audience with King David. Abigail assumed that meant there would be a high-level peace negotiation to end the civil war and perhaps even make David king of all Israel. That would indeed be an event to celebrate.

❧ 61 ❧

On the day that the delegation from the northern tribes was supposed to arrive, Azel, as one of King David's ambassadors, stationed himself on top of the city gate complex where he could see them coming from some distance, ready to go down to greet them when they arrived.

He had already been waiting for several hours, but that did not matter. Nothing could be more important than receiving the representatives of the other tribes of Israel with whom they had been warring for more than two years. Azel didn't doubt some questioned the wisdom of the reception the king had planned for them. Many in Judah undoubtedly felt these ambassadors worthy of daggers to the heart, just as Joab had repaid Abner.

But Azel knew David well enough that he respected his restraint and willingness to forgive. The king had never renounced loyalty to Saul, even when the late king was intent on killing him and all who were loyal to the young hero.

Azel knew many of the men who would soon enter the gate of Hebron, for he had sat in city gate complexes with many of them in Mizpah, Bethel, Dan, even Jabesh-Gilead beyond the Jordan River, where loyalty to the house of Saul was still strong. While many could not know it, Azel knew that this trip and what they would ask of David would be humiliating for many of them.

Finally, late in the afternoon, perhaps as many as 30 men on donkeys appeared on the horizon. Azel descended the steps and went out of the gate to await them. He felt buoyant with the promise of what lay ahead.

"Greetings brothers!" Azel called out when the caravan was still many cubits distant. He knew that they would be relieved to see a friendly face, although Benaiah and a company of the king's personal guard were out of site just inside the gate to deal with any unexpected treachery.

"Welcome, brothers," Azel said when the first riders reached him. After the stragglers caught up, he spoke again.

"Accommodations are ready for you. Follow me to where you can wash and be refreshed. Then we will all gather to sit at the king's table."

The men, some of whom must have been traveling for two days, appeared to be relieved with this reception, and as Azel turned, they followed through the gate.

The evening was mercifully cool, and the banquet room was festive, with colorful drapes illuminated by the firelight from the wall sconces and metallic surfaces of cups and dishes glinting as the light danced across them.

The envoys from the tribes sat at tables near King David. They had just come from their rooms where they had washed off the dust of the road, so they were refreshed. There were murmurs of amazement as they took in the food that was being set before them by young women all dressed in white.

The king himself led them in the familiar prayer.

"Blessed are you, Yahweh, our God, who brings forth bread from the earth, and thank you, O God of Abraham, Isaac and Jacob for this bounty and for this gathering in peace."

That last was improvised for the occasion, Azel knew, and was more evidence of the winsome personality of the king.

Azel and Dani were seated toward the back of the room, so he could not see the faces of the men from the other tribes, but he could guess that, as food was passed and wine goblets were filled, broad smiles were gradually replacing the apprehensive expressions they had displayed when he greeted them at the gate.

❦ 62 ❧

No business had been conducted at the banquet. That waited for the morning.

The men from the other tribes came before King David after having their stomachs filled and after a good night's sleep, aided by the fine wine from the king's table.

The throne room was already crowded with officials of the kingdom when the ambassadors arrived. Azel looked around the room. Ahithophel, counsellor to the king, was present, but Joab and Abishai were also there, representing the military wing of David's government. Standing on either side of the throne were Benaiah and three other members of the king's personal guard in full arms and armor to leave no doubt that they would protect the king no matter what.

Azel wondered who would speak for the men, many of whom had come from far away. When all had made their way into the room, the king spoke.

"Good morning, brothers. I hope your accommodations were agreeable and your sleep refreshing."

The men standing directly in front of the king looked at one another, then one of them took a step forward.

Azel was pleased to see that it was Hezron of Mizpah.

How appropriate that their spokesman would be from Saul's tribe.

"We are grateful for the generous reception you have given us, who have been your enemy," Hezron began.

"We are all sons of Israel," the king answered. "We will ever be brothers, regardless of the family squabbles which may arise."

Hezron blinked then smiled before continuing.

"We are indeed your very flesh and blood. When Saul was king, you were the real leader in Israel," Hezron continued.

Azel was certain it was a rehearsed speech, but he did not doubt the elder's sincerity.

"The Lord said to you, 'You will shepherd my people Israel; you will rule over Israel.'"

Azel saw David's head nod ever so slightly as Hezron continued.

"Samuel was our prophet, priest and judge, and it was he who anointed you to rule over all Israel. The house of Saul is no more. It is time for you to inherit his crown."

Azel knew that diplomatic language often took the long way around to the truth. His recent experience had taught him that, but he knew there were others in the room, like Joab, who would be impatient with this speech, which was careful not to offend anyone.

"So now," Hezron continued, "We ask you to rule over us. We pledge ourselves to you as our king; king of all Jacob's tribes and clans. Be our protector and provider. Make an agreement with us."

The king did not speak immediately, but Azel thought he might have seen tears in King David's eyes as he stood from his throne. Everyone knew how long he had waited to hear these words while others fumed with impatience. David stepped forward and embraced the elder from Mizpah, then finally spoke.

"Blessed are you for making this journey. We who worship the same God will always be brothers. Yahweh did indeed have Samuel anoint me to be king, but I have never taken that for granted or seized the throne by force. God works in His own time. And thanks you to, that time is now.

"I will make an agreement with you. I will be protector and provider, but also your servant. Together we will build a kingdom that stretches to the boundaries promised to father Abraham a thousand years ago."

Hezron smiled as did the others. Azel realized David's words had been what they wanted to hear.

"We have taken the liberty of writing a document that we can discuss, which can be the starting point for our agreement," Hezron said, as another of the envoys handed him a rolled up-papyrus.

David took the scroll from Hezron. Azel knew that David should have been the one to set the terms, but there was no hint in David's smiling face that he would press the point. Rather, the king likely knew how important it was to let these men feel they had a measure of control. Even now, David was refusing to take the kingdom by force, even in the negotiation, but letting them save face.

"I'm sure we can reach agreement with this as a beginning," the king said, gesturing with the scroll. "Have the chief among each of the tribes remain to go over details, while the rest are free to enjoy our hospitality. I will gather my advisors and we will read and discuss until we have reached an accord."

"Gratitude, my king," Hezron said, bowing slightly.

Those not included in the discussion then filed out. Azel, Ahithophel and Joab remained, along with the ten heads of the northern tribes.

Also still in the room were Benaiah and his guards, but it appeared there was no cause for concern.

❦ 63 ❧

Eliel's heart had only partially mended, when his mother surprised him with a suggestion.

"I think you'll like her," Dani told him.

"I don't know her."

"She is granddaughter to an elder of Hebron. Very pretty."

Eliel wasn't sure. His attraction to Sela had been spontaneous and powerful. Then she was taken away. He didn't think anyone else could approach that attraction.

"I have arranged an introduction," Dani continued. "The family will come to the evening meal tomorrow."

Eliel felt his stomach tighten. He knew better than to challenge his mother. She was wise and often right about things, but also capable of getting her way about whatever she set her mind to.

It was a great meal with the two families crowded around the table. Eliel sat across from the girl his mother had picked for him. Her name was Carmela, and her mother had been right; she was pretty. She was quiet, but the room lit up with her smile. When Eliel locked eyes with her for a brief moment before she looked down and away, he could see the same strength and humor his mother had.

Maybe this wasn't such a bad idea.

The baby kicked again, and as always, a thrill went through Sela's heart. She was pregnant with the king's child, though as a concubine, her child would not be a candidate for the throne. It didn't matter, though, because she was well taken care of and had the responsibility of the other concubines, which now numbered five.

Some of them had already borne children to the king and the king's wives had been fruitful as well, so there were many children in the king's household.

One of the king's concubines was related to the family of one of Hebron's elders and Sela overheard her talking about a wedding of a granddaughter of the elder. She was only half listening until the name of the groom was mentioned: Eliel.

Sela thought back to the encounters she had had with the young man who was son to a close confidant of the king. She wondered how her life might have been different if she had been able to develop a relationship with him.

Then the baby kicked again, and she was brought back to her present reality.

❧ 64 ❧

"What do you mean, 'Why?'?"

The girl didn't expect the question. She thought it perfectly normal to ask "Why?" when you didn't understand something, but from her mother's tone she understood her mother was telling her how it was done – had always been done – so there was no answer to a question like "Why?".

The nine-year-old was bright and inquisitive, her curiosity caused her to ask "Why?" about many things, but she understood by her mother's reaction that some things just were, and it was her responsibility to simply accept them.

The mother and daughter were standing at a stone oven in a corner of the courtyard of their home in Hebron.

"There is no reason," Batya continued, "except long ago someone figured out the best way and it would be foolish to do anything else."

Bathsheba watched as her mother continued to show her how pita was made, kneading the flour and water and olive oil in a glazed-clay bowl until it was a gooey mess of dough. It was not the first time her mother had shown her this process, so she knew enough that questions occurred to her, but she understood now that her lot was to simply accept what she was told and do it as it had always been done.

Just then, Bathsheba's father, Eliam, entered through the gate into the courtyard and set down his weapons and pack. He was obviously weary.

"Father!" Bathsheba ran and embraced him warmly.

"My dears! I'm so glad to be home!" Eliam said.

Batya came over and joined the embrace.

"How long can you stay?" Batya asked.

"I have a week before I have to go back."

Bathsheba frowned on hearing that, but she quickly smiled again, choosing to focus on the time they would have together. She didn't really understand what her father did. She just knew he worked for the king and was one of his "Mighty Men," and that must be important.

She just wished he didn't have to be gone so much, and that his privileged position didn't put him in harm's way, but what could a nine-year-old girl could do about such things?

A week later, Eliam, rested and refreshed, left Hebron again, riding his donkey to the north and west, where he was posted when the king's army was not actively fighting battles.

That didn't mean there was no danger. His posting was at Sha'araim, the town situated just west of the spot where a young David had killed the giant from Gath. He commanded the garrison there and was tasked with protecting the workmen who were shoring up the fortifications.

Sha'araim, whose name meant "two gates," was closer to Gath than it was to Hebron, so there was always a threat of Philistine incursion. In fact, if David had not killed the giant, Sha'araim would no doubt be a Philistine town, but King Saul had wisely secured it after that glorious victory and now Eliam was helping carry out King David's intention to hold the town and make it a formidable outpost that would be an obstacle to any invasion the Philistines might mount.

Another town David continued to hold was Ziklag, which had been given to them by the king of Gath during their exile. He had placed a garrison and workmen there was well, and it was completely rebuilt after the sack by the Amalekites and now had a proper wall and gate complex.

Eliam wondered how long it would be before King Achish of Gath figured out that David no longer considered himself to be an ally.

❧ 65 ☙

Two young men stood looking at the sealed tomb. As of yesterday, their mother had joined their father inside the cave. Their parents now belonged to eternity.

"There is nothing keeping me here now," the younger of the men said.

"You still have family here; my family," his older brother answered. "Your nieces and nephews love you."

The younger man turned and looked across the valley. The walled city on the mountain across from him was the only home he had ever known, but he felt estranged from it now that both his parents were dead.

"I must go see what else is possible."

"Where will you go?"

"To Hebron, if they will have me."

"Well Uri, if you are determined to go, you always have a home here, if you are not welcome there," said the older brother.

Uri shouldered his backpack, which contained the belongings he had decided to take with him.

"Good-bye."

"Good-bye, brother."

They shook hands and Uri wondered if they would embrace, but his brother did not initiate it, so he walked away, beginning the trek down the mountain to the road which passed through the valley and turned south.

He had grown up among the Canaanites in the city on the hill, but he was not one of them. His grandfather's family had migrated to the city from far to the north of Lebanon many years ago. They had come from what had been the majestic capital of a great empire; the city of Hattusha.

But then disaster had struck. The great empire had fallen, conquered first by famine, then by the Assyrian empire to the east, and the once proud people were scattered. Now, many years later, they were blending into the other people groups in the many lands where they found themselves and, in another couple of generations, would likely be lost as a distinct people.

The young man had heard many things about the new kingdom to the south; the kingdom of David. Everyone had heard of David. His strategic genius in battle was legendary, but just as famous was his loyalty, even when people turned against him.

The kings and gods with which Uri was familiar had no such loyalties; the capriciousness of the gods was rivaled only by the fickleness of the monarchs who purported to inherit their authority. A king who had a moral north star guiding him was a new idea; one that the young man wanted to learn more about.

He did not just want to learn from the king, but from his god too.

❧ 66 ❧

It was early evening when Uri arrived at the gate into the city of Hebron; late enough he worried they might have already closed the gate for the night. He had considered that he might not have a friendly reception, so he had devised a speech that he would make to whatever guard he encountered.

"Stop!" said a soldier just inside the gate, his hands holding tight to a spear. "State your business!"

"I wish to serve King David," Uri answered.

"Who are you? Where are you from?"

"I am Uriah, recently come from Jebus."

The young soldier looked Uri up and down. "Wait here."

Uri walked over to the wall just inside the gate to get out of the way of the merchants and travelers coming and going. The men passing by looked at him curiously, but kept going as he waited.

Finally, the soldier returned.

"Come with me," he said.

Uri followed him through a door into a room built into the casemate wall. Uri wasn't sure what would happen next. It wasn't long before a man came through the door from an inner room.

"You come from Jebus?" he asked.

"Yes."

"And you want to serve King David?"

"Yes."

"Why?"

Uri wasn't prepared for that question, but his young mind quickly found an answer.

"I have heard many good things about the king. I want to learn his ways and serve him."

The man looked him up and down once and then said, "I am Abishai, one of the king's generals. Do you have military training?"

This was a question Uri *had* anticipated.

"No, but I am young and strong and I learn fast."

Abishai turned to the soldier who had met Uri at the gate.

"Take Uriah to Eleazar and enroll him in the company that is being trained."

"Yes, general," the young soldier answered, then he turned to Uri. "Follow me."

"Thank you, sir."

Abishai said nothing else to Uri, but turned to go back into the inner room.

Uri followed the soldier out the door into the gate complex once more, but instead of turning into the city, he turned to go out of the gate. In the late twilight, Uri saw what he hadn't noticed on the way in: an encampment with rows of tents. Campfires were illuminating the tent walls.

The soldier led Uri into the camp and men sitting at campfires eating or sharpening weapons watched them curiously.

Finally, they reached the center of the camp, where a large tent was lit by torches and several men stood around a table. Uri followed the soldier inside.

"Commander, we have a new recruit," the soldier announced. A tall man, surprisingly young, turned to see who spoke and then his eyes rested on Uri.

"What is your name?" Eleazar asked.

"I am Uriah of Jebus."

"You are not Hebrew? You are Canaanite?"

"No, I'm actually of Hittite heritage. My grandparents fled the great famine."

The commander had a puzzled look for a moment then asked another question.

"Why do you want to volunteer to fight for Judah?"

"I want to serve King David any way I can. Word of his leadership has traveled far, and I have been inspired by him."

Eleazar sized him up, then he spoke to Uri's guide.

"Take him to the fourth squad. They have a vacancy."

"Yes, lord ," responded the soldier, and he wordlessly directed Uri to follow him once again.

"Thank you, lord."

When they arrived at the tents of the fourth squad, the men were engaged in training with swords. The swords were made of wood, so there would be no fatal wounds. Uri watched for a while as the soldier who brought him spoke to the squad leader. They both approached him.

"Welcome, Uriah is your name?"

"Yes."

"I am Eliel. Welcome to the fourth squad. We have a place you can bed down in the second tent. Put your pack away and return to watch the training."

"All right. Thank you."

Uri stashed his things in the space that was available in the second tent and rejoined the men observing the training.

Four men were paired against one another and were violently sparring with the wooden swords as if they were mortal enemies. One tripped and fell back and the other put the sword to his throat. The men watching cheered.

"Remember men," Eliel shouted. "Be aware of your surroundings. Nature can be your enemy as surely as Philistines or Ammonites!"

The men laughed and clapped.

"Let's change partners," Eliel said.

The four who had been sparring handed the wooden swords to others, but there was an extra.

"Uriah, are you ready?"

Surprised, Uri recovered and jumped forward accepting the "sword" one of the men handed him.

"Show Uriah a proper welcome." Eliel called loudly. "He has just volunteered from Jebus."

This elicited a mixture of good-natured jeers and cheers from the men, who then laughed and began rooting for one or another of the men.

The man who squared off against Uriah was tall, but Uriah was broad shouldered and quick, so while he hadn't trained as a soldier, he gave the man a good run, as they battled back and forth.

Finally experience won out and the man pinned Uriah to the ground and held the "sword" to his throat. Then he released him and gave him a playful slap on his chest with the flat of the wooden sword. This caused the men to cheer.

His opponent held out his hand and Uriah took it as he pulled him upright.

Uriah smiled. He felt he had passed his first test.

❧ 67 ☙

Azel and Dani marveled at their good fortune. How things had changed since they had been running for their lives with David and his band of fugitives!

Today, seven years after Dani and Adriel had been almost taken into slavery by the Amalekites, Azel and Dani were sitting in a cart pulled by a team of donkeys. It was decorated with colorful flowers and garlands of green, plus bright, cloth bunting fitting for the celebration which was about to begin. Dani straightened seven-year-old Elisheva's head covering. This would be her first experience of being the center of attention of so many others.

Azel had been accorded this honor because of his status as the king's advisor and envoy to the other tribes. While the other tribes' decision to make David their king had not been due to Azel's efforts alone, he had had a large role in convincing them to come on board. Without his playing his part, this day would not have been possible.

Azel's and Dani's cart was fourth in the procession after the king, who rode a white donkey, colorfully decorated, followed by his nephews, Joab and Abishai on their own donkeys, then Ahithophel and his wife in another cart.

Behind Azel and Dani were many more carts, one for each of the tribes, containing the elders from each of the 12 tribes. Each cart was decorated with flowers and cloth died with colors which each tribe had adopted as its own.

Soon they would begin the journey from the army's camp outside Hebron's city gate to the heart of the city where King David's government complex was located. There they would stand for a ceremony which would finally make David king over all Israel's tribes.

On either side of the caravan marched the soldiers of the king's personal guard and, after them, the officers of the army, especially "The Thirty" mighty men. Azel knew their son, Eliel, who was a member of that elite group, would be in the ranks somewhere.

As they approached the gate of the city, they could already see many people on the walls, cheering and waving banners. When Azel's and Dani's cart passed through the three-chambered gate, people were everywhere, crowded along the route, hanging out of windows and standing on the roofs of houses, waving and calling out blessings on the king.

Azel looked in the crowd for Adriel, because he knew he would be there with friends, though EVERYONE was there, so it was hopeless to spot one person among the throng. The population of the city had swelled with people from other towns of Judah, as well as the entourages from the other tribes. Hebron had never seen an event like this!

The caravan moved slowly, but they finally arrived at King David's government complex. A platform had been erected outside the compound wall, and the king, joined by his seven wives and many children, mounted the steps to stand on the platform. All were dressed in the finest apparel the tribe's designers could create.

Standing nearest the king was David's wife, Ahinoam, and her son, the crown prince, six-year-old Amnon. Azel knew there were many of the king's concubines and their children present in the throng as well. He had long ago lost count and stopped keeping track of their names.

Benaiah and "The Three" mounted the stairs and stood at the corners of the platform, dressed in full armor and holding spears. The members of the king's personal guard took their places on the ground in front of the platform, facing the gathering crowd. Even though the tribal leaders had agreed to make David their king, his security detail was taking no chances that some individual might be tempted to act on the treachery in his heart. The civil war and the assassination of Abner would still be fresh in the memory of some.

Also joining them on the platform were the king's nephews, Joab and Abishai, and their families. There was no more space after that, but Azel, Elisheva and Dani were ushered to the space immediately in front of the platform, along with the king's other advisors. Ahithophel and his family were there, except for Ahithophel's son, who was one of "The Thirty."

The people who had lined the street for the procession followed and stood as near the platform as they were able. No one would miss this great event, marking the end of seven years of estrangement between the tribes of Jacob. Finally, everyone was in place and the ceremony could begin.

❧ 68 ❧

Abiathar, the priest, and Gad, the prophet, stepped to the front of the crowded platform. Gad offered the invocation.

"Yahweh Elohim, our Father, bless us this day and bring shalom to your people Israel. May we unite in the knowledge that you alone are God, and your hand will uphold us in righteousness. Strengthen us to do your will and fulfill that which has been promised to this people through our father, Abraham. Bless our king this day, that he may know your ways and walk in your paths. Amen."

Then the sound of singing came from the left of the platform, as musicians the king had organized and trained sang one of his psalms of praise.

> *"Lord, the king rejoices because of your strength;*
> *He is so happy when you save him!*
> *You gave the king what he wanted*
> *and did not refuse what he asked for. Selah.*
> *You put good things before him*
> *and placed a gold crown on his head.*
> *He asked you for life,*
> *and you gave it to him,*
> *So, his years go on and on.*
> *He has great glory because you gave him victories;*
> *You gave him honor and praise.*
> *You always gave him blessings;*
> *You made him glad because you were with him.*
> *The king truly trusts the Lord.*
> *Because God Most High always loves him,*

He will not be overwhelmed."

When the musicians were finished singing, Gad read from the scroll of the Torah, from Bereshit, the first scroll:

"The scepter will not depart from Judah,
*   Nor the ruler's staff from between his feet,*
Until the coming of Shiloh;
*   The one whom all nations will honor and obey.*
He ties his foal to a grapevine,
*   The colt of his donkey to a choice vine.*
He will wash his garments in wine;
*   His robes in the blood of grapes.*
His eyes are darker than wine,
*   And his teeth are whiter than milk."*

Azel wondered how those from the other tribes were reacting to this scripture selection, which seemed to be saying that Judah would be the ruler of Israel forever. Coming from the tribe of Benjamin as he did, Azel knew that tribal rivalries could raise their heads at any time, and that wasn't what was needed now.

But everyone knew the words and they respected them. Perhaps they could agree that the words of Father Jacob so long ago were finally being fulfilled.

Azel also wasn't sure of the meaning of some of the words in the text the prophet read. He understood the references to the donkey, but who was "Shiloh" and what did it mean that he would wash his robes in wine?

He stopped thinking about his questions, because it was now time for the king to be crowned, then he would speak.

David was struggling a bit, for his mind and heart were full. He maintained a solemn expression as Gad read from the

Torah, but scenes from his life flashed in his memory in quick succession.

Twenty years. That's how long it had been since Samuel came to his father's house in Bethlehem because Yahweh had told him the successor to Israel's throne would be one of Jesse's sons.

David had not even been there. He had to be fetched from watching his father's sheep while a brother who had been rejected by the prophet relieved him. When he arrived back at his father's house, he had wondered why the rest of the family looked at him as they did. He was the youngest of seven brothers, but the prophet said he would be the one to rule all Israel and he anointed him with the oil which symbolized God's Spirit.

Then, in quick vignettes, he remembered the day God led him to kill the giant whose threats had paralyzed Saul's entire army, then his instant celebrity as Saul's champion and his marriage to Saul's daughter, followed immediately by Saul's turning against him.

For nine years he fled Saul, when he knew he could seize the throne whenever he wanted; it was his right, but he would not rule as conqueror over Yahweh's people.

The same restraint had postponed this day for another seven years after King Saul's death. His desire had always been to rule only when the people desired it and God opened the way.

Today was finally the day. He blinked to keep tears from coming as he stepped forward.

As they had rehearsed, Abiathar the priest stood before him holding the crown of King Saul, which brought forth another emotional memory. Abiathar's father had helped David with a gift of bread and the sword of Goliath when he had finally fled Saul's wrath. He was repaid by Saul with death, including the slaughter of his entire family and the destruction of their town. David still felt guilt about that, but he could not be responsible for Saul's murderous anger. Abiathar alone had escaped, and his first impulse had been to join David and his band of outcasts in exile.

Abiathar smiled at David, obviously unaware of the emotions jostling one another in David's heart. David returned the smile.

"Kneel."

David obeyed the priest, kneeling on the wooden platform and bowing his head slightly. David felt the pressure as Abiathar placed the crown on his head. It seemed heavier than usual; it was the weight of responsibility for all Yahweh's people that David felt acutely at this moment.

"Bless your servant David today, O Lord," Abiathar prayed, still with his hand on the crown. "May he lead your people, Israel, in justice and mercy. May he be your Anointed One to see your promise to Abraham, Isaac and Jacob finally realized indeed. May he save our nation in righteousness, that all people may be blessed. Amen."

Finally, Abiathar let go of the crown and David raised his head. He stood as Abiathar, still smiling, embraced him.

David then took a few steps forward to address the people.

"People of God, you honor me by making me your king. I will do my best to lead as Yahweh leads. I will do what is necessary to strengthen the borders of our land and extend them. I commit to you today that, in the strength of the Lord who commands armies, I will defend our united nation, so that no enemy can oppress and enslave us.

"We are one people, the children of Israel. I will not favor one tribe over another. No tribe, including my own, will lord it over the others. I will truly be king over all the tribes."

This brought spontaneous applause from the crowd standing before the platform. David knew the majority of the crowd were of the tribe of Judah, and there could be those who looked forward to lording it over the other tribes, after suffering Saul's favoritism toward Benjamin for 40 years. David wanted to nip that impulse in the bud today.

"I have ruled from Hebron for seven years," he continued, "but as king of all the tribes, I will move my capital."

David saw many in the crowd look at one another with questions on their faces. He had told no one of his intentions, but a plan had been developing in his mind for some time.

"I cannot say yet where I will put my capital, but I will select a place which will be acceptable to all the tribes. That decision will be made very soon."

Azel was surprised by this announcement. As David continued speaking, he wondered what he was planning.

Where could David put his capital that would not favor any one tribe?

As one of David's counsellors, Azel was surprised he had not heard of his plans. He supposed he would learn soon what the king was thinking. He looked forward to it.

✎ 69 ✎

Eliel marched at the head of his command as they made their way from Hebron to the northwest. His men had not been told where they were going, but Eliel knew, only because his father was an advisor of the king and had been in the council when this mission had been planned.

They were marching in the general direction of Saul's former capital of Gibeah in the heart of the territory of the tribe of Benjamin, but that was not their destination. The king and his generals were planning to take Jebus and make it the capital of David's kingdom.

Eliel's father, Azel, had explained the king's reasoning to him and his brother Adriel.

Jebus was on the border of Judah and Benjamin, but it was not an Israelite city. The Jebusites were a mixture of Canaanites and a few Hittites who had fled the famine which had been the undoing of their once-great empire a couple of centuries before. When Joshua conquered Canaan, Jebus had not fallen and so it remained a Canaanite city.

But the connection between Jebus and Israel went back much further; a thousand years. Abraham, after turning his shepherds into a fighting force which won a victory against a coalition of minor kings threatening southern Canaan, paid tribute to the ruler of Jebus, which was known then as "Salem." The ruler was both a king and a priest of Yahweh, which was unusual for a Canaanite.

Eliel thought all that history probably contributed to King David's desire to make it his capital. He wondered what they would find when they got there.

❧

Joab rode his donkey at the head of the column beside his uncle, King David. On the other side of the king rode Joab's brother, Abishai. They were the top generals of the army of Judah, although Joab, the older of the two brothers, was commander-in-chief.

Their force had been augmented by the remnants of the army Abner had created after the death of King Saul, but the deaths of Abner, King Ish-bosheth and the generals Rekab and Banaah had left the soldiers in the army of the northern tribes without leadership.

Nothing had been done to reorganize a fighting force in the North for five years. Joab was making sure those who wished to serve were vetted and trained the way David trained his fighters.

Joab had never been inside Jebus, since it was not an Israelite city, though he grew up just a few miles away, in Bethlehem of Judah. Somehow the city had escaped attack from Israel and Philistia alike.

But that would change today.

He could see the formidable walls of the city in the distance now. It was easy to see why his uncle wanted it for his capital. It sat atop a high mountain with deep valleys on three sides. A frontal attack would be difficult indeed.

Eliel directed his men to set up camp across the valley east of the city in a grove of olive trees. An alarm had apparently been sounded, so the gates of the city on the opposite hill were shut. This city was unusual in that it had multiple gates. Eliel couldn't be sure how many, but he could see three from his vantage point.

The men had established their camp in about an hour and had hastily eaten some of their rations to await orders they were sure would come.

Eliel surveyed the hillside and the smoke of campfires wafting up into the sky. The sun was now low in the sky, and he had to squint as he then looked again at the walls of the city. The approach to the walls was difficult. They would have to descend into a deep valley and then climb a steep incline. It would be difficult for any army to breach those walls. Apparently, not many had tried.

The city stretched from a higher mountain in the north to the convergence of two valleys in the south. The drop from the top of the wall to the valley below at the southern end of the city must have been more than 100 cubits. Eliel was sure anyone falling that far would not survive.

"Captain, may I have a word?"

Eliel turned to see who spoke. It was the new recruit, Uri.

"What is it?" Eliel replied.

"If I may, I have a suggestion about a way to take the city without bloodshed."

Eliel looked at his soldier with a raised eyebrow.

"I had forgotten you came to us from Jebus, right?"

"That's right," Uri said. "I grew up here."

"And you would help King David conquer the city?" Eliel looked at him, trying to gauge his sincerity. "Should I wonder where your loyalties truly lie?"

"I am loyal to King David," Uri insisted, "but I also have family in the city, and it would be best for everyone if the city could be taken without bloodshed."

"How?"

❧ 70 ❧

The order had come down. They would not wait until morning to attack. Eleazar, commander of the company on the Mount of Olives, sent messengers to his unit captains. As one of "The Three," he reported to Abishai. The King was in the ranks with his men east of the city walls.

Eleazar surveyed the ground over which they would have to travel to approach the wall. They would descend into the deep valley and then ascend to the wall. The approach to the wall was very steep and the ground in front of the wall was covered with plaster: smooth, hard and white. It would be difficult for the men to keep their footing, and they would be dodging arrows and spears and stones and they went. Eleazar could see why the king wanted this city for his capital. Once it was theirs, it would be a virtually impregnable fortress.

"You men fall in behind that unit," Eliel ordered. "Uri and I must take a message to our commander. We will be back as soon as we can."

Eliel then motioned to Uri to follow him. If the intelligence Uri had given him was correct, it was vital that the commanders have it and be able to act upon it.

The men were almost to the bottom of the valley, which was littered with broken pottery and other trash that had been thrown from the top of the wall. There was a trickle of water flowing south that the men had no trouble crossing before beginning the ascent to the wall.

Eleazar saw that there was a road cut into the steep hillside that led to a gate.

"This way men," he ordered and those near him followed him up the road, which was much easier than going up the steep incline.

Just then a man gave a choked cry and fell with an arrow stuck into his torso, having pierced his shoulder from above. The other men raised their shields just in time, as a hail of arrows fell from the walls.

Eleazar looked around until he saw the king. He and Abishai were shielding themselves as well. They were about midway back in the column heading up the road.

"You can't come up here!"

The shout came from high up on the wall. Eleazar was unable to make out who spoke or even where exactly they were, with the sound reverberating in the valley.

"You can't come up here! The walls are too strong!"

Eleazar looked at the men around them. Their faces made it plain that they didn't know how they would take this city with its ideal situation on top of a mountain.

"Do you know who is at your gates?" Eleazar shouted in answer. "It is King David of Israel, the giant slayer!"

There was silence for a moment and Eleazar wondered if that might have given them pause, but then came their answer.

Once again arrows rained down and the men struggled to avoid being hit. Eleazar looked in the direction of the king and Abishai, wondering if they had a plan he wasn't aware of.

"Commander, may I speak to you?"

Eleazar looked and saw it was Eliel, one of his unit captains.

"Can it wait?"

"No, sir. This man grew up here, and he may know a way we can enter the city without breaching the wall."

Eleazar looked at Eliel and the man with him and recognized the Hittite who had recently joined their ranks.

"You grew up in Jebus?"

"Yes, sir."

"What is your idea?"

"There is a water shaft which opens in the valley. It leads into the city under the wall. It is large enough for several men to go up and overcome the guards to open the gate."

"How do you know about this?"

"My brother and I played in it when we were boys. It is a favorite place for children to play."

Eleazar looked at him and then at Eliel.

"Do you trust him?"

"He has been loyal and has distinguished himself in the games," Eliel answered.

Eleazar took another look at the wall high above them and said, "Both of you, come with me."

He then led them back down the road to where the king and Abishai were.

The men of Israel tried to answer the arrows with arrows of their own and stones from their slings, but the mountain and the wall atop it was too high, so most of their arrows and stones did not reach their targets and fell back harmlessly. Eliam's frustration was growing, and he knew the men in his unit were feeling the same. They had not been given leave to retreat and so they remained where arrows and stones could rain down on them, keeping their shields ready.

"The blind and lame could keep you from entering the city!" came the voice from the top of the wall. Laughter from other voices wafted down from the high walls and echoed in the valley.

Finally, the order was given to pull back.

"Thank you," Eliam said to the messenger who brought the order. "Fall back men!"

Eliam's unit and the unit captained by Eliel went back down the road together. Eliam wondered why Eliel and Uri had left and not come back.

It was a couple of hours before dawn of the next day when seven men quietly descended into the deep valley. Led by Uriah the Hittite who had known the city since boyhood, they found the outlet of the water shaft.

There were walls built in a square around a spring, which was the city's main water source. However, the walls were unguarded. This surprised Eliel, because the Jebusite defenders high above them must have known it would be a vulnerability. The only thing he could think was that they didn't believe anyone would know to exploit it.

The seven special operators climbed the wall with no problem because the stones were not dressed, but were rough with large gaps where they could get a toehold and climb to the top. They went over the wall and down inside.

That's when Uri pointed out the shaft. It was a tunnel cut into the bedrock. They wasted no time, but went in and climbed part-way up and settled down to wait.

The shaft was barely wide enough for two men to pass and not quite tall enough for a man to stand to his full height.

Eliel looked around at the others. Joab had made clear he wanted the most elite among them for this mission, so his brother Abishai was there, plus "The Three," Adino, Shammah and Eliel's commander Eleazar, plus Uriah, their guide. Eliel was there only because he was Uriah's captain.

He had no idea how difficult their task would be.

❧ 71 ❧

King David would be leading the assault himself. Eliam didn't know for sure what was going on; he had only received orders to go to the gate like they had done yesterday, but this time, the gate would be opened. Eliam had no idea why that would happen, but as the sun was coming over the mount to the East, turning the walls of the city before them to gold, they descended into the valley to once again meet the hail of arrows that was certain to come.

Eliel's unit was there next to Eliam's, but Eliel himself was again not present. Then Eliam realized their commander, Eleazar, was absent as well. Obviously, something big was happening. Then Eliam remembered something: Uri had grown up in Jebus. Did he know something?

"You cannot come up here!" came the mocking voice from the wall. He had begun before they even reached the valley floor. "See? We have put the blind and lame on our walls to defend us!"

Eliam looked at the wall and there were men holding up crutches to mock them. Eliam scowled.

"Forward men. We will wipe the smiles from their faces!"

"They have begun the descent!" Eliel whispered. He had been dispatched to the mouth of the shaft in the valley to see when the army's diversion had begun. That was to be the signal for the seven commandos to go into action.

"Let's go!" Joab ordered and the seven men began the ascent up the water shaft, led by Uriah.

It was dark, so the men had to feel their way, keeping a hand running along the rough-hewn stone. They struggled to

196

keep their footing, especially since there was a trickle of water in the center of the rounded floor of the shaft, Occasionally, one of them would slip, the leather sole of his sandal having grown wet and slippery.

It took a couple of minutes, but they reached a point where the shaft went straight up. Uri whispered that they must use holes cut into the rock for feet and hands. He started climbing upward and Joab followed immediately after him. Eliel once again brought up the rear. It took several minutes of climbing but they finally got to the top of the shaft.

They could hear muffled shouts above them and they knew their army was being taunted by the Jebusites manning the wall. Eliel was uncertain how much resistance they would encounter when they reached the summit, but Uri had given them a good idea of the layout and the distance to the gate.

When Eliel climbed out of the vertical shaft, he saw they were in an enclosed space. Double doors opened to what Uri had described as the street which led to the gate.

"Ready?" Joab whispered as he looked back at the men behind him. They all nodded. Each had his favorite weapon in his hand.

"Go!"

Uriah pushed open the door and the others followed him into the street. A couple of women with water jars on their heads screamed and dropped their jars, which shattered on the ground.

The men rushed past them. Joab led the way with Uriah close by, pointing in the direction of the gate, but his description had been accurate enough all the men knew where to go. Eliel brought up the rear, ready to fend off anyone who was armed and gave pursuit.

Their advantage of surprise was complete. Joab startled a couple of soldiers who were about to mount the stairs to the wall. He and Uriah killed them quickly then continued on.

The Eternal Kingdom

Eliel moved forward while looking back and to the sides for anyone approaching, but the street had the feeling of a sleepy town without a care, instead of a city under siege.

When Eliel rounded the corner and entered the gatehouse, the others were inside, and Uriah and Joab were lifting the heavy bar off the double doors. While the others stood guard with weapons ready, Joab and Uriah pulled the gates open.

"Forward men! Charge! Through the gate!"

Eliam could hardly believe his eyes. The gate had indeed opened as the messenger had said it would. He led his men toward the gate as fast as they could go up the hill.

As if surprised by the sudden burst of activity, the defenders on the wall belatedly began firing arrows down from their lofty walls. Eliam's men were by then at the gate.

When he went in, he was surprised to see the generals of the army as well as Eliel and his recruit Uriah.

How did they get here?

Eliam didn't have time to think further, because the seven men were now meeting soldiers who had come down from the wall.

"Forward, men!"

Eliam led his men forward and they met a few unprepared defenders and made quick work of them.

❧ 72 ❧

A week later, after David's army had secured the city and the defeated residents had agreed to be ruled by Israel's king, the elders of Israel's tribes gathered in Jebus. A platform was built so King David and his advisors and generals could stand before the people.

Azel stood on the platform with others who served the king, most for many years going back to when Saul was king: Joab, the king's nephew and his brother Abishai; Benaiah, the king's friend and bodyguard; Abiathar, the last surviving priest of the house of Eli; the prophets, Nathan and Gad, who gave the king words from the Lord.

Besides the elders, many people from the surrounding towns attended the ceremony as the city was christened "the city of David."

The victorious army also stood before the platform, with "The Three" and "The Thirty" at the forefront.

With the people gathered, King David made a speech.

"I have chosen this city as my capital, because it has not been a city of Judah or of Benjamin. My kingdom will be a kingdom for all the people of Israel – a united kingdom.

"A thousand years ago, the city on this mountain, Mount Zion, was called 'Salem.' Abraham, the father of us all, gave tithes to the priest of Salem. It is from the same word we use to greet one another – 'Shalom' - which means 'peace.'

"I shall call my city 'Shalom' once again, but with added meaning. It shall be called 'Jeru-salem' because it will be a city that will teach peace to the nations."

The Eternal Kingdom

It would be several months before David was actually able to reign in Jerusalem. The army occupied the city while some of its original inhabitants were pressed into readying a dwelling for the king.

Eliel spent his time patrolling the walls with his unit. Occasionally they also were assigned duty to guard those workers assigned to remodel the house which had been chosen as the house of the king.

It was smaller than the house in Hebron and everyone knew it was only a temporary dwelling for the king and his household. Plans were already underway for a much more imposing, permanent palace for King David, along with a government complex.

❦ 73 ❧

"Why do we have to move?" Bathsheba asked her father.

"Because David is now king of all Israel," Eliam answered. "He has chosen Jebus – I mean Jerusalem – as his capital."

"Hebron won't be our home anymore?"

"No, we are going to have a new beginning. You will like our new home."

Bathsheba wasn't so sure. Hebron was the only home she had ever known. She didn't really remember Ziklag. She had only been three when they left there.

Now, at 11 years old, she wasn't interested in politics, though she knew that her father was one of the king's "Mighty Men" and her grandfather, Ahithophel, was one of King David's trusted counselors. She knew enough to know that meant her family would go wherever the king went.

Bathsheba's mother, Batya, was busy packing up the household. Already a wagon was parked outside their home in Hebron and was gradually being filled with the family's belongings. Bathsheba did her part, folding clothes and wrapping kitchen utensils for the journey.

Finally, the day came for the move to Jerusalem. Eliam sat at the head of the wagon holding the reins tied to the donkeys which would power their trip. Batya and Bathsheba rode in the wagon behind him. Though her mother sat on a blanket, not watching the road ahead, Bathsheba stood looking forward, not wanting to miss anything.

They had gone just a little way, when a young man rode alongside them on a donkey.

"Is everything all right? Do you need anything?" the young man asked Bathsheba's father.

"All is well," Eliam answered.

"Do you have a house yet in Jebus – I mean, Jerusalem?"

"Yes, I have found a place adequate for our needs during the army's time there," Eliam answered. "Do you still have a place there, Uri?"

"Yes, my brother will let me live with him in our ancestral home for now."

"It must be strange for you returning under these new circumstances."

"I am glad to be going home, and I support the new government," the young man said.

During her father's conversation with the young man, Bathsheba had not taken her eyes off him. He was obviously a warrior like her father, but he was younger.

He was very strong and handsome; words Bathsheba had never in her life used to describe anyone. Her father had called him "Uri" and it sounded like he had family already in Jerusalem.

She had many questions about this fascinating young man, but she dared not interrupt their adult conversation. Yet, she wanted more than anything for him to notice her.

"How much further, father?"

She directed the question to Eliam, but she was watching Uri. He turned to look at her when she spoke and her young heart thrilled when his eyes met hers. She had never felt this way before, and she barely heard her father's answer.

It wasn't important anyway. She had what she wanted from her question.

❧ 74 ❧

Six months had passed since the fall of Jebus. Now they were all moving to the renamed city, where Eliel and Carmela would begin their life as husband and wife.

Eliel drove the donkeys pulling the wagon that held not only his and Carmela's belongings, but also some of the overflow from his parents' wagon, which carried his father and mother as well as his siblings, Adriel and Elisheva, now seven years old.

Carmela put her head on Eliel's shoulder as the wagon bumped and jostled on the rutted road, and he felt that life would be very good from now on.

Uri approached the house he grew up in and wondered if he should knock. He decided against it, and went right in.

He closed the door, set down his pack and looked around.

Not much had changed since his parents died. He knew his brother and his wife would move into the main bedroom, so he made his way to a secondary bedroom he assumed would be his. That's where he found his sister-in-law, Yael.

"Oh, Uri! You're here! I have your room ready," Yael said, as she hurriedly arranged things on the table beside the bed.

"You don't need to go to any trouble. I'm at home."

"Welcome," she said, and slipped out the door.

"So! You're back." Uriah's brother frowned at him from the door. "And death and destruction came with you."

"Things will be better now," Uriah argued.

"We'll see about that."

Uri was glad his brother didn't know the role he had played in causing Jebus to fall.

❧

Azel had never been to a city like this. Tyre was a city on the coast of the Great Sea, just north of the territory claimed by Israel's tribe of Dan. He wasn't sure what kind of reception he was in for here.

He understood why King David had sent him to Tyre. The people were seafaring, befitting their location, and David knew them to be a powerhouse of international trade. Azel had heard that their trading posts were as far away as Tarshish, but he had no idea where that was or what the people were like there; he had only heard that Tyre's ships returned laden with silver and gold.

As a metalsmith, that interested him, more because of the practical uses of these valuable metals than because of the wealth that came to those who possessed large quantities of them. Azel saw great value in creating an alliance with Tyre, despite their differences in religion, culture and language.

A messenger had preceded him, so when Azel arrived at the palace of King Hiram, he was immediately ushered inside. The opulence of the palace recalled for Azel the palace of King Achish in Gath, although the decor was very different.

Following the soldier who was leading the way to the throne room, Azel encountered many people who eyed him curiously. Some of them had skin that was as black as night and others had coloring lighter and pinker than he had ever seen, with hair that was nearly red and even white. Tyre was indeed a crossroads of the world.

The residents of Tyre spoke a dialect similar to the Canaanite language Azel had known growing up, so he had little trouble understanding the soldier when he ushered him into the throne room.

"Bow when you approach the king." the soldier said.

Azel nodded, then turned to look around. There were many men in the room, standing in small groups whispering as the business of the court proceeded before the throne.

204

Azel looked and saw that the king's throne appeared entirely overlaid with gold. The cushions were purple, and the king's robes were very ornate and of a fashion foreign to Azel's experience.

Azel was suddenly aware that most of the people in the room had stopped their conversations and were looking at him. He thought to slip behind a tapestry hanging from a balcony, but then he heard his name.

"Azel son of Eldad, envoy of the house of David. Step forward and bow before King Hiram of Tyre!"

Azel didn't see who spoke, but all activity had now ceased, and he did what the voice said. He stepped quickly to face the throne and bowed from the waist.

"Welcome," King Hiram began. "I have looked forward to your arrival."

"As have I, your majesty," Azel replied. For the first time he looked closely at the face of the monarch and saw a young man with bright eyes and an easy smile.

"I have watched with interest as your king has established his rule over the territory which adjoins my own."

"Your majesty, be assured, the house of David intends nothing but the peaceful coexistence of our two nations."

"I have no doubt of it," Hiram said. "What business do you desire with my kingdom."

"Sire, your kingdom is blessed with the most unique, desirable timber in the world. My king plans to build a palace and would like nothing more than to line its rooms with the finest, most sweet-smelling paneling anywhere. You may name your price and we will pay it."

"You are correct that our cedar forests are magnificent, and the aroma of the wood taken from them is most pleasant," King Hiram said, smiling. "I and my subjects are honored that you would come to us.

"But there is much more I can do, and I hope your king will be agreeable. I love a challenge and would like to provide stone for the project as well as wood. I have many artisans who have the skill to give the king of Israel a palace that will be the envy of empires!"

Azel was surprised by this. He had come merely to establish a relationship and buy some cedar.

"You wish to participate in the construction of the palace?"

"And in its design, if your king will have me."

After a moment's consideration and a glance around him at the luxurious throne room, Azel answered.

"I believe King David would welcome your counsel. I will arrange for a visit to Jerusalem from your artisans – and even yourself, if you desire."

"Yes, I would like to see the new 'city of David' very much. Arrange a time and I will come to Jerusalem."

"I will convey your desires to my king immediately upon my return," Azel said, bowing low once again.

❦ 75 ❦

King David arranged for the largest house in Jerusalem to be turned over to him as the whole government prepared for the coming of Hiram of Tyre.

A banquet to end all banquets was staged as the two neighboring kingdoms celebrated their alliance. Speeches were followed by raised goblets of wine. The two monarchs publicly pledged loyalty in an alliance that had great promise.

But it wasn't all celebration. Much time was spent with the two monarchs and their advisors going over plans and discussing possible enhancements for the palace. King Hiram showed himself to be very knowledgeable about the art of constructing great buildings.

Immediately after King Hiram's visit, a seemingly never-ending train of supplies and workmen began arriving at Jerusalem from Tyre. The ground that had been prepared for King David's palace was soon a hive of activity as expert builders went to work, each well-versed in his trade.

Azel's job was to coordinate all the artisans, making sure their housing and food was taken care of, and that the plan for the building was being followed. He also was tasked with sourcing great quantities of stone and metals. Expeditions to the Negev found abundant sources of copper which could be used in many ways, not the least of which was alloying it with tin to make bronze. His own forge was kept busy as both Eliel and Adriel worked to supply the bronze needed for sconces, hinges and various fasteners.

Great wagons burdened with cedar logs pulled by teams of oxen made their way to the city and were brought down from the north to the building site.

The Eternal Kingdom

The ground selected for the palace was actually outside the northern wall of the city, on a prominent hill overlooking the whole city. So far, the only way to reach it was from the north, where an even higher summit, known as Mount Moriah, commanded the horizon.

When large foundation stones had been positioned, the walls began going up, made of dressed stones which shone in the sun. The plan called for the entire building to be lined with the fragrant cedar wood that had prompted David to send Azel as his envoy to Tyre.

Besides the palace itself, a substantial wall and gate complex needed to be built to enclose the palace in a new city perimeter. Also, a road and steps were to be built up to the palace from the lower city. The existing wall and its northern gate would remain in place so the palace would be entirely enclosed and could be separately defended if need be.

Azel stood on the hill watching the workmen busily laying the chiseled stone in neat rows, then he turned and looked south. The entire city was visible from here.

What a great site for a palace!

❦ 76 ❦

"I don't understand."

"Our family loyalty remains with the House of Saul."

Azel looked at his cousins, Elihu and Shallam, trying to see past two impassive faces.

"David is the son-in-law of King Saul. Even now, the daughter of Saul dwells in his house," Azel pointed out.

"A wife he stole from a Benjamite," Elihu insisted.

"Saul gave him Michal, then reversed himself. Michal was originally married to David, and she is again."

"No matter," Shallum said. "Our father was loyal to Saul and so are we. We cannot help with the project."

Azel was exasperated. "Your father is dead and so is Saul! David is your king now."

"We have said what we have said," Elihu said and the two went back to the work of their forge.

Azel had come to enlist the help of his relatives in the work that was going forward on the king's palace. His own forge couldn't handle all the work that was coming from the king right now.

If Misha'el had been here, he would have agreed.

Azel's nephew was gone on a trip to find tin and other metals required for their work and wouldn't be back for weeks. He would have been more agreeable, Azel was certain.

He had thought to give his close relatives a good opportunity for a kingdom contract, but they had refused.

No matter. There are many forges in the kingdom.

Azel didn't know if he would return to Mizpah any time soon.

❧

It took a couple of years before the palace was completed. That was record time to Azel's way of thinking. The new palace and associated government buildings were a wonder and a testament to the skill and organization of the workmen brought by King Hiram of Tyre.

The palace bore many evidences of Israel's association with Tyre. The abundant, fragrant cedar paneling was a given, but the palace also had numerous pillars with distinctive, red-trimmed capitals, not unlike those Azel had seen at the royal palace of Tyre. Azel marveled at how different things were from when they sat in the ashes of Ziklag just 10 years earlier.

❧ 77 ❧

"What is the meaning of this?!"

King Achish was shouting at the messenger before him.

"Our troops have been driven from Bethel, sire, ending our ten-year occupation."

The messenger trembled as he spoke the words. The king of Gath of the Philistines was growing old, but it was not good to be the bearer of bad news.

"Who has done this?"

"King David, I suppose."

Achish was trembling as well, but not with fear; with rage. *David was to be my ally; my vassal*, he fumed.

"We'll see about that! Summon the army commander!"

"The Valley of Giants?"

"Yes, your majesty, they are at the very gates of Jerusalem."

"King Achish wants to draw us out," King David said to Benaiah, his longtime friend and bodyguard.

They meant the Valley of Rephaim. "Rephaim" was the plural of Rapha, a famous giant of old, so it meant "Giants."

The valley indeed came right to the gates of Jerusalem and stretched southwest all the way to the Philistine lands. It was a natural conduit from Gath to Jerusalem.

"Tell Joab to prepare to march. I prefer to meet them in the field than be holed up here in the city and suffer a siege."

"Yes, sire," Benaiah said, turning to execute the order.

"Oh! And send for Abiathar. I wish to inquire of the Lord."

"I thought you might," smiled Benaiah. He turned once again to go carry out David's requests.

Benaiah rode his donkey at the very head of the procession, with trusted lieutenants to his right and left. They watched the horizon for movement indicating they were near the camp of the Philistines, which scouts had said would surely be there. It was late; the sun would set soon.

Behind them marched King David's elite personal guard; men sworn to protect the king with their lives. In their midst rode the king, now almost 40, and still a strong and able warrior, but too valuable to be endangered on the battlefield. Beside him rode his nephew and commander, Joab.

They had gone about five miles, when Benaiah held up a fist, which caused the men marching behind him to stop. He silently consulted his two lieutenants, who nodded. They heard it, too: the unmistakable sounds of an army in its encampment. Muffled voices and the sound of cooking utensils carried down the valley, and smoke rose into the sky.

Benaiah turned his donkey and rode back to where the king sat on his own donkey.

"They are ahead," he began. "They don't know we're here."

"Yahweh told us to march against the Philistines and he would hand them over to us," King David said in a loud whisper, then he looked at Joab. "Launch the attack."

The Philistines would not be expecting an attack this late.

The element of surprise favored Israel, and the Philistines were driven back, out of their encampment. Joab only halted the attack when it was too dark to tell friend from foe.

"They left everything, even their 'gods.'" Joab smiled.

"Good," King David said, "Burn them. It will send a message that Yahweh is the real God, unlike Dagon."

"Yes, sire. Our scouts say they did not return to Gath."

"So, we will meet them again tomorrow," the king said. "Abiathar, ask the Lord what we should do tomorrow. Should we march against them tomorrow?"

The priest stepped forward and consulted the precious stones on the ephod that was never far from him.

"Yahweh says, 'Do not march straight up to them. Instead circle around behind and come against them opposite the trees," Abiathar paused, as if hearing additional instructions. "When you hear the sound of marching in the tops of the trees, act decisively, for it will be at that moment that the Lord will go before you to strike down the Philistines."

The men standing facing one another in the command tent looked at the king for his response.

"Then that is what we will do," the king said. "Joab, devise the battle plan and share it with our commanders."

"Yes, sire."

"You are all dismissed," the king said. As the men started leaving the tent, he added, "except Benaiah."

Benaiah hung back as the others filed out.

"I wanted to share something," David began. "You may have already thought of this, but this battle may be different."

Benaiah cocked his head a bit as David continued.

"When we went to Gath and then received Ziklag, King Achish was convinced we were allies. I never looked at it that way, but I also didn't argue with him. When we left to go to Hebron, he believed we would continue to be allies, and he didn't interfere with our civil war, because he still considered the house of Saul to be his enemy. I didn't know how long that could continue.

"Now that we have control of all Israel, he realizes I don't intend to be his ally, thus we have this present battle.

"What I'm saying is, this is personal for Achish. You as my armor bearer and bodyguard should be aware that he may intend to send a party after me personally."

"We will be ready for whatever they do," Benaiah asserted.

"I know you will, but he may plan a surprise."

"Understood, sire."

❧ 78 ☙

The next day, Benaiah rode his donkey ahead of his elite troops in the king's personal guard. The army had marched around the Philistines to get to their rear, a maneuver suggested by the word of the Lord from Abiathar. The Philistines wouldn't be expecting that, because this meant David had left Jerusalem undefended.

Benaiah didn't give that much thought, because the priest had interpreted the ephod to say they were to circle around the Philistines and wait until they heard the sound of marching in the treetops, whatever that meant.

The king had two ranks of soldiers on every side of him and a broad front line prepared to stop any attack. Each man was heavily armed and well trained by Benaiah himself. He was confident they would be successful, but the conversation with the king the night before was on his mind.

The army waited in silence in a stand of trees where they were concealed by the shade and the underbrush, waiting for the signal the priest had specified. Benaiah wondered if he would recognize the "sound of marching."

Then it came. After being calm all morning, a strong wind began blowing, and the treetops began rustling and swaying.

The sound of marching in the treetops!

A signal was sent down the line and the army of Israel went forward. For the second time in two days, David's battle plan caught the Philistines by surprise. They were turned to meet an attack from the other direction. The Philistine officers hastily ordered the disciplined veteran soldiers to move to the new front and the two sides traded volleys of arrows before moving forward to the inevitable clash.

214

Then something changed.

A number of chariots appeared on the Philistine side. That was nothing new – the Philistines always used chariots when the terrain allowed it – but this time it was different. The outer chariots raced ahead of the others and converged on the middle of the Israelite line, coming straight toward Benaiah – and the king.

Like a flash, Benaiah realized what they were doing: the first chariots would break through the line and the next ones would go through the breach, driving deeper toward the king on his donkey. A third wave would follow immediately and there would be no way to stop them.

"Tell the king to withdraw!" Benaiah called to the soldiers nearest the king. He could see them run to tell him, but he didn't know if it would be in time.

The first chariots struck the line of infantry with terrible effect as men were trampled or knocked down. Few were able to stand and defend themselves.

Benaiah maneuvered his donkey to pass between the first two chariots. He injured a driver with his sword as he went by, but the second wave was already upon him.

Before he knew it, his mount fell as an archer in one of the next two chariots found its mark. Benaiah tumbled to the ground, dropping his sword. He got up, looking to retrieve it, but the time it took to do so put him at a disadvantage and another arrow sliced through his shoulder. It didn't hold, flying past him, but it opened up a gash from which blood flowed profusely. There was no time to be concerned with his wound. A third pair of chariots was already arriving.

Benaiah could not find his sword, so he picked up a thick branch which would serve as a club. He glanced back and was glad to see the king pulling back as the remnant of his guard fought hard to cover his retreat.

It was then that Benaiah realized he was alone as the last of the chariots went past, and Philistine infantry was coming after them. He would soon be overwhelmed. He steeled himself for what was coming.

Then he saw what might be the surprise the king had foretold. The Philistine infantry paused and then parted as a huge, dark-skinned man walked through the opening.

Benaiah gasped and thought of running, but then realized he might be able to delay these soldiers by meeting this giant long enough to allow the king to escape, whatever it might cost him, so he gripped his club tightly and waited for the giant to come to him.

As the man approached, Benaiah saw he was at least five cubits tall, half again the size of most men, with broad, dark shoulders with muscles and sinews glistening with sweat. In one hand he carried a large sword and he had a massive spear strapped to his back. He wore a bronze pendant around his neck which caught the sunlight as he walked.

He is Egyptian!

That seemed odd, because Benaiah knew there were giants in Gath; they had fled there from towns in Canaan when Joshua led the tribes to take the land, but Benaiah had never seen a giant from Egypt.

The Egyptian was upon him and Benaiah hurried to dodge the first swing of his massive sword.

Benaiah rushed in before the arc of the sword was complete and swung his club at the giant's thigh, landing a good blow, but the Philistine conscript responded by slapping the side of Benaiah's head with his left hand. He tumbled head over heels, landing in a heap.

The Philistine infantrymen stood laughing as Benaiah recovered, jumping to his feet, but he realized he was without the club. Seeing it a few cubits away, he ran toward it, but the Egyptian pulled the huge spear from the strap across his back and hurled it at Benaiah.

Benaiah saw just in time and was able to stop so the spear struck the ground just in front of him. Without thinking he grasped it and, with some difficulty, lifted the heavy weapon and turned its sharp point toward the giant, who was walking toward him, sword raised.

That stopped the Egyptian, who threw back his head and laughed a deep, mocking laugh. Benaiah took advantage of his distraction by charging, driving the spear deep into the giant's midsection, below his breastplate.

The giant's eyes grew wide and he roared in anger, raising his sword, but Benaiah jerked the spear back and ran to his left side away from the large sword. There he drove the spear into the side of the Egyptian's leg, just above the knee.

The giant cried out in pain and anger, dropping the sword and putting a hand on his leg. He looked for Benaiah, who was already moving behind him, where he ran the Egyptian's spear into the back of the same knee. This time the giant cried out, from pain rather than anger. His disabled knee collapsed and sank to the ground.

With the giant's height advantage gone, Benaiah rammed the spear into the back of his neck between his helmet and armor. No longer in control of his limbs, the Egyptian fell forward with an earth-shaking "thud."

In an instant, Benaiah was atop him and, with all the strength he had left, drove the spear through the giant's armor, into his back. The behemoth would not move again.

Benaiah collapsed off the back of the giant, his chest heaving with the exertion. He knew the danger was not past; scores of Philistine soldiers were standing there, though they didn't immediately move, apparently stunned by the unexpected outcome.

Suddenly a wave of Israelites ran past, shouting loudly. Units from both flanks converged on the site of Benaiah's desperate battle and drove back the Philistine infantry.

Benaiah was able to relax, leaning back on the body of the giant Egyptian he had managed to kill with his own spear.

❦ 79 ❦

The sweet smell of incense filled the air. Ahio swung the censer on its three chains as priests had done for centuries. In a tent a few cubits away sat the Ark of the Covenant, the gilt box with its pair of beaten-gold angels atop it that symbolized the religion of Yahweh. It was the most precious artifact from their people's 40-year journey from slavery in Egypt.

He had just finished the morning ritual sacrifice and was completing the process as his brother, Uzzah, worked to gather the meat from the altar. The priests were allowed to eat parts of the sacrificial animals, so it was vital for the welfare of their families, since Levites had no region of their own in Israel and they didn't have farms or work in trades.

That was because of a curse which later turned into a blessing. When Father Jacob had blessed his sons on his deathbed, Levi and Simeon received a curse rather than a blessing because of their crime of the massacre of Shechem and other mischief. Jacob, who had been renamed "Israel," had pronounced them cursed and said they would be "scattered in Israel."

It was true in the case of Simeon that the tribe had mostly been absorbed into the tribe of Judah, with no boundary between the two and the tribe had never had strong leadership, so it was now virtually indistinguishable from the largest of Israel's tribes.

For Levi, the curse of Israel had manifested differently.

Hundreds of years after the curse, when Aaron, brother of Moses and member of Levi's tribe, was designated as the first priest, it was declared that the priests would always be from the tribe of Levi and they would own no property, but would be assigned to cities throughout the land to administer the religion of Yahweh. Direct descendants of Aaron served as priests, whereas other Levites played supporting roles, but there was no territory of the tribe of Levi, like that of the other tribes.

That is how Ahio and Uzzah, descendants of Aaron's son Eleazar, came to serve before the Ark of the Covenant in the small town of Kiriath-Jearim on the outskirts of Judah. It had come to their father's house in the dark days after the disastrous battle of Eben-ezer, when the Philistines had taken the Ark. Miraculously, the Gentiles had returned it voluntarily, and it wound up here in a tent at the house of the priest Abinadab. Though it was just a short walk to the Philistine lands, the Sea People had never shown any interest in taking it back.

That was almost 70 years ago. Ahio and Uzzah had grown up knowing they would serve before the Ark. Their father had been dead for some time and the sons of Ahio and Uzzah were trained to follow him in this important work.

Today, though, things would finally change.

"I have a message from the king."

Ahio turned to face the messenger, who had been brought to him by Ahio's eldest son.

"Yes?" Ahio answered. The king had been there before. He had passed by several times when he was exiled by King Saul, including when he took refuge in nearby Gath, so Ahio was not surprised the king would send a messenger. He was not prepared for the message, though.

"The king desires to bring the Ark to Jerusalem," the messenger continued. "He intends to reunite the Ark with the Tent of Meeting."

Ahio's mouth dropped open. It hadn't occurred to him that the Ark might someday be taken from his house.

Uzzah came and stood beside his brother.

"The king wishes to take the Ark from Kiriath-Jearim?" Uzzah protested. "But it has been here for many years, since before King Saul was anointed."

"Yes, the king wishes to establish a center for the worship of Yahweh at his capital."

Ahio and Uzzah looked at one another. Ahio could see his brother felt as he did: desperate and helpless.

Perhaps they should have seen it coming, but it hadn't occurred to either of them that the Ark would ever leave the house of Abinadab. A cottage industry had grown up around the Ark, with other Levites and villagers providing goods and services to the pilgrims who came to worship there.

Now that would all come to an end.

But the king had spoken, and Ahio knew there could be no changing his mind.

Ahio held his head high as he walked along. The strong oxen behind him plodded along, pulling the cart with its heavy load as if it was nothing.

On the cart sat the Ark of the Covenant, draped in a colorful, embroidered cloth. All along the road, people gathered to see it go by, singing and laughing and generally celebrating the change that Ahio never thought would come.

He was determined not to let his true feelings be seen. He felt as if his life was ending, and in a way, it was. It was at least the end of an era. He had been raised to serve before the Ark, but now others would take that role. Jerusalem-based priests would take over as the Tent of meeting was brought from Gibeon and reunited with the Ark after so many years.

Ahio had to admit it was proper to bring these centuries-old relics together. It would make a statement about the centrality of the worship of Yahweh for the nation, just as King David establishing as his capital the city that belonged to no one tribe.

The king himself was just ahead, leading the procession. He had his lyre and was playing and singing, as well as dancing along the road. The people were excited and calling out to the king and rejoicing at the site of the Ark, as the oxcart ground along, slowly but surely.

Then Ahio turned and looked back, sensing something was wrong. He saw that one of the oxen had stumbled on a stone and the wagon was shifting.

In horror, Ahio watched the top-heavy Ark lurch sideways and his brother, Uzzah, reached out his hand to keep it from falling. His hand caught the wing of one of the golden cherubim under the drape. Ahio and Uzzah looked at one another. Ahio saw the light leave Uzzah's eyes and he fell back on the road.

Ahio rushed to his side, but it was too late. He was dead.

"What happened?!" the king demanded.

"The Ark was falling and my brother reached out to steady it," Ahio answered his voice breaking. "But Yahweh commanded that no one should touch the Ark, so He lashed out in His anger. Now my brother is dead."

"We stop here!" the king said, loudly enough for all to hear. All celebration had stopped when Uzzah fell, so all were able to hear. Then, to himself, he said, "How will the Ark ever come to me?"

Ahio's grief was so great, he struggled to avoid saying what he felt: *If the king had not ordered the Ark moved, my brother would not be dead.*

Somehow, he held his tongue.

❧ 80 ☙

A temporary place was found for the Ark, ironically with the home of Philistine transplant and Israelite proselyte Obed-Edom, who lived between Kiriath-Jearim and Jerusalem.

In the meantime, David tasked Abiathar with researching the Lord's protocol for transporting the Ark, so the tragedy of the death of Uzzah would not be repeated.

After close examination of the scrolls, Abiathar reported that the Ark should be transported on poles, borne on the shoulders of priests. It was not to be moved on a cart, so situations like they had just experienced would not be possible. After three months, David decided to try moving the precious relic again.

To be certain there would be no tragedy this time, King David declared that the priests would indeed carry the Ark on poles, but after every six steps, other priests would sacrifice a calf and an ox. It would slow the procession to a crawl, but the king wanted to be certain there would be no tragedy like last time. He added maidens and musicians to give the parade a festive atmosphere.

Once again people gathered along the road and cheered.

This time there was no incident, and the city of Jerusalem was finally visible in the distance. As they drew near to the city, the enthusiasm of the celebratory crowd reached a fever pitch, and the king abandoned all decorum to celebrate the event, taking off his royal robes and crown, continuing to dance in just his undergarment.

The crowd continued to cheer, happy that their king was so devoted to Yahweh that he would remove his expensive, imposing royal garments and celebrate as one of them.

The joyful procession entered the city of David and traveled through the streets to its final destination at the height above the king's palace, where the Lord's Tent had already been brought from Gibeon and set up in readiness.

More musicians and dancers awaited the arrival of the Ark and the celebrants accompanying it. Soon psalms rose in the air as the priests bearing their precious cargo topped the hill above the palace, waving palm branches and cheering.

Sacrifices were once again offered as the Ark was taken through the veils into the Tent, through the first apartment – the Holy Place – and finally to its resting place inside the inner chamber – the Most Holy place.

The symbols of the monotheistic worship of Yahweh were finally reunited for the first time since the destruction of Shiloh.

King David returned to his palace as the sun was setting, the long day of celebration finished.

He mounted the steps to the broad portico, still feeling the euphoria of joy and glorious worship which had gone on for so many hours.

But his joy was brought to an abrupt end.

"You really distinguished yourself today, dancing half naked in front of the slave girls like a vulgar fool!"

David turned to see who had spoken. It was Michal, daughter of Saul, who had been his first wife.

"I danced before Yahweh!" he retorted. "I was celebrating before the Lord, who chose me over your father and his entire family. I will shame and humiliate myself even more, if it glorifies God!

"As for the slave girls, they understood that I danced to God's glory. Would that you understood!"

Michal frowned and turned away with a twirl of her colorful skirt. David scowled and walked the other direction, his euphoria from the day of celebration gone.

❦ 81 ❦

Several weeks had passed since King David's victory over the Philistines in the Valley of Giants. The king had wondered if they might not attack again, but then word came that the Philistines were on the march. The word of the spies was that they intended to do battle at Pas Dammim.

"It's a good thing we fortified Sha'araim," the king remarked to those standing around the table in the throne room: Azel, Ahithophel and Joab.

"Very true, they likely would have come further, but they would not ignore Sha'araim with its garrison," Joab agreed.

"What will you do?" Ahithophel asked.

"We must meet them. Joab, how long can the garrison hold them?" the king asked the commander of his army.

"Not long. They must be reinforced immediately."

"Then assemble a force and march. Waste no more time. Abishai and I will follow with the remainder of the army we are able to field."

"As you wish," Joab saluted as he left.

Eliel once again marched with his command. They would meet the Philistines one more time. The march would not take long. Pas Dammim was just to the west of the garrison city of Sha'araim, which was itself just west of the spot where King David had killed the giant, Goliath, the fame of which he still carried today. Eliel's father had been there on that glorious day.

"Lord, will the battle have begun when we arrive?" Eliel asked his commander, Eleazar.

"It's very possible. Joab was taking a rapid strike force ahead of our main body, so we should be prepared to enter the fray immediately."

"Thank you. I will relay that to my men," Eliel saluted and rode his donkey back to where his men were marching.

"Men, we likely will charge into battle as soon as we arrive, so be ready."

The men immediately began checking their weapons as they continued to march.

Eliel looked ahead. He could already see the walls of Sha'araim, and beyond the city, a cloud of dust in the air.

The army under the command of Abishai did indeed plunge into the battle as soon as they arrived. It was apparent they were none too early, as the Israelite force Joab had rapidly assembled was being pushed back.

Eliel's men were on the right flank and, they did as they had done before, they whipped around to engulf the left flank of the enemy to surround and destroy them. Eleazar then drove his center through the line to cut them off.

Eliel knew that Adino was on the left of their line and would attempt something similar.

In the center, however, something else was brewing.

Abishai had led the main body into the fight near the center of the line. His brother's spent troops pulled back and Abishai's fresh fighters replaced them, but they were meeting stiff resistance.

"Forward! Hold the line!" Abishai shouted, but he could see the Philistine fighters were too numerous. Abishai swung his sword this way and that from atop his donkey, felling one after another of the horde that was coming at them.

Then the unthinkable happened. A Philistine arrow fell from a high angle and struck his donkey's neck. The poor animal was instantly paralyzed and fell forward, throwing

Abishai, where he rolled over and over on the ground. When he looked back, Abishai saw that his men were retreating.

"Come back! I'm all right!" Abishai shouted, but they kept running. There were several Philistine soldiers running toward him, so there was no time to think.

Abishai picked up a random spear from the ground and drove it into the chest of the one nearest him. The man uttered a guttural cry and fell at his feet. Abishai took the sword from the hand of the dead soldier and parried a blow from the second Philistine he met before ramming the two-edged weapon into the soldier's throat.

He didn't have time to see if the man was dead because two more were coming. He jerked the spear from the chest of the first man and threw it at the one nearest, catching him in his gut, then met the next one with the sword.

His first blow was blocked by the man's shield, but Abishai was able to parry the other man's sword and jab at him high enough to open a deep gash in the man's neck. He reacted by stepping back and Abishai went in to stab him in his midsection.

Abishai had just enough time then to take the man's shield and pick up the spear before he was set up by three more Philistines.

❦ 82 ❦

"Turn around! Your commander fights alone!" Shammah
yelled to his retreating men, as he slapped a man's thigh with
the flat of his sword. "Back! Back into the fight!"

The men had spontaneously retreated when they saw
Abishai's donkey fall and throw him over, but Shammah had
seen that his commander was alive.

Shammah then led the way as his officers in the rear drove
the men back toward the battle line. When he arrived at the
place Abishai stood, he couldn't believe his eyes.

Stretching out before the king's nephew was a string of
Philistine bodies, some in obvious agony, others not moving
at all. Shammah thought there must be hundreds. He
immediately joined the fight.

As Shammah struck down the first Philistine soldier he
came to, Abishai looked his way with obvious relief, but he
had to turn immediately to face another of the Sea People.

Others then joined the fray and soon the Philistines were
routed, leaving behind hundreds of their comrades. A cheer
went up from the Israelite soldiers.

Finally, Abishai was able to rest. He collapsed on the
ground, and for a moment Shammah feared he had been
stricken, but then he saw his chest heaving and he knew he
was just exhausted. Shammah bent over him and brought his
water horn to the exhausted general's lips.

When the postmortem was conducted after the battle,
Abishai's heroism was not the only feat to be honored. David
himself, along with Eleazar, had stood together in a barley
field while others had fled.

Eliel had had to struggle to keep his men from retreating, but ultimately they did return to the fight.

The report was that Abishai had single-handedly killed or wounded 300 Philistines. The wounded ones had been finished off when Shammah and the others returned to the battle, so he was credited with 300 personal kills.

As the commander of the 30 mighty men, Abishai was honored as the hero he was. His brother, Joab, was proud.

Eliel stood with the other members of The Thirty as accolades were passed out. He had mixed emotions, because his commander Eleazar was being honored, but his men had retreated, leaving him on the field. He knew that, while they had ultimately won the battle, the two instances in which the men had fled, were a dark spot on the reputation of the army. Only the heroism of their officers and the king himself enabled them to turn potential defeat into victory.

Uri stood beside Eliel during the ceremony. The Hittite had distinguished himself in many ways during the battles they had fought, since joining them and revealing the secret water tunnel that enabled them to take Jebus – now Jerusalem.

Eliel could see a bright future for him.

❦ 83 ❦

"Go ahead. Do your worst."

"Sire, I do not wish to harm you."

King Achish stood before David with his head bowed.

"You have served your people honorably," King David continued. "I do not wish to further humiliate you, but our victories over these weeks mean that I will set the terms of our peace. You will continue to rule your people, but your city-state will be a vassal of Israel.

"You once suggested that I could be your vassal and you would be my protector," David continued. "Today I declare you to be my vassal. You will pay tribute to Israel and if you dare to attack us, we will bring terrible retribution against you. Your people's oppression of my people ends now."

Achish looked down once again. He had no answer. David's strength and skill in battle had decimated the army of Gath so he could mount no meaningful resistance.

King Achish was tired, and his bones creaked when he sat down and rose up from his throne. His end would be in weakness, and nothing could be done about it.

Gath had been the jewel of the five Philistine cities, although Gaza was a rival for the position of first among equals, and the others jockeyed for position as well.

Now, with David's army occupying the city, Achish wondered why none of the other Philistine cities had come to his aid. Perhaps they saw how David had repeatedly defeated the vaunted army of Gath, each time reducing its numbers and strength.

Is Israel's Yahweh stronger than Dagon and Ba'al?

It would seem so.

Word came to Jerusalem just a month later that King Achish of Gath had died. David had seen how feeble the once proud king had been when he had visited Gath.

David sent Joab and a contingent of soldiers to Gath to secure the city in the wake of Achish's death and install a ruler acceptable to the Israelite king; one that would be unlikely to revolt and would send the tribute on time.

Achish had no son, so Joab chose a member of the noble class, but one who had little personality and posed no threat.

❧ 84 ☙

"Thank you for coming. I wanted to share something that has been on my mind to see what you thought about it."

The prophet Nathan listened for what the king would say next in his throne room.

They were close to the same age and had history together. On the night David had fled for his life when Saul first threatened to kill him, he had gone first to Samuel, the prophet who had anointed him. Samuel had hidden him among the students at his school of the prophets, which is where David met Nathan.

On that night, David had seen a display of supernatural power come over King Saul, who stripped himself, not only of his crown and royal robes, but of his weapons and tunic as well. He lay on the road in a trance, nearly naked for most of the night. The king had involuntarily spoken prophetic blessings as David watched from his hiding place.

Nathan had explained a bit of how "the word of the Lord" came to prophets like Samuel, who often heard directly from God. Nathan also had that gift.

"I've been thinking lately it's not right that I live in this grand house of cedar, but God's presence in the Ark of the Covenant is still housed in a tent after all these centuries.

"As such, I'd like to build a temple to Yahweh. The people around and among us build temples to their many gods; in every city, it seems. Should we not have a temple dedicated to the all-powerful God who made everything?"

Nathan listened carefully to the king before answering.

"That sounds good. Do whatever you think best."

"Thank you," the king said. "I value your good counsel."

❧ 85 ☙

King David and his advisors were gathered around the planning table in a corner of the throne room early the next day. Whereas it usually featured maps, today it had a simple drawing on papyrus.

"I want it to be the grandest temple in all the land – grander than those in many countries," the king said, as he laid out his idea. "It must be a wonder to the world, for Yahweh is greater than all the gods of legend – of wood and stone and bronze."

The advisors, including Azel, Ahithophel and others, listened carefully, letting him talk.

"It is not right that I dwell in this house of dressed stone and cedar while our God dwells in a tent. I want to do something to honor Him; He has done so much for us. He brought us out of Egypt, redeemed us from slavery, and went before us to give us this land. Now he has raised me up and given us a kingdom with stability and prosperity. He is El Shaddai, God our Provider!"

David was feeling eloquent, and he could see that his impromptu oratory was having its effect. His advisors were hanging on his words and being swept up in his enthusiasm.

Then there was a disturbance at the double doors at the entrance to the room. Everyone's attention was drawn that way as the doors opened.

"I must see the king immediately! I have a word from the Lord!" said Nathan, the prophet. Two soldiers were attempting to prevent him from entering, without success.

"Let him pass," David ordered, and the soldiers released their hold on Nathan, who strode over toward the group around the table.

"My King," the prophet said, dipping his head slightly. "The Lord spoke to me in a dream in the night. I have an urgent word for you."

David looked at the prophet and then at those around the table. "What is it?"

"Do you wish to dismiss those gathered here?"

"Should I dismiss them? We are discussing my plan for the temple of Yahweh."

"Perhaps they should hear also, then," Nathan answered.

The men at the table separated to allow Nathan to join them. He wasted no time launching into what he had to say.

"The Lord says, 'Should you be the one to build me a house to dwell in?'"

David first felt confusion, then a bit of embarrassment as the prophet continued.

"'I have not dwelt in a house from the time I brought the Israelites up out of Egypt until now. I have moved from place to place, dwelling in a tent.'"

The prophet paused only long enough to draw a breath.

"'Wherever I have moved among the Israelites, have I ever said to any of their rulers whom I raised up to lead my people Israel, "Why have you not built me a house of cedar?"'"

No, God has not asked for a house, David admitted to himself. He hadn't thought of it that way.

Nathan continued, "This is what El Shaddai says: 'I took you from the pasture, from tending sheep, and raised you up to be ruler over my people, Israel. I was with you wherever you went, and I cut off all the enemies obstructing you. Now I will make the name of David great; the greatest on earth.'"

"Furthermore, the Lord declares to you that Yahweh himself will establish your house."

Nathan continued and David listened intently, realizing the words were significant and life changing, for now the prophet was quoting God concerning David's own destiny.

"The Lord says, 'When your days are finished and you rest with your fathers, I will raise up your offspring to succeed you on the throne, your own flesh and blood, and I will establish his kingdom. He it will be who will build a house for my Name, and I will establish his kingdom forever!'"

"Forever?!" David interrupted. He had barely heard the part about his son building the House of God.

Nathan did not answer the question, but continued relaying what God had told him, as if it was urgent he relate it all before he forgot.

"'I will be his father, and he will be my son,' says the Lord. 'When he does wrong, I will punish him with a rod wielded by men, but my love will never be taken from him, as I took it from Saul, whom I took out of your way. Your house and your kingdom will endure forever before me; your throne will be established forever!'"

Finally, the prophet paused to catch his breath, then spoke again. "This is what the Lord said."

Silence hung in the air. The men around the table looked at David, anticipating a reaction, which came soon.

"Why does the Lord not want me to be the one to build his house?"

"Because you are a warrior, a man who has shed much blood. The son who will come after you, who will build the house of the Lord, will be a man of peace."

Although it was disappointing, David knew Nathan's words were true; he couldn't deny that he had had a bloody career. He had spent years little better than a bandit, or even a terrorist; killing and looting just to survive. Now he was established as king and the wars he would continue to fight would be to achieve peace, but he would have to shed more blood before peace was realized. Of that he had no doubt.

"Men, you are dismissed. I will send for you when I have need of further counsel."

The men around the table looked at him and at one another and slowly made their way out of the room, leaving just the prophet and the king standing facing one another.

"And there was more," Nathan said when the men had left, "The Lord also said, 'I will provide a place for my people, Israel, and will establish them so they have a home of their own and will no longer be disturbed. Wicked people will oppress them no more, as they have always done, and I will give you rest from all your enemies.'"

David was overwhelmed by all he had been told, so he stood looking at the floor, trying to take it all in.

Finally, he asked a key question.

"Did the Lord really say to you that the House of David will stand forever?"

The prophet did not answer immediately, but raised his head and straightened his back before answering solemnly.

"He did."

❧ 86 ☙

When Nathan was gone, David told Benaiah to cancel all his meetings and make excuses to those who planned to come before him with their requests.

He went out of his palace, down the grand stairs to the street below. Then he began the climb to Mount Zion, behind his house, where he had brought the Lord's Tent.

"My King!" Abiathar said when David approached the gate of the compound. "What brings you here?"

"I need to sit and talk with the Lord."

Abiathar watched as he went into the courtyard of the sanctuary. The morning sacrifice had been completed more than an hour ago, so there was virtually no activity. David walked past the bronze altar of sacrifice and the golden laver, the wash basin so important to the purity of the rituals carried on here.

Between the laver and the colorful curtains marking the entrance to the sanctuary he sat down on the sandy earth. He would not go inside; he was no priest. Other kings regarded themselves as rulers of the priests and arbiter of the words of their gods, but David knew the priests served a King who was higher than he; a king's King.

"Who am I, Sovereign Yahweh, and what is my family, that you have brought me here?" he began. "If this were not enough Lord God, you have also spoken about the future of the house of your servant—a mere human!

"What more can I say? You know your servant, Lord. For the sake of your word and according to your will, you have done this great thing and made it known to your servant."

The Eternal Kingdom

David's voice broke. He was overwhelmed with God's love and the prophecy Nathan had shared.

"How great you are, Lord of all! No one is like you, and there is no God but you, as we have heard with our own ears.

"And who is like your people, Israel—the one nation on earth that you, God, redeemed as a people for yourself, to make a name for yourself, and to perform great and awesome wonders, driving out nations and their gods from before your people, whom you redeemed from Egypt?

"You have established your people Israel as your very own forever, and you, Lord, have become their God.

"And now, Lord God, please keep forever the promise you have made concerning your servant and his house. Do as you promise, so your name will be great forever. Then people will say, 'The Lord Almighty is God over Israel!' And the house of your servant will be established before you.

"For you, Yahweh, God of Israel, have revealed this to your servant, saying, 'I will build a house for you.' So, I have found courage to pray this prayer to you.

"Sovereign LORD, you are God! Your covenant is trustworthy, and you have promised these good things to your servant.

"Now be pleased to bless the house of your servant, that it may continue forever in your sight; for you, Sovereign LORD, have spoken, and with your blessing the house of your servant will be blessed forever."

He sat there for a while, eyes closed, simply meditating on all that had transpired and all that it would mean.

After some time had passed, David left the Lord's Tent, but he did not return to the throne room. Instead, he went to the women's quarters and knocked on the door.

Sela opened the door and her mouth fell open.

"David! I mean, majesty!"

"Shalom, Sela. I wanted to see Ahinoam and Amnon."

"Please, come in," Sela said, still seemingly surprised by his unannounced visit. "I will get Ahinoam. I think she's in her room."

David sat in a chair by the door. His wives and children were mostly tending to chores and perhaps at the market, but David was glad that Ahinoam was there.

Soon she appeared, holding the 10-year-old's hand.

"Ah, Ahinoam, my love," David said as he rose and embraced her. "And how is my firstborn son today?"

"Very well, father," Amnon said, smiling.

"What brings you here?" Ahinoam asked.

David knew that he rarely if ever had personally visited the women's house; usually communicating through messengers, but today was different in so many ways.

"I wanted to see you. And Amnon. Especially Amnon, really."

"I'm glad, but why 'especially Amnon?'"

David paused, trying to decide how much to tell her.

"I was excited about something, but I now know I am unable to do it," he began. She looked at him, her eyes being two question marks. "However, along with the disappointment came a very big promise, and it may very well involve Amnon."

"Really?" Ahinoam said. "What promise?"

"A promise God told Nathan to give me; about our future."

Are you the one who will build the Lord's Temple? he thought, as he put his hand on Amnon's shoulder.

"One of my sons will build a Temple for the Lord," David explained. "I had thought to do it, but Yahweh says it will be my son."

Ahinoam's eyes widened as she seemed to understand why David had come to visit her and Amnon. The boy looked at his father as if not quite understanding.

❧ 87 ☙

Years were passing as David strengthened his kingdom. The subjugation of Gath meant Israel was at peace and the centuries-old Philistine threat was neutralized. Progress for the kingdom was now unimpeded.

Eliel was given more responsibility in the army as David and his nephew Joab, his right-hand, expanded Israel's borders. Moab for some reason rose up in defiance, but the noise from the kingdom to the southeast was quickly put down, so the nation that had been the birthplace of King David's grandmother, Ruth, was now a tributary of Israel and David's kingdom became ever richer.

Edom, Moab's neighbor, also rose up against Israel, but Abishai's command was sent and put the threat to rest once and for all, killing more than 20,000 of the soldiers of the Edomites, who were descended from Jacob's brother Esau.

Eliel took part in most of these adventures, but the next war would be sparked by an indignity done to his father.

"How good it will be to be home again!" Eliel said, his mind on his new wife, Carmela.

"Yes, it will be good," Uri agreed.

They were marching back to Jerusalem from Edom where they had finished mopping up after the battle in which they had conquered yet another people group.

Eliam trotted up beside them just then.

"It's good to see you both made it out of the battle!"

"And you, too!" Eliel replied.

"Uri, I've been meaning to talk to you," Eliam continued.

"Oh, about what?" Uriah replied.

"I'd like you to meet my daughter. I think you'd like her. She's 17, so it's time she was married."

Uriah's eyes grew wide. "Well, I met your daughter some time ago, when she was much younger. I mean, I guess we weren't officially introduced, but I have seen her before."

"Good. I'll let you know a good time and we'll have you over for the evening meal. Batya is a good cook."

"I'm sorry, I don't know her name," Uriah said.

"Bathsheba."

"Right."

Bathsheba had grown up since he last saw her. She was now a young woman whose beauty few could match. Uriah was bashful the first time he went to have the evening meal in the home of Eliam.

Batya, Bathsheba's mother, had prepared an outstanding meal, but Uriah was embarrassed to be the center of attention, so the butterflies in his stomach almost prevented him from tasting the food.

Bathsheba, on the other hand, appeared poised and self-assured. Uriah was at least 10 years older, but she had a quiet maturity beyond her years.

They were married six months later. Everyone involved felt it was meant to be. At the wedding, Bathsheba was radiant; she seemed to light up the room and no one who was there could take their eyes off her.

Her grandfather, Ahithophel, counselor to the king, was very proud.

Uriah and Bathsheba moved into a little house within the walls of Eliam's and Batya's compound that Uriah helped Eliam build.

So began their life together.

❧ 88 ❧

"King Nahash is dead," King David announced.

No one in the throne room needed to be told who Nahash was. He had long sat on the throne of the desert kingdom of Ammon, far to the east of the Jordan River. King Saul had defeated them when they besieged the trans-Jordan city of Jabesh-Gilead, but then Nahash had been solicitous toward David when he had been on the run from Saul.

"His son, Hanun, succeeds him on the throne. I'd like to express my condolences to him on his father's death. Ahithophel and Azel, I'd like you to take the message to him."

"Of course, sire," Ahithophel answered.

"Benaiah will select a security detail to accompany you," the king continued. "I will have a document for you tomorrow morning that you can take to Rabbah."

"How long will you be gone this time?" Dani asked.

"We should be back in 10 days. Two weeks at most," Azel answered.

"How much longer will you do this? I miss you when you are gone," Dani sighed, knowing that her husband's work was important, but wishing he didn't have to be away so much. He served as the king's envoy, so he was away at distant capitals often, but he also oversaw the production of metals for the king's many building projects, both of which took him away from Jerusalem often.

"And I miss being here with you," Azel said, embracing her. "I cannot say for how long this will be my lot, but I must do my duty."

"I will have your finest tunic and cloak clean and ready for your journey tomorrow," Dani said, stiffening her jaw. "Now I think there's a little girl that would like some attention from her father."

Twelve-year-old Elisheva was standing in a doorway, looking at them. Dani wasn't sure how much she had heard. She ran and threw her arms around her father's waist.

"Do you have to go, father?"

"Yes, 'Sheva, you know I have a job to do."

"But I don't want you to go!"

"Don't worry, I'll be back before you know it." Azel smiled down at his youngest and Dani had to smile too. "I guess I'd better check with Adriel to be sure everything is well in the forge before I leave tomorrow morning."

Dani simply nodded, for the lump in her throat made it impossible for her to speak.

The journey had been difficult for Ahithophel. He was several years older than Azel. While Azel also had a daughter-in-law now, Ahithophel had a granddaughter who had grown up to be a beautiful young woman and was now married to a man in Eliel's command.

Azel knew that Ahithophel was glad when they finally arrived at Rabbah and found lodging for the night. Tomorrow they would stand before King Hanun.

Four young soldiers that Azel didn't know had accompanied them for security. They were accustomed to long marches in harsh environments, so they seemed none the worse for wear.

Azel had to admit that he was happy the trip was behind them, when he settled into the strange bed that was made available in this foreign city and was soon asleep.

❦ 89 ❦

The palace in the Ammonite capital of Rabbah was rustic and exotic, with plants Azel didn't recognize and fabrics and architectural details of unfamiliar design. The next morning, Azel noted that the people of this place were very different from his own, however they welcomed the emissaries from the House of David, and shortly they were ushered into the throne room of King Hanun.

"Your majesty, we bring greetings from King David of Israel." Ahithophel, as senior advisor to King David, took the lead. "He wishes you the best after the death of your father, the honorable King Nahash."

"Your words are welcome," King Hanun answered. "But what are your intentions in coming here?"

"Our 'intentions?'" Ahithophel stammered. "We convey condolences from our lord and king…"

"Do you? Or do you come to spy on us?"

It was only then that Azel noticed the hard faces of King Hanun and the men who stood on either side of the throne.

"It seems more likely you are here to assess our defenses for a future campaign against us!"

"I assure you, your majesty, nothing could be further from the truth!" Ahithophel insisted.

Azel could see the king was not convinced.

"If I may, our king sent this document expressing his good wishes," Azel broke in, handing the scroll to Ahithophel to maintain protocol. Ahithophel handed it to one of Hanun's men nearest him.

Hanun took the document and broke its seal. He scanned it, then crumpled it into a ball and threw it on the embroidered carpet at his feet.

Azel's mouth fell open. He hadn't encountered this kind of reaction in any of his dealings as the king's envoy.

"This means nothing!" Hanun said. "My trusted advisors assure me that your intentions are dishonorable. So, we will dishonor you!"

Azel wasn't sure what this would mean, but he soon found out. Hanun clapped his hands in what must have been a prearranged signal, for immediately, soldiers surrounded the envoys and all six were forced to the floor.

Azel knew better than to resist, though a couple of their security detail tried, but they were quickly immobilized by blows to their heads. The Ammonite soldiers held them down while other used daggers to hack away the beards of all six men. Then they proceeded to cut their tunics high enough to expose their buttocks.

When they were finished, the soldiers let the men up; two of the soldiers needed to be helped up by their fellows after stunning blows.

Azel's face was red, as much from embarrassment as rage. The Ammonite soldiers, the king and his advisors were all laughing at them.

"Be on your way and tell your king, this is what we think of his greeting!" King Hanun said, continuing to laugh.

They didn't stop until they crossed the Jordan. The men didn't talk much the whole way. They finally had to stop for the night in Jericho.

"I don't want to go on to Jerusalem like this!" Ahithophel said. Fortunately, they all had changes of clothing so they were at least covered below the waist, but there was little they could do about their beards.

None of them had had smooth faces since they had been adults, but the state of their beards was worse than a boyishly smooth face would have been; their beards were a mess, having been hacked carelessly by the Ammonite soldiers, some areas long, some almost shaved.

"It is indeed embarrassing," Azel agreed. "Let us find a messenger to send to the king to inform him what has happened. We will wait for word."

The others agreed.

"How dare that little flea treat my ambassadors that way?!" raged King David. "We will attack Rabbah at once!"

"What shall we tell Ahithophel and Azel, and their escort?" Joab asked.

"Tell them to remain in Jericho until their beards grow back. In the meantime, assemble a force to go against the city at once!"

"It will be done, your majesty."

"How long will he have to stay?" Dani asked the messenger who stood at her door.

"The king has sent word they are to stay in Jericho until their beards grow back."

Poor Azel! He must be humiliated!

So, he would not be able to come home for a while. Then Dani had a thought:

I remember how David reacted when Nabal disrespected his messengers once before. He is so much more powerful now. How terrible will be his wrath?!

❦ 90 ❦

The mood in the palace in Rabbah had turned from mocking to terror, once the envoys from Jerusalem departed. One of Hanun's counselors threw cold water on the initial hilarity by suggesting that David might not take kindly to his official representatives being disrespected so flagrantly. Another commented that David's kingdom had recently subdued Moab, Edom and even Philistia.

The throne room went silent for a long moment, until the king spoke.

"We must send silver to the Arameans to join with us, for David will surely attack."

His counselors proceeded to all talk at once, congratulating the king for having such a great idea.

It WAS a good idea, but perhaps it was the only course of action open to them. Aram was to the north, above Geshur. The latter was allied with David through his marriage to the king's daughter. Aram was also to the east of Tyre, which had provided materials and workmen for the construction of David's palace, and it was known that David had begun a trading relationship with that prosperous city. Hanun could not appeal to the Moabites or Edomites to his southwest, because they had already been subdued by David and there were Israelite garrisons on their borders. Even the Philistines paid tribute to Israel now!

Aram was the only near neighbor able to help them in the inevitable clash with Israel's giant-killer king.

Eliel now commanded a hundred men, so he was in attendance in the command tent which had been set up in the center of the encampment far to the east of the Jordan River, on the hot, desert sand. Joab was speaking.

"Our scouts have confirmed that another army marches from Aram. They are encamped at Medeba, to our north. The Arameans and Ammonites intend to close on us from both directions. Therefore, Abishai, take your command and go to meet the Ammonites. I will command the remainder of our force and meet the Arameans. If one of us falters, the other should send reinforcements."

"It will be done," Abishai nodded solemnly.

No one had to remind any of them how difficult the fighting could be in this harsh environment.

"Be brave and fight for our cities and our God," Joab said loudly. "Yahweh will do what He decides is best!"

Eliel looked at Eliam, who was also a captain who commanded 100 men. Both of their units were in Abishai's cohort under Eleazar, so they would be going to meet the Ammonites. Eliel had no idea what kind of fighters they would be, but he was looking forward to exacting justice. His father still sat in Jericho, waiting for his beard to grow.

The Ammonites marched out of their city to meet Abishai and his troops in the field, rather than remain in the city and be subjected to a siege.

Eliel surveyed the flat, sandy soil ahead of them, where a large dust cloud swirled in a broad circle, kicked up by the horses and camels ridden by the Ammonites. He remembered something he had learned as a boy: the Ammonites were descended from Abraham's nephew, Lot, so they were distant cousins. However, that meant they were not children of Abraham, so the fact of their common heritage made no difference to him.

The fighting was hot on both fronts, but Joab's force drove the mercenaries from Aram back.

Apparently, messengers relayed word to the Ammonites, because once the Aramean line collapsed, the Ammonites withdrew as well, back to the protection of their walled city of Rabbah.

Joab then withdrew Israel's forces to their encampment, instructing Abishai to relay any developments to him, for he and a contingent of soldiers was returning to Jerusalem to report to the king. The army remained camped while messengers and scouts kept Abishai appraised of developments.

And developments there soon were, because Israel's scouts learned that another Aramean army was marching from beyond the Euphrates River far to the north, commanded by Shophach, King Hadadezer's commander-in-chief. The word of the scouts was that, together with the Arameans they had already defeated, this army would be perhaps 100,000 men, all told.

Word was immediately dispatched to Jerusalem, and the messenger returned to inform Abishai that Joab and King David himself were marching to their aid with all the men at their disposal. All of Israel's military might would be in the field to meet this threat.

It was at times like this that King David's natural talent for administration bore fruit, for he had put in place a plan to rotate the enlisted troops, with all the military-aged men of Israel divided into 12 corps. Each corps served one month per year during peacetime, but at times like this, he had an almost bottomless reserve force of trained fighters to draw from. Thousands of those reserves were called up to meet this threat.

The battlefield was broad and flat where the two armies met. The Arameans had literally thousands of chariots, which were ideally suited to the conditions. Each one was pulled by a majestic Arabian horse and carried a driver and an archer.

The Eternal Kingdom

The Philistine chariots had often inspired terror in
Israelite fighters, but ever since Benaiah had killed the
Egyptian giant during a chariot onslaught intended to take
out the king himself, the battle-hardened veterans under
King David's command were not frightened.

The chariots were challenging to be sure, but the men of
Israel were not deterred and met them with disciplined force.

It was a pitched battle for a while, but ultimately the
discipline and training of the Israelite force, together with
their belief in the reality of their God, won out and the
Arameans were defeated.

When the postmortem was conducted after the battle, it
was reported that about 7,000 drivers and archers in the
fearsome chariots had been killed and a shocking 40,000
Aramean infantrymen lay dead on the field. General
Shophach himself was among the dead.

Needless to say, the Arameans surrendered, and King
Hadadezer had no choice but agree to be subject to Israel.

Eliel stood listening to the reporting in the command tent,
as the top commanders passed on the information they had
gleaned from the battlefield. It suddenly occurred to him that
there was a prophecy that Israel's territory would one day
stretch from river of Egypt to beyond the Euphrates. It looked
like the prophecy was at last coming true.

"Now we turn our attention to Rabbah!" Joab shouted.

Eliel knew that would mean a siege.

Once Azel and the others' beards had grown out enough to
trim and look respectable, they returned to Jerusalem,
knowing justice was being meted out for the indignity they
had suffered.

Now Rabbah was a city under siege; it was only a matter of
how long before the city fell.

Azel wondered at the foolishness of the counselors who advised Hanun to respond the way he had. He hoped that he would never be guilty of giving his own king such bad advice.

He very much enjoyed his time at home, but it was not to last. The king needed him to survey the extensive mining operations that were now under Israel's control in Edom and the Negev. The metallic ore they would yield would further enrich David's kingdom, brought out of the ground by the people they had conquered, who were now their slaves.

<h1 style="text-align:center">❦ 91 ❧</h1>

"But why are we going, mother?"

"The king wants to see you. He wants to honor you."

"Are you sure he doesn't see me as a threat?"

The question lingered as Mara considered how best to answer. "The king and your father were best friends," she said, looking at her son's earnest face.

Mephibosheth had missed out on so much of life. His injury when he was five had left him helpless; unable to walk. He used his hands to move about, dragging useless legs behind him. He was now twenty years old but had not learned a trade. She felt guilty about that. Perhaps there would have been something he could have learned to do, but she had been protective. He was all she had of her beloved Jonathan, and she blamed herself for his handicap.

It had been 15 years since Mara and Mephibosheth had fled across the Jordan River to the west. Mara's father had died within two years of when they fled Gibeah of Saul, but there was a civil war with Judah and Mara hadn't gone to see her mother. She had died a couple years after that. With her parents gone, she had no reason to cross the river.

For 13 years, they had lived in the home of Makir in Lo-Debar. She was very thankful for his generosity.

The years had been kind to them. Ziba had married a couple of wives and had many sons. Though he had been a servant himself, Makir gave him his freedom and he had employed servants of his own.

While they traveled, she remembered her son's question about whether David considered Mephibosheth to be a threat. She had assured him that David and his late father Jonathan had been loyal friends, but she didn't know for sure that David would not regard him with suspicion. He was, after all, one of the few living, male descendants of King Saul, who had tried to murder David. She didn't know for certain that he might see Mephibosheth as a threat to the throne.

The thing that made her think all would be well was Mephibosheth's disability. For the first time since it happened, the accident that left him crippled might give him an advantage.

When they arrived at the palace in Jerusalem, Ziba led the way, carrying Mephibosheth up the stone stairs and through the double doors into the palace. Mara realized he had been there before. She wondered what arrangement he may have already made.

An armed guard ushered them into the throne room, where David sat upon a gilded throne. Mara marveled at the ostentatious furnishings and tapestries; the architectural details that were so much nicer than the rustic throne room her father-in-law had built. The difference was striking.

She recognized King David, though she had not seen him for about 25 years, after he fled the murderous threats of King Saul, so he was much older and more mature. She held back as Ziba carried Mephibosheth to a bench which had been placed before the throne.

"Mephibosheth?" the king said.

"Yes, at your service, sire."

"Do not be afraid," David assured him, rising from the throne to come near. David took both of Mephibosheth's hands in his own. "I want to extend kindness to you for the sake of your father, Jonathan. You will be a regular guest at my table from now on."

"How am I, your servant, so privileged that you regard a dead dog like me?"

"Your father was very important to me. He was loyal when others turned against me. I now want to reward his loyalty."

Then the king looked at Ziba.

"Ziba, thank you for being guardian to Jonathan's son. Everything that was Saul's and his house I hereby give to your master's son. You will cultivate the land for him; you, your sons and servants. You will bring the land's produce to be food for your master's son to eat."

"Your servant will do everything my lord the king has instructed." Ziba replied, bowing.

Mara's eyes teared up as she heard the words that meant she and her son would always be provided for. They would be able to return to the ancestral land of Saul in Gibeah.

❧ 92 ❧

The sun was low in the west, casting long shadows on the streets of Jerusalem. King David was on the rooftop of his palace, where he had a view of the entire city below.

He looked toward the sun, which would soon sink behind Mount Zion. His feet followed his gaze, and he walked slowly to the banister on the western edge of his palace.

It had been a light day for official duties. The army was in the field and there had not been much other business. David had decided that there was no need for him to be in the field during the siege, so Joab commanded the army at Rabbah, while David returned to Jerusalem.

The king's mind wandered as he surveyed the western wall and the buildings which were proliferating beyond it, signs of the expanding of his kingdom's capital.

Then he absent-mindedly looked at the streets and buildings inside the western wall, now bathed in golden light, their roofs and west-facing surfaces brightly lit, with northern and eastern planes in cool shadow.

It was truly a beautiful city.

How wise it was to choose it as my capital!

Then his attention was arrested by movement immediately below the palace.

It was the mikveh, the pool where ritual washings were conducted, as commanded in the law of Moses. From his high vantage point, he could see the water, smooth as burnished bronze and the color of that important metal where a narrow shaft of sunlight fell across it. Three women approached and the one in the center opened her large bath sheet. The other women took it, holding it to shield the first woman from the view from the street.

But David was high above them, and he saw what those on the street would not. He sucked in a breath of the cool evening air.

She is beautiful!

He stayed, watching her descend by the steps into the deep pool as required by the Torah to begin the purification ritual. As the daylight faded, the cool light of twilight bounced on the white walls of the Mikveh, filling it with soft, warm light, and the water glistened on her shoulders and arms as she moved in the deep pool.

When the ritual was done, she started back up the stairs, and her friends again stood holding the bath sheet, which she backed into as her friends wrapped it around her. It clung to her wet body, so her friends put a deep blue cloak over her, which she then pulled over her head.

Then the three women were gone, down the street and around a corner.

Her purification ritual is ended, she can have sex again, the king realized.

It was an obvious fact that every Hebrew knew: seven days after the beginning of menstruation, wives must wash in the mikveh before resuming relations with their husbands. Usually other men would not know, but he knew.

Who is she?

He thought he knew that, too.

The oil lamp flickered in the darkness, but she treasured its precious light, however unreliable, because it extended the daylight and the opportunity to complete one more household task before retiring.

Her young fingers expertly moved the needle back and forth across a small tear in one of her husband's tunics.

Without this repair, it would soon become a larger rend, and then would make the garment unusable.

But her husband was far away and would not wear the tunic for a while yet; how long she could not know.

Suddenly there was a loud knock at the door.

Who would be here at this hour?

"Bathsheba! Open the door!" a male voice called.

She was alarmed. Was this bad news from the battlefield? Both her husband and her father were there.

She laid the garment aside and carried the oil lamp to the door, which she opened a little.

"What is it?"

"The king requires your presence," came the answer.

She looked at the men. There were three of them, dressed in the armor of palace guards.

Why would the king need to see ME? And at this late hour?

"Come with us," demanded the man, as he pushed open the door and took her arm.

"Why does the king want to see me?"

"We only know he sent for you."

One of the guards pulled her out of the house and another took the oil lamp from her, extinguished it and set it down beside the door, which he then closed.

❦ 93 ❦

It was not far to the palace, but it was uncomfortable because the men were all business and didn't volunteer more information. The man who had done the talking was no longer holding her by the arm, but he was following close behind while the other two walked one on either side of her. This made her understand she didn't have a choice in the matter, whatever "the matter" would turn out to be.

They reached the front gate and the two guards on either side straightened to attention as they passed through. The three men guided her up the steps to the portico and then toward a set of stairs leading to the upper level.

"You aren't taking me to the throne room?" she asked.

"Our commander will tell you where you are to go."

Bathsheba blinked as they walked her past a torch in a wall sconce and stopped in front of the stairs.

"Wait here," the leader of the trio of guards said.

Bathsheba watched them leave her, standing at the foot of the stairs.

This is odd!

But she didn't have to wait long. She heard footsteps on the stairs before she saw anyone. It was Benaiah.

"Hello," Benaiah said, not really looking her in the eye. "Follow me."

He started back up the stairs and Bathsheba followed, still feeling this was all strange, but supposing she would get answers soon enough.

At the top of the stairs was another portico and Benaiah led her to a set of double doors. The flickering torches on the wall told her that the red doors had gilding which shone like stars in the firelight.

Benaiah didn't hesitate but opened one of the doors.

"Your majesty!"

Benaiah ushered Bathsheba through the door.

Is this the king's private quarters?

Just then the king appeared. He was dressed casually, in only a simple tunic, not wearing his crown.

"Bathsheba! Thank you for coming!"

She heard the door close behind her and she looked back to see that Benaiah was gone.

"Come, sit with me a while," the king motioned to a small table with two chairs. On the table sat a wine jug and two bronze goblets.

"This is the finest wine from the Valley of Jezreel," the king said as he poured from the jug into the two goblets. He handed one to her.

"Please, sit."

"Your majesty, why am I here?"

He smiled before he spoke. "Please, sit."

His smile caused a thrill to go through her. His charisma was well known. His attention was flattering. She felt her face flush. Simultaneously she had impulses to run away and to run to him; such was her confusion.

She sat and took a sip of wine from the goblet, though she eyed him warily. Only then did she see the large bed on the opposite wall.

"I saw you today," he said.

"I don't understand."

"At the mikveh."

"Your majesty!" Bathsheba felt blood rush to her cheeks.

How much did he see?

"Bathsheba…" his voice trailed off. It was a moment before he would speak again. He took a drink from the goblet.

"How could you see...?" She also drank from her goblet of wine, her mind racing. She couldn't finish the thought.

"Bathsheba, today was not the first time I saw you. You are so beautiful!"

She sucked in a breath, looking at him. His eyes were locked on hers and she found she couldn't look away.

"Your majesty, I..."

He took her hand in his with a tender, but strong grasp. He pulled her forward.

"I must have you!"

"Your majesty, I'm married...!" she stood, alarmed.

He stood also and pulled her to him. He wrapped her in his arms and kissed her.

She was screaming inside, but he was the king; what could she do?

Her resistance failed. He was so strong! He quickly removed her tunic and pushed her to the bed.

"No!" she screamed finally, but it was too late.

❧ 94 ❧

Michal tossed and turned, but sleep stubbornly refused to come. She was upset and that didn't help her rest. She had three times requested an audience with the King, her husband, but she was just one of many wives and concubines now, and the women simply did not go before the king unless bidden.

So far, her requests had been met with silence and that had allowed bitterness to grow in her heart. David had not spoken to her since the episode when he danced before the ark in view of the young women.

Finally, she sat up in bed and threw off the bedclothes. She swung her feet down to the smooth, cool stone floor and was soon out of her bed chamber and into the hallway. A quick left turn brought her out the door of the women's quarters to the colonnade, where moonlight seemed to reach deep into the polished stone, a new shaft falling between each colorful, rectangular column. The bright red piping on the Phoenician columns looked black at this hour, but they still contrasted with the light, dressed stone.

She walked slowly, aimlessly, for what else did she have to do? Being the wife of a king sounded glamorous, but most of the time it was deadly dull, and while she had many privileges and comforts as a wife of the king, she could not leave. She suffered in silence the tasks assigned to her by the pushy Abigail, but her mind was often more on what might have been.

What if her father had not hated David? What if her father had not driven him away and consigned her to be the wife of a man she hadn't known? Would they still be together? Would

David have led them to victory and her father would have died of old age? She felt sure if that had happened, she would be the only wife David needed.

Yet there was the matter of providing an heir. She had failed to give children to two men now, whereas David's other wives and concubines were fertile and produced many children. Now her time for childbearing was past.

Her aimless midnight wandering had taken her to where she could see the stone stairs that led to the private living quarters of the king. Would she ever be invited there again?

Wait! What is that?

No one had been about; no one would be at this hour of the night, except those soldiers assigned to keep watch, but she was certain she heard someone coming down the steps.

Then she saw her, hurrying down the stairs, stepping carelessly, pulling her cloak about her and over her head.

She is getting dressed, Michal realized. *Coming from the king's quarters! She has been with the king!*

But Michal didn't recognize her as one of the wives or concubines of the king, and she was practically running, as if fleeing the palace. She did not go toward the women's quarters but made her way across the portico to the stairs which led out of the palace, out the gate and down the street.

Michal slipped between the columns where she could not be seen, and peeked around as the woman quickly moved away, her head down. In a sudden flash of recognition, Michal thought, *I know her! Whose wife? One of David's "30"?*

The Hittite!

❧ 95 ❧

Less than three months later, Bathsheba was trying to go about her household chores, but she kept breaking down, near tears, yet steeling herself to keep them from coming.

She had missed her time of month twice now; there was no mistaking it. She tried to tell herself there could be an explanation other than the obvious one, but no other option was convincing.

I am pregnant.

She had never been pregnant before, but she knew women who had been, and her experience matched theirs closely enough she had no doubt.

My husband has been gone for five months, she thought. There was no way the calculation could make the baby his. She hated that she had done this to Uriah. When it eventually became obvious that she was pregnant, and if anyone learned the baby was not Uriah's, she would be a pariah.

What could she do? She didn't want to tell her parents. They would be crushed. That left just one person she could tell; whom she MUST tell.

David sat staring at the papyrus in his hand. It had been sealed when the messenger had given it to him; for that he was thankful.

He mentally kicked himself for not realizing this would happen. He had acted rashly, out of lust; that's what it had been. Now she was pregnant, and everyone knew her husband had been at the siege for months.

He felt foolish, but also desperate to hide what happened.

But how? Eventually Bathsheba's condition would be obvious and someone would know.

Then he had an idea.

"Scribe. I need to send a message," David said to the court scribe sitting nearby.

"Yes, sire?"

Joab, Abishai and several others of high rank stood around a table in the command tent across the valley and over a dune from the city of Rabbah of the Ammonites.

"The siege is taking longer than we thought it would," Abishai said, stating what everyone at the table knew, but had been reluctant to admit.

"We need new tactics to break through and get into the Ammonite capital," Joab said.

But he was thinking, *I'll be glad when we can leave this cursed desert.*

Just then a soldier came into the tent.

"General, a message for you from the king," the soldier announced, handing Joab the papyrus. He unrolled it and quickly read the message. It contained the expected general greeting and exhortation to victory, but the only specific message was for Joab to send Uriah the Hittite home to Jerusalem to meet with the king.

That's odd, he thought, but he didn't have time to linger.

"Go tell Uriah the Hittite that the king needs him back in Jerusalem," he told the soldier, who saluted and left the tent.

"Now, where were we?"

❧ 96 ☙

The donkey Uriah was riding struggled a bit as the sand shifted under his hooves, but the sturdy animal was now accustomed to it after months in the desert. He was traveling the long, lonely road out of the desert, to cross the Jordan River.

Uriah did not have details as to why he was being called back by the king, but Uriah was a good soldier, often going where he was told without knowing the reason. Since he was one of David's Thirty mighty men, Uriah figured the king must have some important special mission for him.

The terrain was gradually growing greener as he descended into the Jordan valley, for which he was glad. He forded near Gilgal and continued on the road to Jerusalem.

Finally, Uriah topped the Mount of Olives and could see Jebus – now Jerusalem – on the facing hill. He paused only briefly to take in the site, then started down the road into the Kidron Valley, across the brook and up the other side.

King David was on his throne, listening to the presentation of one of Judah's elders about a proposal concerning the building of new housing west of the city. The population of Jerusalem continued to grow, now that Jerusalem was not only the nation's capital, but the Tent and the Ark were there.

David noticed Uriah slip in and stand in the shadows on the side wall. The king was distracted for the rest of the presentation, but managed to comment and issue a decision, which the elder promised would be carried out.

The man who was next in line stepped forward.

"Wait, I believe we have a report from the Ammonite war."

Uriah turned to look at David, who motioned him forward. He came quickly forward and bowed.

"Welcome, Uriah, how is Joab?"

"He is well, your majesty."

"And what of the battle?"

"The siege continues, but there has been little change in a while. I understand the commanders are working to develop new tactics that may break the impasse."

"Hmm," David said, pausing a bit. "Sieges are never easy. How is the morale among the men?"

"It is good. They understand the difficulties."

The king looked down for a moment, then spoke again.

"You must be tired after your journey. Go home, clean up and reunite with your wife. We can talk more tomorrow."

Uriah bowed. "As you wish, your majesty." He turned and left. David watched him until he was completely out the door.

Uriah came to the gate out of the palace, then stopped, thoughts turning in his mind. He was having second thoughts about what the king had told him to do.

"I will be meeting with the king again tomorrow," he said to the soldiers guarding the palace gate. "Is there a place I can sleep within the palace walls?"

"We palace guards sleep inside the casemate wall," volunteered one of them, gesturing to the eight-cubit thick wall which had doors at intervals. "It's not luxurious, but you'll find it better than camping near the battlefield."

"That sounds good. May I stay with you tonight?"

Just then a messenger from the king came out of the gate. "Ah, Uriah! I was to take this food to you at your house, but since you are still here, here is a gift from the king."

"Thank you. Be sure to give the king my thanks."

When the messenger was gone, Uriah held up the basket. "Join me, men, in this feast of the king's food!"

❦ 97 ❦

It was another sleepless night.

Michal tossed and turned after lying awake for some time. Finally, she threw off the covers and rose in the dark room. She slipped into her sandals, wrapped herself in a shawl and tiptoed out into the hallway, through the common room and out the door of the women's quarters.

She stood on the portico, looking at the distant hills in the moonlight. Then she saw movement near the gate below.

Someone else has difficulty sleeping, I guess.

Or maybe it was just the sentry. She watched idly at first, then something caught her attention. She thought she recognized the man who had come out of the rooms near the gate, dressed in the armor of a soldier. He sat down at the cookfire and was soon joined by a lone sentry on watch duty.

It's Uriah, she thought, remembering another night when she could not sleep.

Why is the Hittite back from the battle, but not at home with his wife?

"Uriah sent his thanks for the food last night, sire."

David acknowledged his servant with a nod. "I trust he and his wife enjoyed the gift."

"Oh, he did not go home."

"What?! Where did he go?"

David felt his throat tighten and a bead of sweat form on his temple.

"He stayed here, in the rooms near the gate with the guards," the servant answered.

The Eternal Kingdom

David resisted the urge to say something, fearing he would reveal how dismayed he was at this unexpected revelation.

Later when Uriah appeared before him, King David asked a few things about the battle and the army, before asking what he really wanted to know.

"You've been away on the military campaign for many weeks. Why didn't you go home to your wife last night?"

"How can I enjoy the embrace of my wife when my men and my commander, Joab, are staying in tents far from home? As surely as you live, I would not do such a thing."

David's heart raced. *What can I do?*

Then his nimble mind settled on a course of action.

"Remain with me one more day. You can return to the battle line tomorrow. Not only that, but tonight, you must come to eat at my table."

Uriah looked surprised. "I am just a common soldier, your majesty. How do I deserve such an honor?"

"Nonsense," David insisted. "You are of great value to Joab and to me; one of my mighty men. I expect you to be back here for the evening meal."

"Yes, your majesty. As you say."

That night King David ordered a fine feast prepared with extra wine. Uriah came and was seated at the head table with the king. The table was laden with food, but wine in glazed-clay and shiny bronze vessels was the priority.

"Let me fill your cup again," David said.

"No, I have had enough," Uriah protested as David filled his cup to the brim."

"Drink up! Tonight we celebrate, for tomorrow you return to the battle."

Uriah hesitated, then raised his bronze cup once again as the king smiled.

By the end of the meal, Uriah was pretty far gone. He rose from the table, nearly sinking back to the cushion on which he had been sitting.

"Thank you, my lord. This was indeed a fit – a fit feast for a – feat fist for a king…"

"I'm glad you enjoyed it. Now enjoy a night at home."

Uriah looked at the king with confusion in his eyes for a moment, then looked away as he turned to go.

The next morning, the servant reported to King David that, once again, Uriah had not gone home, but spent the night at the gate with the guards.

It was not yet the heat of the day, but King David felt hot from the base of his neck to the crown on his head. A bead of sweat trickled down his forehead.

When Uriah arrived once again, the king gave him a rolled up and sealed papyrus.

"May Yahweh be with you on your journey," the king began. "Please take this message to General Joab. It is for his eyes only."

Uriah nodded solemnly and bowed before making his way out of the throne room.

Again, David watched him go until he passed through the double doors.

⚜ 98 ⚜

Boredom is a real problem during a siege.

Joab knew this instinctively, but he had not experienced the reality of that boredom until now. Every few days, a few of his commanders took men close to the wall of the Ammonite capital to attack. He did not endanger the whole army; it was just harassment, forcing the defenders to expend resources to keep the Israelites from breaching the city, but Joab knew they would not go over the wall any time soon. A direct attack would be too costly and might not succeed.

No, the prudent course was to wait them out; starve them out. When they had no food and no water, they would invite the Hebrews into the city. It was only a matter of time.

In the meantime, boredom was a problem. He worried about his troops' morale. They staged games of skill and chance to occupy the men, but you couldn't do that all day. Foraging parties kept their own stores of food supplied, but it wasn't easy to find food in this desert. So, the men were on bare minimum rations, even as they waited for hunger to bring the inhabitants of the city to their knees.

He was alone in the command tent in the dark, having sent his top officers away. There was no new strategy to be planned; no new campaign to stage. They were in siege mode. He stared into the dancing flame of an oil lamp on the table.

Then Uriah came in, the dust of the road still on him.

"Lord general, I have a message from the king."

"What is it?"

"He said it was for your eyes only, so I have not read it."

Joab looked at him and the rolled and sealed papyrus Uriah held out him.

"All right, thank you," he said accepting the papyrus message. "You are dismissed."

Uriah saluted and turned to leave.

When he was gone, Joab broke the seal and unrolled the papyrus message. His eyes grew wide as he began to read. The short message was in the king's own handwriting.

When he had finished reading, he frowned, then held the papyrus over the flame of the oil lamp on the table. The fire took hold and slowly burned its way toward Joab's hand. When it was about to scorch his fingers, he dropped it to the sand at his feet and watched it burn until nothing was left but ash, then he kicked sand over top of its blackness.

❧ 99 ❧

"Do you understand your orders, soldier?"

"I understand what you said, but I don't understand why I am to endanger the life of one of my men."

The air was tense. Eleazar waited for Joab to answer, but when the answer came it wasn't reassuring.

"The king commands it," Joab scowled. "He has his reasons. It is not for us to wonder why."

Eleazar saluted and turned to leave.

"Report back to me when it is done," Joab added.

Eleazar did not respond, but turned to glare at the general, then left the command tent.

"Today we are to attack the water source."

Eliel let the words sink in for the men of his company.

"The general believes it is the key to taking the city. We as members of the king's Mighty Men have been given this honor. Eleazar will lead us personally."

Eliel looked at the men before him, especially noting Uriah. He had just returned from leave in Jerusalem.

"It is well defended," another soldier commented.

"Yes, which just confirms its importance," Eliel replied. "Strap on your weapons. We attack in one hour."

Rabbah's water source, essential for any city, was of life and death importance here in the desert. It was outside the main city, but enclosed by a wall with a tunnel leading into the city through which the people came to draw water. Because of its importance, Ammonite soldiers were posted atop the circular walls surrounding the spring.

Eleazar's men, composed of four squads from Eliel's company, moved stealthily behind dunes topped with sparse tufts of desert grass. He led them to a place they had been before, during other forays against their besieged enemy.

"Ready?"

Eliel's men nodded.

"Charge!" Eleazar shouted.

The men jumped to the top of the dune with a shout and ran down the other side and then the short distance to the stone wall which enclosed the city's water source.

Four men from each squad began launching arrows over the wall and others hurled spears.

The defenders rose, startled by the attack after days of inactivity. One stood just in time to be caught in the chest by a spear and he toppled forward off the wall.

Eliel's men ran toward the wall, and several threw iron hooks to the top of the wall with ropes attached. When the hooks held, the men began climbing as the others rained arrows and spears onto the top of the wall to drive the defenders away from the front of the parapet.

The men had to repeatedly throw the hooks to try to get them to hold, because when a hook held, a defender would pry or knock the hook loose and the Hebrew would fall to the sand below, only to try again.

"Keep it going!" Eliel shouted as his men kept shooting the arrows and hurling the javelins toward the top of the wall. When javelins were gone, they resorted to throwing stones. This mostly kept the Ammonite defenders from the front of the parapet, but some loosed arrows from farther back and Eliel's men had to use their shields to keep from getting hit.

A man beside Eliel was hit with a random arrow and he sank to the sand with a cry. Eliel saw it was not a mortal wound so he helped the man get back over the dune to safety.

Again and again, the men at the forefront threw the heavy hooks over the wall and attempted to scale it.

The Eternal Kingdom

Eliel saw that Uriah had succeeded in getting a hook and rope to hold and was nearly to the top of the wall, pulling himself up hand-over-hand.

"Cover him!" Eliel called, and his squad rained arrows and stones on the defenders.

But just then, Eleazar called out, "Retreat! Retreat!"

The men stopped and looked at him with question marks in their eyes as some obeyed and moved away.

"Don't you understand?" Eleazar shouted. "Retreat!"

The men slowly backed away and some looked back at the wall, as if not sure they heard right.

The uncertainty allowed the Ammonite defenders to return to the edge and two of them thrust their spears into Uriah's midsection. He let go of the rope and fell hard to the desert sand at the base of the wall.

Eliel wasn't sure but, as they retreated, he thought Uriah raised his head and looked at them before a trio of arrows from the top of the wall struck him and he lay still. Eliel looked toward his commander, but Eleazar was not looking his way.

Eleazar could not look at his men as they returned to camp. None of them spoke or looked at one another. Eleazar mumbled an excuse and left to go to the command tent.

"I need to speak to General Joab," Eleazar said to the sentry standing at the entrance.

"You may go in."

Eleazar stepped inside and let his eyes adjust to the relative darkness after being in the bright desert sun.

"Is it done?" Joab asked without looking up.

Eleazar found he could not immediately speak.

"War and politics are dirty businesses," Joab said, letting his words hang in the stuffy, desert air while Eleazar tried to find his tongue, not sure what Uriah had to do with "politics."

Finally, he saluted and said, "It is done."

They stood looking at one another sadly for a long moment, then Joab turned back to his charts.

"Will you tell his father-in-law, or shall I?" Eleazar asked. Uriah's father-in-law was another of "The Thirty" mighty men, assigned to another unit.

"Eliam should know," Joab agreed. "I should be the one to tell him."

Eleazar saluted and turned to leave the tent. He hurried away, hoping he wouldn't vomit where Joab could see him.

❦ 100 ❦

Bathsheba heard a voice calling her name and knocking, so she left the bedroom she shared with Uri to answer the door. She was delighted to see her father, Eliam.

"Father! So good to see you!"

She threw her arms around him and then looked behind and beside him.

"Uri couldn't come?"

"I'm afraid I have bad news."

Bathsheba put her hand over her mouth. She had feared that this day would come.

"Uriah was killed during a foray against the enemy."

"Oh, no!" Bathsheba cried and she began to sob. She sat down on the nearest chair. When she realized she had put one hand on her abdomen, she moved it away, lest her father wonder about it, though at this stage no one would know she was pregnant.

"How did it happen? Were you there?"

"No, my unit was not involved in the raid," Eliam answered as he held her close. "Who knows how such things happen in battle? It's always so chaotic. What I've been able to learn is, he was too far forward when the rest of the men withdrew."

Her heart was breaking, but then a thought intruded in her mind. She immediately rejected it, but the seed was sown.

Could my husband's death have been arranged?

Her father continued to speak, trying to say something to ease her grief, and she was indeed grieving, but her mind was also going down a dangerous path, and she was unable to stop it.

She bore the king's offspring in her body. She would not be able to keep the fact of her pregnancy secret forever. The men who escorted her to the king's quarters and the king's personal guard must have deduced what happened behind closed doors.

How many people know about my adultery? Could powerful forces within the government have conspired to remove Uriah and protect the king?

It was too horrible to contemplate. The next thing that would happen, if there indeed had been a conspiracy, would be that the king would take her into his women's quarters as his wife.

If that happens, I will know.

❦ 101 ❧

Benaiah rode beside the king at the head of a column of soldiers as he often did. Word had come to Jerusalem that Rabbah was about to fall, and Joab said the king should come, lest they name the city after him instead of David.

Benaiah thought it snide of Joab to say such a thing, but David seemed unbothered. He had simply ordered the troops remaining in Jerusalem to join him as they journeyed into the desert to see Rabbah fall after the long siege.

The final battle at Rabbah was a formality. The siege had greatly weakened the inhabitants; they were starving.

In a formal ceremony, Hanun, king of the Ammonites, whose outrageous humiliation of King David's envoys had finally led to this moment, knelt before Israel's monarch. David handed the crown Saul had worn to Benaiah, then removed Hanun's crown and put it on his own head.

The Ammonite crown was a marvel. It weighed 75 pounds and had a huge precious stone on the front. David wouldn't wear it daily, of course; it was too heavy. After the ceremony, Benaiah put it in the king's supply wagon.

The next task was clean-up, and Benaiah was not involved in that. Instead, Joab and the other commanders directed their men to force the men of Rabbah to transform the city into a labor camp, where everyone from king to stable boy worked doing carpentry and forming bricks for building projects King David was planning.

The Ammonites became a race of slaves, turning out materials that would make Israel ever stronger.

❧ 102 ☙

It was dark when Bathsheba arrived. When the messenger had brought the invitation, she had felt a certain fatalism, but she couldn't refuse to go to the king when summoned.

She was so conflicted she was afraid she might scream. She had to keep calming herself and telling herself she would need to make the best of her situation.

But there is hardly any good outcome possible, is there?

It had been five months since the king had taken her to his bed. She was dressed all in black, as a widow, so her face was all that would reflect the light of the sconces beside the door. She knocked on the door and it was immediately opened.

"Welcome," said the king. "Thank you for coming."

"Your majesty," Bathsheba answered with as little emotion as she could. Inside she felt everything from embarrassment to grief to rage, but she was determined not to show it as she followed him inside and he closed the door.

"How are you?"

Bathsheba didn't answer immediately, not sure what he was asking. Did he mean Uriah's death? Or her pregnancy? Or was he referring to the guilt she felt? The truth was she was barely holding on, but she wouldn't tell him.

"I'm doing all right."

"I know things have been difficult, with the death of your husband. He was a very valiant man."

Bathsheba studied the king's face for any clue about the circumstances of Uri's death, but she could discern nothing.

"Bathsheba, I know it must be difficult without a husband."

She knew her nerves were raw, but she was surprised at how her heart leaped when he said her name. She barely heard the rest of the sentence, but she recovered enough to answer: "My family and friends have been very supportive."

"That's good, but I want to make things better."

She waited for him to complete the sentence, but he didn't immediately speak again. He approached her and took her in his strong arms, holding her tight.

"Become my wife, Bathsheba. Let me be a father to the child. You can live in the palace and both of you can live as royalty. I will love you and the child will grow up as a child of royalty – my child – as it should."

There it was. She had thought that if he proposed marriage, it would mean Uri's death was not an accident like she suspected. Now he had done it.

But strangely she didn't feel the anger she had expected. Rather he seemed sincerely concerned for her and the baby. Thoughts and emotions swirled like a whirlwind in her mind and heart. She didn't know how to answer.

He released her and looked at her expectantly.

"You have many wives," she said, finally. "What would one more be to you?"

"I love you, Bathsheba. I have been tormented in my soul by my desire for you. Marry me."

"My father is one of your warriors. You could order him to give me to you, just as you ordered me to your bed!"

David now had a look of profound hurt and she immediately regretted saying it.

Does he really love me?

"I – I shouldn't have said that," she whispered.

"No, I deserve it. You are right of course. I could simply take you and demand your father's blessing, but I don't want our relationship to be that way. I want you to be my wife because you want to be."

Again, Bathsheba studied the king's face for any sign of insincerity. She saw only earnestness.

What would her life be as one of David's many wives – would she be number eight?

The other options available to her were to find another to marry her, though with a child, would that happen? Otherwise she would end up a ward of her father, living the widow's life forever.

"Please," David said, "become my wife."

"You say you desire me, but you already have wives and concubines aplenty. Is your passion for me different?"

"Most of those unions were to cement alliances with other kingdoms. I have relations with them to produce offspring that binds those other nations to ours. My first wife was Michal, Saul's daughter. She is here to prove I stand in the line of Saul, but I have never brought her to this bed chamber."

He took both her hands in his.

"My feeling for you is indeed different, stronger, than the others. You are special to me."

She looked away, because the intensity of his gaze made it difficult for her to think straight. Finally, she spoke again.

"If I do, will my child receive the same opportunities and privileges as your other children; the same education...?"

"The same and better, I promise."

"I must remain in mourning for three more weeks."

"Yes, of course, but I want to be married before the child is born," King David said earnestly.

She looked at him and something told her he was honestly showing her his heart. She felt herself on the verge of tears.

"I don't know... I don't know what to do..."

"Say 'yes.'"

"Yes."

Bathsheba heard it, but she wasn't even sure it was she who had spoken. He immediately embraced her again.

"Wonderful! I will begin preparations immediately."

Then he kissed her, and she suddenly felt as if she had had too much wine.

❦ 103 ❧

The ceremony was not as lavish as some of the wedding feasts King David had staged for other wives. Azel and Dani were there, as they often were, now that Azel was a regular advisor and envoy of the king. Other advisors were there too, notably Ahithophel, the grandfather of the bride, seated at the head table along with the bride's parents.

While the tables were laden with wonderful food and there was wine enough to enable the guests to be jovial, to Azel, something seemed off.

He knew Dani sensed it too. She was uncharacteristically quiet and kept looking at Bathsheba. Azel could tell when Dani's sixth sense was on alert, but he didn't know what was in her mind.

Azel was focused on preventing his own mind from thinking that many others died in battle, but and the king had not married their widows.

Joab drank deeply and long from the bronze cup and then motioned to one of the maidens to fill it again. It had been a long siege in the desert with all the privation that goes with such a campaign, and he was glad it was over.

Looking about the room, he saw the guests were enjoying the feast, and the king was holding forth in his charismatic way, but Joab's attention returned often to the bride.

He had never spoken face-to-face with his uncle, the king, about his order to make sure Uriah died in battle. He wasn't worried about it. He had done treacherous things before and would likely need to again in the name of loyalty.

But treachery it was. Did the king order him to facilitate Uriah's death so he could take his wife as his own?

The thought was too horrifying, even for Joab, who was accustomed to executing terrible orders. If what he was thinking was true, his uncle had acted out of character.

The king had angered Joab many times, refusing to kill his enemies, like Saul when the perfect opportunity presented itself, mourning for enemies like Jonathan and Abner. He always seemed to err on the side of being too generous to his enemies, unless he was simply playing for appearances, in which case the king might be more cynical than even Joab.

But if Joab's worst fears regarding Uriah and his widow were true, it would be a dramatic departure from his uncle's customary transparent innocence.

Did he overplay his hand this time? Time will tell.

At another nearby table, King David's wives and concubines largely passed the meal in silence.

Michal looked on smugly, for she knew things the others didn't: The night she saw Bathsheba come down from the king's bed chamber, then, another night, she saw Bathsheba's husband spend the night with the sentries at the palace gate instead of going home to his wife. That was strange enough, but now David had married her.

How convenient for the king that her husband is dead!

Her cynicism was bitter in her mouth, but she relished it. She felt somehow vindicated, though she wasn't sure how.

Bathsheba was again trying to maintain a pleasant expression while a storm of emotions swirled inside her. She was beyond grateful that the elaborate dress that the king had provided for her wedding covered the slight swelling of her belly which had just begun to show. Soon no tunic or dress could hide it.

The Eternal Kingdom

She felt keenly the eyes of everyone in the room on her. She wondered how much they knew; how much had been told. She cleared her throat and forced a smile, turning to look at her new husband, who smiled back at her.

A few days later, Eliel surprised Azel and Dani with a visit. Though the siege of Rabbah had ended, Eliel had been tasked to stay and help with the aftermath.

"There are skilled artisans among them," Eliel said. "We are putting them to work."

Azel and his son exchanged grim smiles, knowing that "putting them to work" was a euphemism for slave labor.

"How long is your leave, son?" Azel asked.

"I have a week, then I must head back."

"To Rabbah?"

"Yes. There is much to be done to secure the city for Israel and make sure the people can't rise up."

"It will be a true blessing," Azel commented. "This will increase the wealth of the kingdom. The other night, we had a banquet to celebrate the king's marriage to Bathsheba. Our kingdom is growing stronger every day."

"The king has married the wife of Uriah?"

"Yes."

Eliel looked down.

"What's the matter?" his father asked.

"I was there when Uriah was killed. I haven't talked about it, but it was strange."

"How so?"

"Just as Uriah was in the hottest part of the fighting, Eleazar called 'Retreat.' We obeyed, leaving Uriah without cover. He was killed almost immediately. Then after we returned to camp, Eleazar immediately reported to Joab."

"Of course, he would report to his commander if he commanded the raid," Azel said.

"Yes, but it just seemed strange. Like something wasn't right. Nothing was ever said publicly about Uriah's death. He was one of The Thirty, father!"

Azel considered what his son said and replied, "Son, when anyone dies in battle it is a tragedy, and it's always tempting to look for a reason, but many times it's just a random, sad outcome. Only Yahweh knows who will live and who will die."

"I hope you're right."

Azel nodded, but he had questions of his own.

❧ 104 ❧

It was late. Michal was prowling the colonnade once again. The session in the throne room had gone long. The elders and counselors of the king were only now departing. Finally, Michal saw the person she had been waiting for.

"Benaiah!"

"What is it?"

Michal always felt he didn't show proper deference to her, probably owing to the fact that he was among those her father had tried to kill, but that was unimportant now.

"I wanted to ask you something. About five months ago, I saw Bathsheba leaving the palace in the middle of the night. What was that about?"

"What? Why would you ask such a thing? What makes you think you saw her?"

"I suppose I could be mistaken. She was still married to Uriah then."

"Of course you are mistaken!" Benaiah insisted.

"You are probably right, of course."

"The king would not have done such a thing. You are wrong about all of it."

"Would not have done what?" Michal asked.

Benaiah stomped off to go home after his long day, as Michal watched him with a sly smile.

"I know what I saw."

"But you can't say you know what it means."

Abigail's jaw was set. She couldn't believe that Michal would insinuate something like that.

"I just know that Bathsheba came down from the king's chambers in the middle of the night," Michal whispered. "Five months later, her husband is dead and the king marries her. Now we learn she's pregnant!"

Those were the facts; neither Ahinoam nor Abigail tried to deny them.

"I don't believe there's a connection," Ahinoam said. "Men are killed in battle often. Bathsheba's baby must be Uriah's."

"Well, you have not known the king as long as I have," Michal shrugged. "But perhaps I am seeing something that is not there. Perhaps it is all coincidence,"

Ahinoam and Abigail looked at one another with distress in their eyes.

"What are you saying?"

Ahithophel looked at his son, afraid to complete the logic in his cryptic statement.

"Just what I said: something isn't right about Bathsheba's marriage to the king," Eliam repeated, not wanting to look at his father.

"What could be wrong?" whispered Ahithophel. They were at his home in Gilo in Judah, many miles from the palace in Jerusalem, but Ahithophel's wife was nearby, and he didn't want to alarm her.

"It doesn't strike you as odd that Uriah was gone for months when Bathsheba became pregnant, and then he dies in battle and the king marries her?"

"But Uriah was home on leave during that time."

"For two nights. Did he go home to Bathsheba?"

Ahithophel thought back. He had been away from Jerusalem about the time Uriah had his leave.

"I wasn't in Jerusalem when he was there, but why would he not go home to Bathsheba?"

"Of course he would," Eliam said.

"If he didn't, that would mean the baby is not Uriah's." Ahithophel wished he hadn't verbalized what had only now occurred to him. They had only learned Bathsheba was pregnant after her marriage to the king.

"Right. So, whose is it?"

"You are making a serious accusation against your daughter and possibly against King David. I am a loyal confidant and counsellor of the king. You were yourself away at the battle when she became pregnant, weren't you?"

"Yes."

"So, you don't know what happened when Uriah was back in Jerusalem on leave either."

"No, I don't. It just seems odd that Bathsheba gets pregnant, Uriah gets killed and the king immediately marries her. A marriage to my daughter doesn't add to any strategic alliance."

"You are one of his mighty men and I am his close counselor. Would the marriage not strengthen those relationships?"

"Yes, but those relations were already in place."

Ahithophel sighed. "Eliam, put these questions out of your mind. You are engaging in dangerous speculation, and you do not have enough information to conclude anything."

Eliam paused, then spoke again.

"Yes, father. You are right, of course."

❧ 105 ❧

The women's quarters once again resounded with the sounds of birthing. The king's newest wife did well in her pregnancy and the birth went smoothly. There were plenty of wives and concubines who had been through it before, so she had no shortage of encouragement and advice.

A son was born to Bathsheba, and it filled her with joy, though he just would be another of David's many sons. She received gifts of everything a new mother and baby could need from the other women. She didn't mind that they were second hand. It meant they accepted her, despite having no trouble calculating the timing between marriage and birth.

Bathsheba did detect side glances from the other wives and concubines, but they did not speak to what was obvious.

There was one exception, however.

"So, I see the bastard is born!"

Bathsheba's eyes widened. It was Michal, the daughter of King Saul and David's first wife.

"I – I don't know what you mean," Bathsheba stuttered.

"Yes, I can believe that!" Michal laughed, walking away.

Bathsheba's face flushed red, and she considered retorting about Michal's failure to give the king a son, or any child whatsoever, but she thought better of it.

"Ignore her."

Bathsheba turned to see Abigail.

"Let me hold your baby!"

Bathsheba handed her son to Abigail.

"What a beautiful child you are!" Abigail said in high-pitched baby talk as she held him at arm's length, then brought him close to her bosom and began bouncing the child up and down gently.

"We all have sorrow in our histories," Abigail said. "Take care they don't make you bitter, as they have others."

Bathsheba saw a deep well of sadness in the eyes of the older woman as she played with her baby.

❦ 106 ❦

Nathan awoke with a start. It was still dark, but the dream was no less vivid now that he was awake than moments earlier when he had dreamed it.

More often than not, when Yahweh spoke to him, it was just an impression, however unmistakable it might be. It might be fragmentary so when he delivered the "word of the Lord," he might not have the full story. The full story might not come out until he relayed it to the intended recipient of the message or it could be left to the recipient to put the message together with circumstances in his life so the word God intended could be received.

But occasionally, God spoke in a dream, and then it was usually a complete message, although it might be symbolic, so it could still require interpretation.

Last night's dream was apparently symbolic, but its meaning came through loud and clear. He assumed God hadn't actually given him a message about a selfish rich man and stolen mutton.

Nathan rose, slipping out of bed to avoid waking his wife and went out the door of the upper floor and around a corner to climb the stairs to the roof where he often prayed.

He wrapped his cloak about him in the early morning chill and looked upward at the king's magnificent palace on its high hill, where the rising sun was beginning to guild its pillars, making it stand out against the gray sky.

It was certainly grand and beautiful, but if he underskood his dream correctly, he had been tasked to illuminate a dark secret inside its walls.

The Eternal Kingdom

He had had no inkling of what had happened until now. Nothing had raised his suspicions until the dream. Now some random pieces fell into place to form an unexpected picture.

He knelt on the rooftop and prayed for clarity and to have the right message to deliver to the king when he went before him later today.

Nathan was immediately allowed into the palace courtyard by the guards, who knew him from previous visits.

He walked to the broad stairway leading to the double doors into the palace. He walked with purpose, for his time of prayer had only confirmed his understanding of the dream that had been given to him.

Dreams that were not of the Lord usually evaporated like the morning dew when he awoke, but this one had stayed with him, just as vivid after several hours.

He was again allowed into the palace through the double doors without a word, the guards being well acquainted with him as a counselor to the king.

Since he had awakened early, Nathan knew exactly how he would approach the subject with the king. King David was always receptive to a story, and he had a keen sense of justice. People who appeared before him to air a grievance were often generously rewarded.

He was a truly good king overall, so this mission grieved Nathan, but it must be done.

King David stroked his beard as he listened to one of his subjects from the tribe of Ephraim relate an injustice.

"Has this matter been brought before the elders of your town?" the king asked.

"Yes, but they could not reach a consensus," answered the Ephraimite with a frown.

"Perhaps that is because your claim to the sheep you say were stolen is weak."

This caused the man's frown to turn to a scowl, but he did not speak.

"You have not provided adequate proof as far as I can tell," the king continued. "I'm not surprised the elders could not agree. I need to hear the other man's side of this question."

"He is a scoundrel and a thief!"

"So, you've said, but I would need to hear from him to render a decision. I'm sorry this can't be resolved today.

"Next!"

The man grumbled and turned to go.

Nathan stepped forward to be heard.

"Nathan, how good to see you! What brings you to my court today?"

"Your majesty, I have a matter of injustice to bring before you. It regards the ownership of sheep as well."

"Go on."

The others in the room were only partly paying attention as Nathan began his story.

"There were two men, one rich and the other poor. The rich man had a great flock in his sheep pen, but the poor man had just one little ewe lamb which he had raised from birth. It grew up with his children and would eat his food, drink from his own cup and sleep in his arms like a pet.

"When a traveler came to visit the rich man, he desired to stage a banquet in his honor. He needed a lamb for the feast, but instead of taking a lamb from his own flock, he took his neighbor's ewe lamb, his only lamb, and slaughtered it."

How dare he do such a thing! David thought.

"As surely as Yahweh lives, this man shall die for what he has done!" David said loudly. "But first he must restore what he hast taken fourfold for his cold-hearted crime!"

As David finished, he saw Nathan's face grow hard.

What is happening?

"YOU are that man!"

David's mouth fell open.

The Eternal Kingdom

"Thus says Yahweh, the God of Israel, 'I anointed you king over Israel and I delivered you out of the hand of Saul. I gave you a house full of wives and the house of Israel and Judah. And if that was not enough, I would have given you more as well.'" Nathan paused only long enough to take a breath.

"'Why have you shown contempt for the word of the Lord by doing evil in my sight? You struck down Uriah the Hittite with the sword of the Ammonites, but you may as well have held the sword yourself. Now the sword will never depart from your house. You then despised me by taking Uriah's wife as your own!'"

David looked around the room at his trusted advisors, like Azel and Ahithophel, his bodyguard, Benaiah, and the subjects who had come to air grievances today. All whispered conversations had stopped, and their wide eyes were all on him. Finally, he saw Joab in a dark corner of the room.

David could not breathe. For a year he had believed he could keep his secrets. Bathsheba had given birth to a son and he had believed the baby would be seen as adopted by him. No one would know the baby was actually his. And certainly no one was to know that he had given the order to see to it that Uriah was killed. Only God himself could have revealed this to the prophet.

But Nathan was not finished.

"Moreover, Yahweh says: 'I am about to bring disaster on you from inside your own house. Right before your eyes I will take your wives and hand them over to another and he will have sex with them in broad daylight! You have acted in secret, but I will do this in the light of day in the site of all Israel!'"

When Nathan ended his statement, no one moved or spoke for a moment that seemed endless. It seemed no one was even breathing.

Suddenly Ahithophel stormed out of the room. That broke the spell, though still no one spoke until the king responded.

"I have sinned against the Lord!" David cried, burying his head in his hands. He felt as if his heart might break. He had convinced himself that he as king could do what he had done and not be found out, but his grief now was not because he had been exposed. That was bad, for sure, but somehow, he had forgotten his deeply held belief that Yahweh was the King of kings and he, the king and anointed one of Israel, must answer to Him.

"Yes, and the Lord has forgiven your sin," the prophet continued. "You are not going to die."

David raised his head in surprise.

Yahweh has forgiven me, though I have not asked?

"However, because you have treated Yahweh with such contempt, the son who has been born to you will surely die!"

Once again David lowered his head and put his hand to his chest, feeling pain in his heart.

Bathsheba will be devastated!

❧ 107 ☙

The baby was sick, and Bathsheba was very concerned. When the king told her the prophet had said the baby would die, she had refused to believe it, but now he was sick.

Although Abigail was helpful and understanding, having lost her own son to illness, Bathsheba felt very alone as she cared for the child, fearful that the prophet's words would be proven true again.

Then Benaiah came to the women's quarters and asked to see Bathsheba.

"What is it?" Bathsheba asked when she went to the door.

"The king lies on his face before the Lord, begging for the child's life."

Bathsheba looked at the hardened soldier and saw sad eyes. Her own eyes filled with tears.

"Perhaps Yahweh will hear his prayer," she said.

Benaiah simply nodded and said, "I wanted you to know."

"Thank you."

Bathsheba closed the door and returned to sit with her ailing baby.

The throne room was dark. The sconces had not been lit for several days. No one stood before the king. There were no grand meals. The royal kitchen continued to produce food and those who sat at the king's table, his wives, concubines, many children and close servants and counselors continued to eat, but the mood in the palace was dark and the halls were quiet.

Joab continued training the military part of the kingdom, Benaiah saw after palace security and personnel and Abigail managed the king's wives and children, plus purchasing for the palace, so all continued to function as before, but the king himself was not as visible as he had been.

All who were close to the king felt the darkness that had settled in the king's heart.

"Sire, please come and eat," Benaiah pleaded. "You have been here night and day."

King David lay with his face to the ground on an embroidered cloak, which was now caked in dust. His head was toward the door of the Lord's Tent and it was also covered in the dust of his grief. The priests had to step around him as they performed their duties.

"I will eat when I know the Lord has answered," the king replied without looking up at his bodyguard.

"But I worry that your own life is in danger the longer you stay here exposed to the elements and without sustenance."

"I will remain before the Lord."

Benaiah sighed and shook his head. He then left to return to the palace.

The boy died just as the prophet had said he would.

When they told him, the king arose from his place of prayer before the Lord's Tent and returned to his duties.

Joab was glad to see his uncle back on the throne, but it irritated him that the king fixated on things and allowed his grief to immobilize him when there were greater issues which demanded his attention.

I hope he appreciates all I do for him.

❧ 108 ☙

Life was good in the palace. There was always abundant food and creature comforts. Everyone was deferential and sought favors from the royal family, even from the children of the king.

The crown prince, Amnon, had heard the stories of deprivation suffered by his mother and father during their exile, but he had experienced none of that. When he was a young child in Hebron, life had been fairly rustic, but the kingdom had grown richer with every passing year and now, few luxuries were denied him.

At eighteen, he was strong and confident of his place as heir to the throne. It flattered him when men much older bowed to him and his mother, soliciting their help to obtain access to the king with issues of concern. He watched as his father administered the kingdom, and looked forward to the day he would inherit the unquestioned power to order men to do this or that. He already experienced it to a limited extent, because he knew his father would back him up when he wanted to do anything.

A major perk of which he was only now becoming aware was the attention given to him by women, mothers to daughters of marrying age. He was unquestionably the most eligible bachelor in the kingdom. He had his father's good looks, which only enhanced the appeal of his social position. Fathers also hinted that their daughters would soon be available for marriage. When he wished, he would have his pick of the most beautiful, intelligent wife in the realm.

As the firstborn son, he and his mother enjoyed a generous section of the palace. Their quarters were larger than any other of the king's wives'. Larger than Maacah's even, though she had two children.

Amnon had played with them as a child, because they were almost as old as he. Now that they were all adults, they were not as close as they had been. Absalom, the brother closest to him in age, was a social dynamo. He was often out in the city, getting to know everyone, regardless of social status. He could charm anyone and get them to do anything he wanted. Amnon thought Absalom would be an asset when he became king. Perhaps he would be best utilized as a royal ambassador; that would likely suit his talents. Since his mother was not a Hebrew, he might have all the more credibility in dealing with leaders of other countries.

Tamar, Absalom's older sister, had been a gangly, skinny girl when they were growing up, and Amnon didn't see her too often anymore.

Then, at a state dinner to honor some dignitary, Tamar had entered the state dining room of the palace with her mother and the sight took Amnon's breath away. She was dressed as the princess that she was, the oldest of David's daughters. She was blessed with the best of her father's and mother's physical attributes. Her dark hair and eyes were mesmerizing, and her young form was detectable under the fine fabric of her gown. Amnon had never seen her like this.

As she and her mother sat at the same table as Amnon and his own mother, she smiled at him, and he felt a thrill for which he was completely unprepared. He had flirted often with many girls eager for his attention. It was great fun and flattering, but this felt different.

He had lived in the same household with her all his life, but had never considered his half sister as a potential lover, until now. He had difficulty not staring at her for the rest of the dinner.

❧ 109 ❧

Bathsheba was following Benaiah after having been called to the king's bed chamber. For a moment her mind went back to the night when she had first been summoned by the king when she had no idea what lay ahead.

So much tragedy had transpired since then.

She was glad for this opportunity, though, for she had news. She hoped the king would agree that it was good news.

"Welcome, my love," the king said warmly, and he came close to embrace her.

"I have something to tell you."

He released her so he could look into her eyes. She saw apprehension there, for there had been so much bad news between them.

"I'm pregnant."

The king's face lit up with the bright smile that caused everyone who knew him to fall in love with him.

"How wonderful! You deserve some joy after all that's happened."

She returned his smile. She would not point out that much of the sadness in her life had been caused by him. She wanted more than anything to give him an heir, even though there would be six sons in the line of succession before her new baby, if it was even a son.

"I hope it is a son," she whispered.

"No matter. It will be a child of our love."

"His name should be Jedediah," Nathan insisted. "'Beloved of the Lord' is what it means." He was standing before the throne. David and Bathsheba sat facing him, the only other people in the room.

Bathsheba had not spoken, but she sat on a stool next to the throne, stroking her expanded belly. The child would not be born for a couple more weeks, but the prophet seemed to know the baby would be a son. He was rarely wrong, so her heart was bursting with joy, though she didn't reveal it.

"I know what 'Jedediah' means," King David retorted, "but once you told me the son who would come after me would be a man of peace, so I think his name should be 'Solomon.'"

Bathsheba shot a look at her husband, the king, but remained silent. Did he mean that her son would be king after him? What about David's other, older sons?

Azel entered the palace for the first time in several weeks. The king had been reclusive ever since the prophet had exposed his adultery with Bathsheba and his part in the death of Uriah. He had been surprised when he was called to stand before King David again, as he often had before.

When he entered the throne room, he was surprised again to see Ahithophel there at the planning table with the king and Benaiah. He wondered if their relationship had healed after all that had happened, but he wasn't about to ask.

"Welcome, Azel!" David said. "Now we can get started."

The king unrolled a papyrus which Azel had seen before. It was the plan for the temple of Yahweh.

"I want to resume planning the temple. The prophet said my son would be the one to build it. I want to give him every advantage, so there will be few obstacles preventing its construction.

"Azel, there will be a need for a great many bronze, silver and gold utensils, fixtures and furnishings for God's service; more than can be produced by your shop alone, but I'd like your family to oversee the work."

The Eternal Kingdom

"As you wish, sire. It would be our honor," Azel answered, his mind racing ahead to think of what this task would entail. Likely he would first try again to enlist the help of his nephews in Mizpah, but he would need to reach out far beyond them to meet the demand of this project.

"It will also require great stones to be quarried and set in place," the king continued, "as well as great quantities of timber. Our friend in Tyre will be able to help with supplies of cedar, but we will need many artisans to help with dressing the stones and milling the wood. I'm open to suggestion about the best people to put on this."

The others at the table began discussing people who could handle the tasks, but Azel looked down at the plans. It occurred to him that the massive building the king was planning would be a wonder of nations. The preparations the king had already begun and then the building project itself would continue for many years into the future, likely past the end of his own life.

My son will carry on my work, he thought proudly.

The End

The Story Continues...

Children of the King

In the fourth novel of the "Age of the Kingdom" series, King David continues expanding the kingdom and preparing for the construction of the Temple of Yahweh, which the prophet said his son would build, but his moral failing bears fruit in tragic violence among his own children.

Can the kingdom survive treachery, violence and insurrection within David's own family?

About the Author:

Gary L. Ivey wrote *Quest for a King* and *Exile of the King*, the award-winning first two books of the "Age of the Kingdom" series, as well as *The Eternal Kingdom* from his home in Hawaii. He is a husband, father and grandfather.

He has written two other novels in the "Backlash" series: *Backlash* and *Backlash 2: Justice Denied*.

He has also written a number of screenplays which have been honored at a variety of film festivals.

He has been a music minister, a pastor, a Christian magazine editor, media producer and a TV ministry director.

He is Vice President of a marketing and web development firm based in Georgia, which he co-owns with his wife of 51 years.

www.ageofthekingdomseries.com www.garyivey.com
www.backlashbook.com www.studioiv.productions

Subscribe to the **Age of the Kingdom YouTube Channel** at www.youtube.com/@ageofthekingdomseries

Go to **www.garyivey.com** for blog posts about his projects, freedom and the free market, and random thoughts and to order from the online store.

Follow Gary L. Ivey
Facebook: **@GaryIveyAuthor**
Instagram: **@garyivey**
X (Twitter): **@gary_ivey**